Amanda S. Holiday

One for an Old Friend

revised edition

One for an Old Friend
revised edition

iUniverse books may be ordered through booksellers or by contacting:

iUniverse
1663 Liberty Drive
Bloomington, IN 47403
www.iuniverse.com
1-800-Authors (1-800-288-4677)

ISBN: 978-1-4502-9833-9 (sc)
ISBN: 978-1-4502-9834-6 (e)

Print information available on the last page.

iUniverse rev. date: 02/25/2015

No Place for a Lady

"Damn it!" To punctuate the expletive, I tapped the enter key sharply. That woke my computer from its third nap since I sat down after supper four hours earlier.

I had a Thursday noon deadline for the next week's issue, but a compelling finish for the story eluded me this Tuesday night. As on the previous two nights, I admitted writer's block. I saved the paltry output of my evening's work, shut down, then slouched deeper into the chair to gather my thoughts for a moment. My mood was as dark as the moonless night beyond my window.

The ringing phone disrupted my mild funk just before a thunderous tantrum to vent my frustration. That outburst could have rivaled the fury of the driving mid-October squall outside. I composed myself and answered, "Hello?"

"Oh, thank God! … Mickie, this is Norma. I'm so glad you're home."

Although I barely recognized her voice above the background noises of a boisterous crowd, I noted an edge of fear in it. "You're calling late. What's up?"

"I need your help! I have to talk to you, but not on this phone. Too many ears are too close, and some aren't friendly. Meet me in the Blue Onion in an hour. Okay?"

Norma Winslow, probably my best friend, called for help. She didn't usually ask for help for little things, so I knew she faced a serious problem. Still, I needed a bit more than an hour. I had to put on my face, dress, and then drive there. "I'll try to get there in an hour, Norma, but it's 10:30 already. Best I can promise is that I'll be there by midnight." While surprised by her call, I knew and respected the Blue Onion's reputation as the roughest of rough places around the docks. "But let's meet some other place, any other place, than the Blue Onion. The Silver Sloop, maybe?"

Norma held firm. "No. We have to meet here. I'm supposed to meet Sid here later, and I can't reach him to change those plans."

I understood the importance of Norma's other appointment with the other private detective I respected, so, despite serious misgivings, reluctantly agreed, "Okay. Before midnight, in the Blue Onion."

"Get here as soon as you can. And Mickie, dress 'loose' so you blend in. Pack your gun because it's dangerous. If I have to leave before you get here, check with Gwen, the bartender. Hope to see you later. Bye!" Norma hung up.

My thoughts, now personal, strayed far from my current assignment. As I combed my hair and put on my makeup, questions came rapidly and regularly as waves driven before an on-shore wind, but the answers hadn't yet left their secret port.

If you ever read the *National Rag*, you may have seen my column, <u>Muddy Skirts</u>. My byline reads Michelle Stevens, but my friends call me Mickie. I earned my pay. I was often first to report a scandal or tragedy, or to uncover a desperate life at the dark fringe of life. To get such scoops for the tabloid that paid me, I constantly jousted with rivals, out thought and outmaneuvered them, pushed back other pushy people to be the first to poke through the wreckage of a ruined reputation or an ended life.

Certainly, paychecks earned as a professional busybody housed me in modest comfort, fed me, kept my bills paid with a bit to spare, and put clothes on my back without making me get on my back. While researching the story about pimps and prostitutes along the waterfront, I met some people who did just that to earn a living.

On the face of it, I had it much better than the men and women who worked the streets. Their trade in transient pleasure acquainted them with severe risks, and not just that they might catch some disease. Many were assaulted by the Johns and even by a few of the Jills. Some were injured seriously. For a few, the need to make a living by selling their services brought crippling injuries or death. In fact, a dozen had been murdered and another half dozen just disappeared so far this year.

Still, I wasn't overly fond of my job. I worked on the dark and dirty side of life, so feared the depressing darkness and dirtiness would stain my soul indelibly. Sometimes, I felt that I had become unforgiving, unyielding, unrelenting, as hard and cold as the concrete, asphalt and steel of my world. It's a world that I wanted to escape, if only I could find a way that wouldn't make me a good story in my own column.

As I rolled black thigh high hose up my legs, I again conceded that each column printed betrayed a person. Some secrets were shanghaied when I invaded someone's privacy. Others were shared because a person trusted me to honor their confidence. Every story exposed someone without concern for the effects. I wasn't raised to be so callous, thus each column cost something of myself that I loathed to pay.

Had I walled away my emotions and integrity forever? Or did I just leave them hanging in the closet when I dressed for work? During that morning's staff meeting, my editor revealed that he thought of me as just another of the hacks who wrote for the paper. While unintentional, it was an insult nonetheless, and fueled my fears and concerns that I had lost my way just to earn some money. I never felt this way when I was on the police force, because then the search for truth served justice and the community. Reporting for the scandal sheet merely served the perverse curiosity of the readers. It made me a Judas to anyone who trusted me.

As I selected a low cut white blouse and black leather miniskirt, another question haunted, taunted, me. Would I ever have a real life? Whenever that thought invaded my meditations, especially on quiet nights at home, it started me crying into my cocoa. Tonight, those quiet tears freely would salt my drink, but it would be a proper drink at the Blue Onion. I was on a mission.

By the time I put on some gaudy jewelry suited for bar hopping along the docks, it was time to leave. I felt a sudden gnawing uneasiness as I pulled on my 4 inch heels and got my coat and purse. Only later did I understand the premonition came because Norma said, "Hope to see you later." As I pulled the door closed behind me, I thought, "I should have my head examined for going to the Blue Onion. I must have an extra, make that an excess, hole in it somewhere. If it was anyone other than Norma, I'd sit this one out."

* * * *

Across town, in a small booth across from the Blue Onion's bar, Norma sat alone. Despite efforts to direct her thoughts in other directions, the sense of imminent peril persistently invaded her consciousness. Unable to ignore it, she examined it as she nervously nursed her drink.

Early this afternoon, she snapped surveillance photographs related to the case she and Sid worked. The pictures incriminated dangerous people who would kill her rather than let her share those photos with her partner or the police. At first, she believed that her subjects didn't notice her. The growing dread began just after she retrieved the developed prints, when she saw one of the photographed men behind her as she pulled away from the parking spot. She lost him in traffic, but she knew that's when her status changed. No longer prowling huntress, she was herself hunted now.

That origin for her tension determined, she returned to the present. The first two phone calls she just made were but one-way speeches to answering machines. In a perfect world, one or the other, maybe both, would have been home. Neither call would be of any use if Sid or Chet didn't check his machine in time. The information had to be passed along before her pursuers caught up to her and silenced her.

Uninvited, apprehension and fear now sat with her. They had been Norma's escorts during quiet moments for these last six hours. At first, they kept a polite distance. Now they crowded her to make room for a foursome at a small table for two, to make space for regret.

A nagging second thought, a realization, was seed of her growing remorse. Norma knew before she dialed that her third call entangled and endangered Mickie, her closest friend, but she saw no other option. If neither Sid nor Chet arrived before Mickie, well then, so be it! Regardless of risks to her friend, Norma must draft her, convince her to deliver the information to the others. In her favor, Mickie would be quite capable to complete the task against opposition, if she hadn't gone soft.

Still, Norma's regret sprouted from understanding that her friend shouldn't be exposed to such hazards without full explanation. Norma wanted to tell Mickie the whole story, tell her why she was picked to be a courier, and to become a target, before the end of the night. The new arrival, entering through the back door, made a silent threat that her wish might not be possible.

She recognized this tough from her earlier surveillance. He was one of the thugs involved in the evil plot. As he stalked toward her, Norma went out the front door and turned left as soon as she reached the sidewalk. She spotted another lurker, a shadow under the neon cross marking the mission soup kitchen.

He anticipated her flight, positioned himself to block escape to the left along the street. To the right, the sidewalk was open, but her next possible sanctuary would be too far to reach before he could shoot her in the back. The first thug came through the door behind her. He'd catch her easily if she stood flat-footed. Left no time for careful plans, Norma kicked off her heels, charged forward, then made a second sharp left to run down the gangway between the Blue Onion and the mission.

Norma knew that she took a calculated risk. If there were three, the third could already block the gangway. She would be trapped between enemies. She could only hope to get a head start before the two on the street reacted to her maneuver.

She hoped to cross the alley, and reach her car parked in the lot behind the bar. Once in her Corvette, she could outrun them easily.

But indeed, a third man waited at the end of the gangway. The thug moved confidently to intercept her flight, but she was more ready, more determined to escape than he was to catch her. Her path opened because he didn't block the unexpected blow from the purse she swung as a bat after a low pitch. Surprise etched his features as his knees buckled from the blow directed below them, but the thug wasn't done yet. As she tried to get past, he grabbed her coat. Norma kneed his nose hard enough to drive a ball through the goal post from fifty yards. His head snapped back and his grip loosened as he passed out. She nearly got away, except now the other two reached her, grabbed her, punched her.

No scenes from her past flashed before her eyes. She was far too busy for that. Norma fought for her life as a cornered bear turns on tormenting hounds. She was outnumbered and knew that she fought a lost battle if she couldn't disable one or both. Norma maneuvered to face only one attacker at a time and kept the wall at her back. She struck them as hard as she knew how, with no rules save her own survival,

If she couldn't win, at least she could mark them. Besides the bruises and scratches she would make them wear, samples of their blood and skin under her fingernails would be clues to their identities. If she could tear off an attacker's ear, thumb out an eye, crush a larynx, side-kick a knee to rupture ligaments, or drive her heel down on an instep hard enough to break a foot, the police might even catch the thugs at the nearest emergency room.

Suddenly, she fought only one, then none, but felt the presence of a third. She tossed the hair out of her eyes. Through the haze caused by her assailants' punches, she recognized a friend and ally. "About time you showed up, Sid!"

"Got your message. Looks like I found you just in time." her partner answered. Sid surveyed the sprawled antagonists, "Let's go. They're starting to come around." He grabbed her arm, briskly led her to his car, and they sped away.

A block into the trip, Norma said, "Oh shit! Sid, head for the hospital. This isn't all their blood. I'm cut. I'm bleeding. I feel kind of woozzzz …" She passed out.

"Damn it! Hold on, girl. We're only blocks away!" Sid dialed 9-1-1 to let the emergency room know he was coming in fast and laden with a stabbing victim so they'd meet him with a Gurney.

* * * *

In the gangway, Nick's head cleared slowly, inexorably. The last remembered image of the brick wall rushing toward his face faded. The darkness which followed the pain of impact was replaced by fresh view of a narrow corridor which opened onto a lighted parking lot across the alley. As he regained his senses, he felt himself stumbling along, moving at a quicker pace than his uncoordinated legs could manage.

He realized Stretch had him under the arms, partly carrying, partly dragging him from the scene of the skirmish. Nick checked that his jaw wasn't broken, then whined, "That son-of-a-bitch rammed me into the wall! Damn near broke my head." His words echoed faintly in the narrow brick canyon of the gangway between buildings.

Nick breathed with difficulty. He experienced this before, after other fights. As they reached the lighted alley, he saw the blood on his left hand, wiped from his face when he checked his jaw. He knew his nose was broken again. He asked Stretch, "How'd you do?"

"Didn't do no better than you. Almost had her before that other guy jumped in. But we're both better off than Curly. He's still out cold. We need to get him to Doc's." Tall, thin Stretch broke the news with the subtlety of a left jab to an already broken nose. It staggered Nick like another punch to his head.

The lingering fog lifted from Nick's dazed mind. He knew bruises from a lost fight were sure to show within the next few days. They always seemed to hurt more than those he got when he won. Nausea flooded and ebbed, so he knew that at least one punch had been to his stomach. But Stretch was right. No matter how he felt, he was moving. Curly was hurt seriously if they needed to get him to Doc's place.

With effort, Nick remembered their ambush. They had planned it well, and it promised to go well at the start. How, why, had it gone so badly at the end? Images formed, became ordered in correct sequence. Nick remembered, then admitted aloud, "She was pretty tough herself. Never figured she had the nerve to fight us."

Stretch, stooped and breathing deeply under his burden, noted, "Smart, too. Took on Curly to open an escape route rather than trying to fight three of us at once. Just a good thing we caught her or she'd have got away clean… Shit! She did get away, … I must still be a little loopy from the fight."

Despite feeling only half alive himself, Nick tried to break away. "Can't leave Curly. Got to take him with us."

"We won't leave him. After I get you to the car, I'll go back for Curly. We need to clear out before the cops get here. Then we'll go to Doc's. See if he can help Curly, get you patched up." Stretch outlined his plan as he restrained Nick. He leaned Nick against the car, opened the door for his comrade. As he turned away, he noticed his friend's bleeding nose, "Nick, try not to bleed all over the seats, huh? Vonnie will kill me if I get blood on the seats."

Stretch dragged Curly to the car. As he crossed the alley, he paused to take a few breaths. Before he restarted, he ordered, "Nick, open the back door. Spread that blanket over the seat so I don't get Curly's blood on it."

Nick did as instructed, then rested alongside the car for only a moment. He thought he rested only a minute, not even enough time to completely stanch the flow from his bloody nose before he sat inside, but it must have been longer than it felt.

Too, while quite thin for his height, Stretch was a lot stronger than he looked. He was back already and propped Curly in the rear seat. He arranged Curly to look like a reveler with a snoot full, just in case a passing patrolman eyed them while they drove.

Stretch took a final look back at the site of their defeat as he put the car in gear, then eased toward Doc's. He didn't want to be stopped for a minor traffic beef with an unconscious man in the back seat, especially when that man bled freely on his shirt.

Nick was characteristically silent, so Stretch was free to think. As guests of the state, the four of them shared a cell some years ago. He was caught driving a stolen car. Nick and Curly were caught during an attempted armed robbery at a convenience store. Only Doc could claim that he got a raw deal. While Doc saw combat as an Army Medic, the jury didn't buy the Post Traumatic Stress Disorder defense presented by his Public Defender. The jury found, and the judge concurred, that kicking the other guy in the head a half dozen times after he was down turned the bar fight into attempted homicide. That made it serious enough to land in prison, even for a first offense.

Doc worked his six years in the infirmary. Almost an extension of his training to treat soldiers wounded in battle, he mastered the useful specialty of patching other inmates injured in fights at Gray Stone U. Curly and Nick needed him now. As an extra benefit, Doc wouldn't ask embarrassing questions like a hospital would, just treat them. He'd know what to do with Curly's body if he died. And, they could call the boss without being overheard by anyone outside the gang.

Stretch looked at Nick, stated the epitaph for their thwarted effort, "At least we got away before the cops showed up… We need to tell the boss it went wrong."

Nick understood clearly. When they reported failure, the boss would be furious. Just maybe, the fact that some guy jumped in would explain their failure well enough that the boss would only bellow his wrath at them. But, a huge but, if they failed to report at all, they would be killed. Whatever else they did, they didn't want the boss to think they went to the police. The boss was just paranoid enough that any failure to report raised that suspicion. The boss never let anyone live to cut a deal with the District Attorney, certainly not long enough to be a State's witness. Between the two fates, Nick preferred to face an angry boss rather than death.

Thoughts of dying depressed Nick, so he turned his mind to another question. He wondered which of the others would get the job next. Maybe the boss would go outside the gang to hire a specialist.

Casper came quickly to mind. Casper was no friendly ghost, but a deadly dangerous man who secured his moniker because he slipped in and out like a ghost. Typically, the only evidence of his visit was a body to bury. For local talent, he was very good at this sort of thing. Some even said he was the best in his trade. His reputation was that he got the job done, even under the nose of the police if he had to, provided you paid him enough.

Some of Nick's bruises-to-be acted up. The twinges brought back thoughts about the recent battle. It should have gone their way. They had been three men to one woman. Who would have supposed that thin woman would be so hard to silence, even after that other guy stepped into it on her side?

* * * *

As I drove to my rendezvous on a lonely dock area street, my rational mind argued against it. It was already much too late at night to go there by myself. Any sane person would just turn around, go home, apologize later. Still, I pressed on despite growing misgivings. When I finally asked myself, "Why am I doing this?" the answer was simple. I would meet Norma at the Blue Onion for that one reason which outweighed all my fears. My friend asked me to meet her there and to help her.

That resolve had baser reinforcement. I wanted an important story badly. If the story were as good as Norma hinted, the payoff would be huge and not just in money. Sure, I'd be paid well for a good article, but this meant more than just a paycheck. This could prove I could make it as a serious investigative reporter. With that, I'd get to write real exposés rather than fluff pieces. If it worked out, I could leave behind anecdotes about someone having their 'fifteen minutes of fame'. I wouldn't live for insinuations of brewing scandal. Those only revealed the famous sometimes have feet of clay supporting them on the pedestals that we build for them. I'd get to cover hard news.

As thoughts of duty to my friend and professional advancement muted my fears, the rest of the drive seemed short. I found a spot and parked a half block down from the meeting place. Warily, I stalked up the street, past dark stores and neon-lit bars, finally to stand under the designated marque. A stray thought sprang from ambush.

Standing under a street lamp at Midnight in this neighborhood might earn an unwanted proposition. Uneasily, I caressed the can of pepper spray carried in jacket pocket, and tried to convince myself that I was ready if any passerby's advances persisted after initial rejection. Notwithstanding preparations to discourage and defeat close encounters of the unpleasant kind, I felt every muscle and nerve ready for flight or fight. I paced to release the energy. That's when I spotted the shoes in the gutter.

During an anxious slow lap between lampposts, I glanced down the gap between buildings to ensure no threat lurked there. Nearly to the far end of the gangway, a dark bundle showed against light brick, even in the shadows. Reflexively, since I have been paid to be nosey for many years, I walked down the passageway to investigate more carefully. Closer to the item, I recognized it for what it was, so picked up the purse to look inside.

Besides the honest intention to return the handbag to its owner, once her identity was known, I also grasped the identification might steer me to a worth-big-bucks juicy, sleazy story about some celebrity who had been slumming it down here. Almost as soon as the thought crossed my mind, I scolded myself. I still looked for muck despite hopes that I could raise myself from the mire. When would I stop muddying my skirt while snooping for the mud on others' skirts?

While searching for the driver's license, I noted the purse's contents.

Soon, I found the wallet, extracted and read the identification. Disbelief washed over me. I reread the driver's license, now held with trembling fingers, to confirm the discovery. This was Norma's bag!

Worry for Norma's safety shouldered initial disbelief out of the way. She would never abandon her purse willingly. Where was she? What happened to her?

I fought the panic of uncertainty and willed myself to become calm. I had to be in mental state to help. I called up the professional detachment developed on my last two jobs. Whatever the story, finding Norma's bag in this grungy alley in the most notorious quarter of town meant she was in serious trouble.

Even as I asked the questions, I knew that I wouldn't find the answers outside. Though I explored a story in this neighborhood for some time now, I never visited the Blue Onion before. Its reputation was an inviolable taboo, a breach-proof barrier, against casual sojourns, even against official visits for minor causes.

With a deep breath to steel my nerve, I crossed the threshold. The barroom was ominously darker than outside under brightly glaring streetlights and multicolored flashing neon marques. As my eyes adjusted, the stench of stale beer and smoke assaulted my nostrils immediately.

With each following breath, fainter but conspicuous odors of grilled burgers, french-fried onion rings, and the crowd-pungent cacophony of hard-worked deodorants and competing too-strong perfumes invaded my consciousness in subsequent waves. Once my eyes adjusted to the dim light, I surveyed details of these new surroundings.

Judged by their work clothes, male patrons were seamen, stevedores, and laborers. Assessed by their 'uniforms', several women-of-easy-virtue loitered alone along the bar, or in pairs or threes at booths and tables. Others openly negotiated with the men who wanted no long term involvement, only short term companionship at reasonable hourly rates.

I once heard an account of a British regimental reunion held some years after the Battle of Waterloo. The announcement invited, "Officers and their Ladies, Sergeants and their Wives, Other Ranks and their Women." Those words came to mind, seemed strangely appropriate in this realm. Clearly, this was no place for a lady, nor for an unescorted wife, but women were here.

Two barmaids, dressed to the standards of the female clientele, scurried to and fro, like cargo lighters from ship to shore and back again for yet another load. They ferried a seemingly unending stream of drinks from bar to patrons, trays laden with empty glasses and bottles on the return passage.

Once my eyes fully adjusted to the dim lighting and I could identify smaller details again, I couldn't just stand in the doorway all night. I must either retreat or move deeper into this lair, become another face in a faceless crowd. Mission dictated move forward, but the spilled-beer-sticky floor tried to snatch the shoes from my feet as I gingerly negotiated an obstacle course of tables, chairs, and people I really didn't want to meet. At last, I reached the dubious refuge of a stool at the better lighted, thus vacant, end of the bar near the grill. I checked my watch. It was five minutes to midnight, five minutes that would seem to last an hour each in these environs.

From her back, the bartender seemed to be an attractive woman, albeit now mature, matronly. While her waist was no longer of girlish proportion, still, she had curves enough to bewitch at least one grizzled old sailor. From his post at the grill and french-fryer in the back corner kitchen, he stared openly, watched her every move while he turned raw meat, onions, and potatoes into food which passed, barely, as edible.

As she approached, though, something discordant struck me. Was that a hint of stubble under her powder, or merely a trick of light and shadow? Did she have a hormone problem, or was she a he? Early in this assignment, I met some she-males and other Trans-girls who, despite the dangers, plied their trade along these streets. Sex paid much better than any other job they could find and keep because employers and fellow-workers would not accept them as capable though admittedly quite different people. I wondered whether one of them, aging, no longer favored by her former clients, retired behind the bar after a career on a stool before it.

With whisky-and-cigarette-husky voice, the bartender smiled and offered a first beer, "First time visitors get one on the house, doll. Are you here to meet Norma? She said she was going to meet a girl friend here around now." As she stood before me, I examined her face more closely, then decided the fleeting first impression that the bartender had a beard stubble was merely some trick of the lighting. Close up, her looks and speech patterns were female, but the gnarled hands which placed the napkin and small glass before me showed signs of long years of hard physical work, possibly boning fish at the cannery not far away.

"Thanks, Gwen. She told me your name when she called. And yes, I'm supposed to meet Norma. " I quickly quaffed a full swallow of the amber draft. Despite years as a reporter, and those on the force before that, I felt a sudden, urgent need to fortify my will. The liquor-courage afforded by a beer or two, not so many that I would forget my purpose, would quiet the nerves and dull the apprehension. I feared the answers to my questions would prove disquieting.

"Then you're Mickie Stevens?"

"Yes again, Gwen. Have you seen Norma lately?"

"Before she left, about an hour, maybe two, ago, Norma said to tell you she'd be back soon, so just relax and enjoy the beer." Gwen turned away to answer the summons for refills at the central waitress station.

I had to wait until she returned to ask more questions, but I couldn't wait patiently if I let my mind wander onto Norma's fate. Instead, I sipped the comforting potion and studied my surroundings. The Blue Onion was done in typically nautical motif - fishing nets fouled with seashells and dried starfish, oars, and such. Framed prints, artists' renditions of great and famous ships and sea battles, hung at irregular intervals along the walls. They shared space with framed photos, some of warships, others of merchant ships. A few photos showed the ship's company, or at least a part of her crew. I read the hull number in the nearest photo. I knew about that ship. My dad served aboard her, the USS Yorktown. He survived his war, but she sank from damage received during the Battle of Midway, June 1942. Without asking, I understood that the black ribbon tacked to that frame, and to other frames, marked lost ships. By extension, each ribbon also memorialized the shipmates and friends lost with them.

Clearly this was a hangout for the working class of the docks, but that didn't make it the worst place in the world either. I framed a new lead for the story. At worst, it could open a later article. "Perhaps unsavory characters mingle with working stiffs, as in all such rough places, but this is no sinister den of international intrigue despite it's location on the docks. Rather, this is a blue-collar bar, peopled by those who work and live in a rough neighborhood. It showcases ships that ride at anchor in the harbor near, or still proudly sail the seas in its patrons' hearts and memories dear."

Smoothly, the second paragraph formed. "The schemes and plots hatched here won't topple any governments, or threaten rival gangs. Most likely, the larcenies concocted here will divert a television or two from the cargo nets to rooms for personal use, or sale from the back of a van for a few extra dollars."

As I sipped my beer, I concluded that the real danger here was physical and proximate. Any argument that broke into a fight could, probably would, instantly involve everyone in the place, not just the originating combatants.

I understood that quite well and personally. I still nursed ribs bruised when a hurled beer bottle blind-sided me during a fracas at another bar visited earlier in this assignment. Such missiles could be lethal to an observer, even if thrown without overt intent to harm a bystander. And, it would be a safe bet that this crowd bristled with knives. Undoubtedly, some packed a gun. A few would carry both dagger and pistol, advocates of escalated responses to a threat, whether real or merely perceived.

As minutes passed, such meditations ended when bottom showed as the glass left my lips. I pushed the empty glass to the bartender's edge of the bar in the universal signal, silently flagging the innkeeper to bring another beer.

After a few more beers, I might even start to like this place. Really, it wasn't so bad. In fact, it was like my favorite hangout while I was in college. What did I say? I needed to stay focused! I recognized sidetracked purpose, struggled against pleasant memories, refocused on present details.

Despite World War Two vintage posters that warned, "Loose Lips Sink Ships!", I hoped the double sawbuck, a $20 bill, dropped on the bar would buy the answers to asked, perhaps even unasked, questions.

That seemed to be the standard fee for information, rumor, and gossip from bartenders and others up and down this strip. At least that had been the case during initial research for the current assignment.

While I waited for the bartender to deliver the refill beer, and confident that other patrons ignored me, I more carefully considered the items in Norma's shoulder bag.

A matching leather wallet and key case were carried in a small, zippered outer pocket. The center section held a hairbrush and three small leather-look vinyl totes. One contained those cosmetics needed to put on a new face. Another embraced dental floss, travel toothbrush, and small tube of paste. The third, for serious emergencies, contained a small sewing kit and spare pantyhose.

All were ordinary things that single career girls carried because they can't always make it home after work before going out on an early date. If working in the oldest profession in this neighborhood, a woman faced the same time constraints.

But ordinary items shared space with the unexpected. The purse also held what looked like a nickel bag of wacky tabacky, a folder of rolling papers, and a dented metal pint flask that still held a few more swallows of something that smelled like peppermint schnapps. It also held a half dozen factory-fresh Trojans® in a zippered compartment on the side.

On the back, the side nearest the person who shoulders the bag, a concealed pocket hid a small .357 Magnum revolver with live cartridges in the cylinder. The troubling question repeated itself, "What happened out there?" I knew that whatever happened must have been total surprise or gone down too quickly for her to use the gun in self-defense.

The bartender neared with a fresh brew as I completed the mental catalog. This time, now that I paid rather than drank for free, Gwen served my beer in the middle size of glasses displayed on the back bar. Before she turned away, she probed, "Honey, do you always carry two purses?"

"Only when I find one in the street. There's a pair of heels, too." Given an opening, I quizzed, "Driver's license in it belongs to Norma Winslow. How well do you know her? Do you know what happened to her?"

Gwen's eyebrows arched ever so slightly on an otherwise emotionless face as she answered with affected lightness, "Sure, doll, I know her. She's been a regular in here since somebody bought her detective agency."

Even though expected, the reply troubled me. Nothing I knew about Norma hinted that she would be known by name in this place.

The taller barmaid called Gwen to the other end of the bar to restock her tray with freshly filled mugs of beer and glasses of mixed drinks. They spoke briefly, but longer than it takes to order a round of beers for a table. At her return, Gwen continued, "With nothing better to do with her time, Norma started to hang out in here. When her money went south with a crooked investment advisor, she started to drink - heavily - and to take on odd Johns to make ends meet."

Dazed, feeling my jaw sag open, I spoke to disguise my surprise, "Thanks, Gwen. Watch my beer while I make a call, Okay?" When Gwen nodded assent, I slipped from the stool, threaded through the throng to the phone on the back wall, dug needed coins from the bottom of my bag, and called Sid. Speaking to his machine, I reported the call from Norma, and the unkept meeting after I found her purse, and possibly her shoes outside. As postscript, certain that Norma would not disappear without cause, without sinister outside intervention, I asked him to search for my body, drag the bay, if I didn't call again by breakfast.

* * * *

Short blocks away, Sid and Norma sheltered and regrouped in the Emergency Room at County. After surgeons repaired her minor wound, CSU technicians scraped tissue samples from under her fingernails into evidence bags. Finally, Norma's head cleared as the fear and adrenaline and anesthetic ebbed enough that she missed her purse. "Sid, where's my purse? And my shoes?"

"Probably back where you had the fight." Sid offered. He probed, "I'll go back and find it, but only after you tell me what the hell is going on. What did you find out that nearly got you killed back there?"

She asserted, "I'll tell you what I think is going on, but I'll tell you while we drive back. I've got to go back to the Blue Onion. Mickie will be waiting for me there. I'm late now. And I left my notebook with Gwen." She got off the bed.

He replied, "You're staying here until they say it's OK to leave. I'll go. Just tell me what is going on. And why did you bring Mickie into it?"

Too weak to argue the point, Norma merely stated, "No. I'm going." but relented and related her suspicions. "I think that at least some of the coeds recently reported to be missing were kidnaped into white slavery." She watched his eyebrows, noting his surprise registered in them.

"Some of the missing hookers too. I don't have hard evidence of that, but I've got a lot of notes that show circumstantial facts to support my theory." She paused to breathe against the constricting bandages. "Those facts include the attack on me after I took photos of them dragging a girl into a house on Calabash Street. That might have silenced me except you jumped in."

"But what about Mickie? What's her involvement?"

"When I got your answering machine instead of you, I called her. Somebody had to hear my theory and safeguard my notes if I got killed before I spoke to you. She's at the Blue Onion by now, waiting for me."

He grunted, "Stay put until the doctor says you can leave. I'll talk to the Chet and arrange a guard for you."

He spun on his heel and went out, nearly running over Detective Chet Grabowski in the hall. "Chet, Norma needs a guard, and you need to get the Crime Scene Unit to the Blue Onion."

"What the hell are you talking about, Sid?"

"Norma thinks she was attacked there because she busted the lid off some white slavery ring that could explain the unsolved cases of missing girls. I have to get there fast. She called in a friend who doesn't have a clue what she faces."

"I'll take care of it. I'll be along shortly. Meet you there!" Chet called at the back of the departing.

Sid paused before starting the car. He dialed his cell phone. Gwen answered when the phone on the back bar rang. Sid explained as much as he could as he drove. No one heard what she said, but any who watched would note that she gave the short answers required by yes or no questions. Once, Gwen glanced in Mickie's direction, and gave the only long answer of the call.

That's when she got the instructions that changed the night, "Have Bruno watch over her until I get there, but don't let her know that he's with us. She thinks she can handle anything and everything by herself." Gwen made a trip to the ladies', paused beside the big sailor on her way back to the bar. She spoke briefly. The old salt nodded affirmation of his duty, understanding of his task. Then he faced the phone and saw the woman he was to guard. The smile on his lips told Gwen plainly that he had more than duty on his mind as he rose and walked toward Norma's friend.

* * * *

As I finished narrating the message to Sid's answering machine, someone grasped my shoulder. The rush of adrenaline raised hackles, made me light-headed for a second. Believing that I was doomed, I turned hesitantly, quite reluctant to rush the outcome I fully expected would be my untimely end.

A large, tanned hand extended from the worn, weathered-blue wool sleeve of a deodorant-and-sweat-perfumed peacoat. Less-faded spots, where once were sewn service stripes, rating, and grade patches, led my eyes around and up to rest on the face of the big fellow who stood so close behind.

Trim gray-flecked beard did nothing to soften the impression that a pirate accosted me. A scar extended from brow to cheek beyond edges of a patch over his left eye. He would have looked fierce with both eyes visible, so looked fiercer still behind that patch. A gasp escaped through my parted lips.

He growled, "Take it easy, lady. I won't hurt you. Let's go back to the bar." He severed my connection to the outside with one great forefinger, then indicated the way back to the bar with his other hand.

I felt like a movie spy caught at a covert radio behind enemy lines, cut off from escape by the Gestapo. Exercising the only peaceful option, the one that would buy the most time, I yielded and hung the receiver in its cradle.

As we returned to the bar, I felt his hand, nearly large enough to span my back at the waist, silently, firmly guide me to my stool. Norma's purse was gone. I mentally kicked myself for leaving it behind. I should have taken it with me when I phoned Sid. Now, it's gone. Dumb move.

Gwen delivered two beers this time. Obviously, the mug was mine and the schooner for the great hulk who sat beside me. He stood about a half-foot taller even though I was 5' 13" when I wore these heels, easily weighed at least 75, maybe 100, pounds heavier on an athlete's frame, but was only a few years older.

Gwen winked, smiled, and nonchalantly explained, "Doll, Bruno here took a shine to you. Bought you a beer. He looks like a rough one, but he's a gen'leman." She faced the just introduced sailor, skewered him with her glare, and sternly demanded compliance, "Ain't ya, Bruno?"

"Indeed, Lady Gwendolyn. No lady ever complained that I behaved badly, particularly not one under your protective wing." Bruno spoke with an unexpectedly gentle voice after the unwelcomed self-introduction at the phone.

Fear of instant disaster dissipated as I perceived a different dilemma. My mind reeled as I assessed the complication this turn presaged. I came to report a story, not to be the story. I had to talk my way out of this - muy pronto! Instinctively, I bought time to think. Insincerely, I gushed, "Well, thank you for the beer, Bruno."

My brain raced. Whether single or married, I wouldn't be here alone, seated between hookers and Johns, unless I, too, worked this bar, or had some other very good reason. He'd never believe the usually saving lie that I awaited my husband. Even with just one eye, he'd see I wore no ring, not even that one of paler skin left when wedding band is slipped from the finger for an evening's dalliance.

I didn't know how he'd react if I admitted that I was here for a story. I might anger him, so rejected the truth ploy as too dangerous. A polite counter offer might buy the time needed to think of a safer alternative rejection. I demurred with half-truth, "Let me buy you a beer when you finish that one. I'm waiting for a friend."

Bruno swivelled on his stool to face me. His great paw gently rested on my thigh as he asked, "Does that mean you're not interested? Even if I paid you well?"

While I knew that question, or some variant, would come, I blushed. I stammered the half-lie, "I'm flattered you're interested, really, but I came here only for a few drinks with a friend." I braced against an outburst that never came, then continued, "Besides, I don't do one-night stands, not even for a lot of money. I have to know a guy, and like him, and get some commitment from him before I do anything."

Crestfallen, Bruno removed his hand from my thigh. He softly grunted his apology, "I see. Sorry for jumping to the wrong conclusion."

In a blink, Bruno heartened. He laughed, "Well then, this time I'll take the beer you offered!" After a moment's thought, he offered a rain check for his proposition with good humor, "You know, I'm not a bad guy after you get to know me. Maybe you'll feel differently next time you come here, and accept my offer later."

Something in his forthright manner, in his uninhibited spirit, appealed to me, stirred my soul. I smiled as I raised my glass, "Maybe." And I was surprised by the realization that I meant it. Certainly, it wouldn't be later tonight, but it was not necessarily so very far into the future.

We drank our first beers while Bruno narrated an enchanting and exciting yarn of a sailor's life and travels. In just a few minutes, we became comfortable with each other. Finally, without gory details, he described the shipboard incident when he and other crewmen saved the lives of their ship and shipmates alike. While the Board of Inquiry ruled it had been an accident, a fluke occurrence, his bravery scarred him, cost him an eye, and ended his career too early.

I felt rather than heard him sigh as he interrupted his tale. His empty glass clunked gently to the bar. I admitted my attraction to the large sailor, "At least it didn't kill you before we met."

Gwen came at the summons. When I ordered the second round rather than Bruno, Gwen asked with seemingly genuine concern, "Lover's spat already?"

"No, just my turn to buy." Somehow, I didn't mind the intrusion. I felt that Gwen stood in for the favorite aunt who had been my confidante during my teens, the one who listened to those things I couldn't talk over with my mom. For some reason, I felt among friends despite the recent meeting.

When Gwen delivered the refills, I added, "But you were right. He is a gentle man, and, I think, a good man too." Gwen smiled as she turned away. Bruno blushed faintly.

During his second brew, Bruno related that he alternated between anger and depression as he healed from his wounds. Then he revealed how, with the help of family and friends, he ultimately accepted his life as it is, not as he wished it were.

In this too-brief time together, he stirred something cached so deeply within me that I feared I would never feel it again, not after the last time. The chemistry between us, or maybe it was just the beers and the hour, swayed me.

Maybe because I needed it, I ruled out the effects of alcohol and the early morning loneliness of a woman with no one to love. I touched his arm gently, offered sincerely, "Maybe next time, Bruno, now that I know you." I felt the muscles beneath his sleeve tense, ripple, relax. I, too, relaxed because I liked him very much.

Bruno peeked at me from the corner of his glistening, sparkling, twinkling hazel eye. With broad grin at once roguish, wistful, playful, warm, he toasted, "For old shipmates and new bunkmates!" and drained his glass. His grin spread into full smile. He gently lowered the empty schooner to the bar. As if to accept the promise, seal the bargain, he lightly squeezed my thigh, then rose and left.

Whether or not Norma arrived, I knew I had a great story to show for this night's foray. Just as surely, I knew that my new friend's story would be one kept to myself, for myself, if only to prove that I could still keep a confidence. More importantly, I admitted I owed him that much for awakening, renewing, those softer yearnings and feelings too long absent from my life.

Gwen's approach brought me back from my daydream. She winked, "Even with that eye patch, ain't he enough to make a girl's heart pound?" An involuntary smile confirmed my agreement. Gwen removed the empty glasses to the sink near the grill, where she leaned close to the old sailor who always watched her. Both smiled as they spoke briefly.

Gwen drew a fresh mug, brought it to me and placed it on a dry napkin. Pushing it across the bar, she introduced herself more formally, "So, honey, I'm Gwen White. Do I call you Mickie, or would you like to be Michelle in here?"

Because I hesitated, Gwen prodded, "Come on. I read it in your face, doll. Bruno will bring you back here, whether he brings you in on his arm, or you come in looking for him. And I just hate to call a regular customer 'Hey, you'!"

Her direct manner broke down residual reserve, the walls erected against casual contacts initially breached by Bruno and unrepaired. I smiled, answered, "Glad to meet you, Gwen White. I'm Michelle Stevens. My friends call me Mickie."

"Very glad to meet you, Mickie." Gwen pushed away the offered money. "Keep your money, honey. You listened to Bruno when not many women do, and made him happy. That made Harvey and me happy, so you drink free tonight."

"Won't your boss get angry that you give away free drinks?"

Gwen slyly chuckled, "Mickie, I am the boss… At least I'm one of them." She glanced over her shoulder toward the cook and reported, "Own this bar with my husband, Harvey. He's the old geezer who does the cooking."

Gwen again faced me, "Have a good time tonight. I'll be by now and again to see how you're doing." Gwen hesitated as she started to turn away, "Oh! Sid called. He asked me to tell you that he's standing in for Norma. Something came up and she can't make it. He's sorry to be late, but should be here soon. He'll explain all about it when he gets here."

Gwen resumed her task of sating her other customers' thirsts, or in some cases, helping them drown their woes. She was gone before I could ask another question. Well, it sounded like Norma was alive, and Sid would be here soon, so I'd wait in the company of my new fantasy - maybe Bruno would rejoin me yet tonight.

I noticed when Gwen answered the phone again and had equally as short a conversation with the caller.

* * * *

At the gangway, Sid slowed and shined a flashlight into the dark. The attackers were gone, and he didn't see the purse either. Maybe somebody found the purse and took it to Gwen. Norma was out of the picture for at least a day. He parked next to her Corvette and went in the back way. Barely through the door, Gwen met him in the back hall at the foot of the stairs.

Gwen reported, "Woman, calls herself Mickie, brought Norma's purse and shoes in a few minutes ago. She's at the bar now, but just got off the phone. While she was talking, I took the chance to grab it and take it upstairs. Left it in room 6. I put the notebook inside, too. Here's the key. Hoped she'd be back for it, since we didn't find her body outside. Is she all right, dearie?"

"Thanks, Gwen. Yes, she's all right, but she'll be laid up in the hospital for a day or two. " Sid peeked around the corner, then confirmed, "That woman, Mickie, is a friend. Norma said she asked her to meet here."

Sid took the key and started up the stairs. Before his foot hit the second step, he paused, turned, and outlined, "Let me check if everything is still in the bag. I'll call you on the house phone when I'm ready to come down."

Upstairs, Sid took fifteen minutes to review Norma's notes. At sixteen minutes, he grumbled to himself as he called the bar. He had questions, mostly about her sanity, but he admitted a few doubts about his own sanity as well. At the hospital, she narrated a crazy, hardly believable scenario. The part that scared him most was that he almost believed it himself. He could think it over later. Right now, he had a different duty. Right now he needed to watch a friend's back.

Thanks for the information

WHILE DOC TENDED NICK'S WOUNDS, STRETCH called the boss. He was surprised. The tirade was mild compared to what he expected. Maybe the boss figured the unexpected interference explained their fiasco, at least mitigated their debacle.

After the torrent of expletives dwindled, the boss paused. He asked, "Stretch, do you want Casper's help?"

As a matter of pride, Stretch usually finished what he started without help, but Norma Winslow had been alerted by the failed attempt to silence her. She'd be much more aware of the threat, and forewarned is well armed. Casper could prove useful.

Two more factors favored accepting outside help. The boss suggested that he call in Casper. By itself, that was good enough reason. You opposed the boss at your own risk. Besides, neither he nor Nick would get close to her before the identifying scratches and bruises healed, and they couldn't wait for that. In the time it took to take a shallow breath, Stretch decided to accept the offer without argument against it. "Sure, boss, we can use his help. Do you call him, or do I?"

"You screwed up. Take care of it!" the boss ordered. "Tell him for me that she's good, but not that good. Tell him that I'll pay double if I read her obituary in Friday's paper. That will put it on the front burner for him."

While the boss didn't threaten to eliminate them, he slammed the phone down hard enough that the sound hurt Stretch's ear, and pride. Stretch called Casper, and then told Nick.

* * * *

Casper accepted the assignment, especially eager after promised double pay for a fast, drop-everything-else-priority job. Other contracts could wait until he finished this one. He recognized the name, Norma Winslow, as a private eye who nearly caught him once. He was confident that he would recognize her from the photo Stretch would deliver. He wouldn't hit the wrong person, not this time.

Back when he first perfected the skills of his trade, he sometimes killed the wrong person. He nearly convinced himself that, even if they sometimes starred in his all too frequent nightmares, the half dozen innocent people killed before he got those targeted added to his experience. Like the military, he defended the acceptability of extra dead as merely collateral damage, but even his own subconscious mind protested that claim was unjustifiable. After all, he used a weapon effective against individuals, point targets, rather than area targets like airfields or groups of enemy hiding among civilians. He steadied himself with the thought that he had progressed beyond such errors at this stage in his career.

Those ghosts laid to rest once again, Casper prepared his weapon of choice for close-quarters work. After he watched a wildlife short, he adapted a spring-driven syringe, similar to the darts used to capture bears alive for scientific study. After modifications, it worked whether pushed into his victim and triggered manually, or if shot into his target, triggered automatically by the impact.

Once triggered inside the target, the dart quickly injected tranquilizer. Casper used the same dose that knocked down an angry 750, 1000 pound grizzly bear, made it lie quietly while one of the biologists stuck a hand into its mouth without losing fingers. Such a large dose proved quite lethal to ordinary people.

It was an extremely effective weapon, and, he rationalized, caused a humane death, too. His victims just went to sleep and never woke. Far better than the fear, pain, and agony that knife or gunshot wounds caused.

It also gave him time to become scarce before the police began an investigation. If a pathologist noticed some bruising at the injection site, became suspicious, and ordered tests, screening blood and tissue samples for drugs and poisons took time. Sometimes, because non-specific screening tests didn't always detect this drug, the pathologists found no specific cause of death. Frequently, the technicians didn't even test for the specific drug he used because it was so uncommonly found to cause human deaths. After all, it was labeled and sold 'For Veterinary Use Only'. Even if the investigators suspected poisoning, they had a hard time connecting him to the crime.

Casper concluded that it was a very good choice of weapon, indeed, although it lacked the spectacular impact and social statement of a car bomb.

* * * *

Before Sid left the room, there was a light knocking. He peered through the crack he opened, then swung the door open wide. "Norma, what the hell?"

"Relax, Sid. Doctors gave me a choice whether I stayed the night or left. I left."

"Well, you'll need these." he said as he handed her purse and shoes to her.

* * * *

Nearly finished with my second beer and a cigarette, I saw Gwen glance toward the back and followed her gaze. I couldn't tell whether the new arrival came through the door or down the stairs, but the tall, dark-haired woman lurked in the dimly lit hall. She moved nearer hesitantly, like a deer left the safety of the woods to feed in an open hayfield at dusk. She scanned for someone in the crowd, as if she would flee in a heartbeat if she didn't see the right person, or did see the wrong face. A few steps behind, Sid followed.

While a little gray streaked her hair and fatigue showed obviously in her face since our last meeting, even in the dim bar lighting, I recognized her. As our eyes met, Norma's tension ebbed visibly. She smiled and started across the room.

Another movement caught the corner of my eye as a drunken sailor rose from his stool. He staggered noticeably, steadying himself by running left hand along the bar until he reached the corner and headed for the men's room on a zig-zag course. Their paths intersected, and as he passed, bumped Norma's shoulder hard enough to deflect her from her path. He withered under her glare and whatever she told him.

As she took the seat next to me that Bruno left vacant, she said, "I nearly got drunk from his breath when he apologized. Did you notice that he pinched me? He has his nerve." Norma took a breath to compose herself, then greeted , "Thanks for coming and waiting for me, Mickie. I need your help."

"You're welcome, Norma. I see you got your purse back. Talk to me a bit?"

She laughed quietly, "Shush, Mickie! Around here, the going rate for talk - or anything else you want - is $100 an hour, just like at your shrink's… I'm really glad you came."

Before we could order, Gwen served a Manhattan for Norma, another draft for me, and a whiskey and water for Sid who sat next to the left. She glanced over her shoulder, then passed the cryptic message, "Norma, he hasn't been back - yet. Be careful though. We'll keep watch, but he may get in anyway."

Norma nodded, but her smile failed as Gwen returned to mid-bar to watch the front. Harvey, her husband-with-the-ever-watchful-eye, reluctantly resumed surveillance of the back door rather than watching his wife.

Norma took a long, shallow sip, more as if taking time to compose her thoughts, steady her nerves, than to guzzle the drink. I commented, "You don't knock them down like a boozer would."

My friend breathed deeply, then submitted, "I need to keep my wits about me to do my job down here. I allow myself only two drinks a night. This is just my second one. The rest of them are just colored soda water." After another sip, she asked, "Do you remember the medical problem that I helped you through? I need your help now as badly as you needed my help when you were recuperating after your surgery."

"Yes, Norma, you have it. But what's wrong?"

"Well, shortly after you went overseas on that story, things started to go wrong." Norma detailed bad luck with love, work, and money. She recounted loss of her lover, old clients, and the unsuccessful search for new ones. Then she took the advice of an accountant who was a part-time con man and lost much of her money. Depressed, she abused alcohol, eventually relocated to this neighborhood to stretch her money.

She never admitted that she turned to prostitution, but it was a logical extension of the path she traveled. At least that was what I heard after being set-up to believe the worst by the bartender's anecdote. The details fleshed out the summary that Gwen related earlier. I listened intently for any hint that my initial conclusion was wrong. Norma never gave me any reason to think otherwise, but her story raised a last question, "So, Norma, what now?"

She recounted, "Well, Sid - you remember Sid Koenig, don't you?"

"Yes, I remember Sid." I confirmed. I leaned over and said, "Hi, Sid. Haven't seen you for a while."

He answered, "Hi, Mickie. You're looking good." As an afterthought, he quaffed his drink in one swallow and continued, "Well, since you're here, I need my beauty sleep. Had an early reveille yesterday and I'm tired."

I and Norma both said our good-byes. Then Norma continued,"He bought into partnership with me. Saved the business, and ran it while I dried out. That saved me." Before she continued, Norma looked around warily, then leaned closer and emphatically whispered just loudly enough for me to hear her above the jukebox, "I had a close scrape earlier, a scuffle with some toughs. I got away only because Sid stepped into the fight. He probably saved me from a beating or worse. I lost my purse then." She patted her bag, and finished, "I got this back only because you found it, brought it inside, and asked Gwen about me."

"I'm glad you're safe. I was worried about you when I found your purse. I thought you disappeared like some of the other women reported missing from this area."

"That's the story I promised you. I think I know what happened to at least some of them." Norma entreated, "Do something for an old friend, huh?"

"Sure, Norma. What?"

Norma slipped a thick envelope into my hand under the edge of the bar. She both charged and warned, "I'd guess that they're still after me. Work with Sid if anything happens to me. And be careful. This is big enough to get us all killed."

Satisfied after I concealed the envelope in my bag, Norma said, "Now that notebook is safe, I'll tell you what's going on." Norma paused. "At least I'll tell you what I think is going on. But first," she raised her glass and toasted, "One for an old friend." She sipped, leaning back slightly, no longer burdened by her secret's weight.

Surprise flashed across Norma's face as she fell backward. Blank stare succeeded surprise after her head hit the floor with that nasty sound of a dropped melon bursting against hard surface.

Instantly, I dropped to Norma's side to comfort her, aid her, but was pushed aside by other patrons, drunk and sober, who tried to help, or just to gawk. Behind the bar, Gwen called 911, demand ambulance and police, but Norma already lay still.

Shocked immobile, I could only kneel at the margin as Bruno came back from wherever he had been. He bulled through the crowd to cover Norma's legs with his coat, as if to defend her modesty more vigorously in death than her short skirt had done in life. Then he returned to my side, helped me to my feet and guided me a few steps away. Once sure that I could stand on my own, Bruno again waded into the crowding shadows. The retired Master Chief Petty Officer barked, "Give her air! Move back!" He enforced his order with a nudge here and a shove there to move the crowd away. The three who remained gathered closely around Norma seemed to know first aid appropriate for a concussion.

Officers from the first squad car and the ambulance crew stormed through the door mere minutes after Gwen called them. Even with their hustle, they were too slow, too late for Norma, already dead before the ambulance squealed to a stop out front.

Still, these first-responders carried equipment to resuscitate, stretcher, blankets and such to comfort the victim. Trained to work until a doctor signed the death certificate, they rejected the finality of my friend's passing, worked feverishly to save her long after she was beyond earthly cares.

I looked around. The bar was far less congested. I didn't notice who left, yet knew many had gone. One police officer herded the now sparse crowd to the opposite corner. He told us to wait until the detectives questioned each of us.

No longer able to watch from close range, I found a seat at an empty table that still allowed me to observe as the scene played out. When the patrolman asked, I gave name and address, then waited for a detective to take my statement. Shocked, numbed by the incident, I regarded the paramedics' futile efforts to revive my friend with detached objectivity.

During the confusion, Bruno retrieved his coat after the paramedics removed it to cover Norma with a blanket. As he hovered near the bar, Gwen surreptitiously slipped my bag to him. Using the activity of rescuers and police which diverted attention from him, he maneuvered stealthily across the room to deliver it.

He hovered beside as I fished for cigarettes and lighter, moves which disguised the search to ensure the costly envelope still resided within even from him. When I raised a cigarette, Bruno winked, then gently squeezed my shoulder as he passed behind. He slipped out the back door while Harvey, Gwen's husband, dropped a glass at the front to distract the officers.

As I smoked that first cigarette since Norma fell, I noted Gwen's short, surreptitious phone call. After she hung up, she reached a few inches farther and silenced the jukebox by pushing the master reset. It was almost as if she deliberately delayed muting the music to mask her conversation.

Three cigarettes later, Max, editor of the *National Rag*, brandished press credentials to bluff his way through the door as the paramedics carried Norma out. I waved to attract his attention.

He found me, sat in the chair across the table, and explained, "I've heard about this place. I didn't want to wait for a call at breakfast that you'd be too dead to make. Came here to watch your back, get you out alive." He shook his head, resumed, "When I saw them carry somebody out on a stretcher, I thought I was too late. What's going on?"

Usually unflappable, Max fidgeted in his chair as he listened to the short version. Then we sat, another silent couple in a muted crowd, and watched the macabre floor show as crime scene unit technicians gathered evidence. Other than working officers, no one spoke except to answer direct questions.

Now seven cigarettes, mere stubs smoked down to the filter, lay in the ashtray. The crime scene technicians had nearly finished their work when the detectives arrived at our table.

When asked, Max told the detectives that he arrived to meet me as the victim was being carried out. After the officer at the front door confirmed Max's recent arrival, the detectives' interest in him waned quickly.

In my turn, I became the focus of their scrutiny. In the room since before Norma's arrival through her departure on the stretcher, I made a full, detailed statement. Yet I feared I didn't tell them much they didn't know already from the other witnesses. I wished with all my heart that I could have been more help. More fervently, I wished that Norma had not died, that I didn't need to make a statement at all.

After they finished questioning Max and me, the detectives conferred, compared notes, and, satisfied we could add nothing more, told us that we could leave. We joined the minor rush of other witnesses through the front door into the cold, fresh near-dawn air. As we walked away, I looked back over my shoulder. Police cars formed a hub of activity on an otherwise still and empty street.

* * * *

No one in the joint paid attention to yet another drunken swabby, so Casper just staggered in, blended into the crowd. He watched for a while, then did the job he had been hired to do. Getting out was a little more ticklish. The police arrived more quickly than he expected. He had to carry on his drunk act until the detectives dismissed him as an unreliable witness.

Casper laughed to himself. As the perpetrator, who would have been a more reliable witness to Norma Winslow's demise? But then, invisibility always had been his trade mark.

His only distinguishing mark not hidden by the disguise was the tattoo of his old service number on his wrist. The only flashy object was the POW-MIA bracelet he forgot to take off before he went. Next time, even for another rush job that paid double, he'd slow down enough to take care of such little details. Still, he was certain no one noticed. He knew The Chair or The Needle awaited him if they ever caught him, and he planned to die in bed from old age rather than by the Executioner's hand.

Long before he neared his home, he stopped at a pay phone. It wouldn't be a long conversation, but he needed to call Cheese.

That brought another smile. To all the rest, Art Limburg was 'The Boss'. Casper was the only person alive who scared him badly enough that he got away calling him Cheese. Lesser threats tried it, and Cheese personally fed them to the fishes.

In prison, Casper called him Cheese for the first time, then creamed Cheese in the fight that followed. Casper laughed aloud at his own small joke as he found the change and fed the phone.

Too, Casper had been hired to kill Cheese's parents before they could change their will. While he couldn't do the job personally because he was Cheese's neighbor in prison, he sub-contracted the job. Casper's attorney held a signed confession which implicated Cheese in his parents' deaths. If turned over to police, that letter ensured Cheese would get the death sentence. It was Casper's insurance policy.

Casper instructed his attorney to turn the letter over to the District Attorney if he were killed, murdered or disappeared. Even though the nickname rankled him, it was in Cheese's own best interest to allow Casper to die of old age.

Casper finished his call, told Art he expected the first half now, the rest after the obituary showed in Friday's paper, and drove home. He smiled again. By Friday afternoon, he would have enough money in the bank to live well for a full year, and he had a short list of jobs still to finish, including additional contracts on others that Cheese wanted eliminated. If he bothered to report this income, he would owe the IRS a bundle next April fifteenth. Casper laughed aloud once more. Better a stretch at one of the Federal country clubs for tax evasion than have to explain the source of his freelance income.

* * * *

As Max escorted me to my car, he tried to console, "Don't let it get you down. We all die sooner or later. At least, since she was unconscious, she wouldn't have felt much pain in those last minutes."

Reflexively, I glared at him, snapped, "Your bedside manner stinks, Max. I really don't want to hear that now. If you can't do any better than that, just shut up!"

Once invited to join us, silence walked between us until we neared my car. As I fished keys from bottom of my bag, in answer to my unasked question, Max decreed, "Norma Winslow has been inside pages for a long time now. Nobody but you cares that she died because she fell off a barstool in a dockside dive. Our readers just won't find it as interesting as another front page report of an Elvis sighting at a shopping mall. If you write the story, I won't run it, not unless it was murder."

"Oh, Max, you don't understand." I pled my case. "We are … were close friends. Do you really object that I follow up on this? I have to do it, you know. I owe her that, even if you won't print the story."

Max considered, then sighed grudging consent, "Okay! You'd just quit if I said no." But he constrained my efforts, "You have a month of vacation due. Take it. If you have a printable story by the end of it, I'll count it as time on assignment instead of your vacation. Otherwise, you've used your time finding out about a friend. And you won't argue when I pick your next story."

Max imposed a final condition, "Before you start Norma Winslow's story, finish the item on the dockside sex industry. I want that story on my desk by Friday noon. Understand?"

I nodded to accept the constraints without further argument, and affirmed, "Okay, Max."

Like a "B" movie head coach who sends a substitute player into the big game, Max sent me forth into the fray with a reassuring remark and pat on the shoulder, "Okay, then. Go get 'em, Tiger!" He turned away abruptly, strode vigorously to his car two spaces farther down the street.

I called after him, "Thanks, Max! You won't be sorry. This story could take us both to the big time." Without looking back, he waved over his shoulder as he unlocked and opened the driver's door.

As he drove away, my reporter's impulses screamed that this would be a really big story, but I knew that finding a big story was only shallow motivation, a veneer worn over my emotions. Only a thin layer deeper down, I really wanted to find out what had happened to my friend. Preserving the movie metaphor, I felt the heavy burden to play above myself, and, despite daunting opposition, to save the game.

One consuming question needed an answer before I headed home. I returned to the ebbing confusion, hailed the nearest policeman before he closed his door to drive away. "Where did they take her?" Smiling I explained away his suspicious frown, "She doesn't have anyone else close. I need to let somebody know that I'll take care of funeral arrangements."

He pointed vaguely toward the other cars, directed, "Talk to Detective Sergeant Grabowski. He's in charge of the case." I studied all the cars still parked, evidently uncertain which one he meant, so the patrolman specified, "He's the big guy - looks like he should be a linebacker - talking to his partner, next to the blue sedan right in front."

I pointed at the tallest suit next to a blue sedan, "Him? The tall one?" When the driver confirmed my choice, I moved toward the pair, then stopped at a polite distance, but within earshot. After too many years as a reporter, I eavesdropped on their conversation as I waited my cue to approach.

The bigger man was animated, serious, and recently arrived, or I would have noticed him before. He listened and questioned as his partner brought him up to speed. When the exchange of information appeared completed, I spoke, "Sergeant Grabowski? A uniformed officer said that you're in charge."

He glanced over his shoulder, located me, and closed to less than arm's length in two strides. "Yes, to both your questions. I'm Detective Sergeant Grabowski. This is my case." He paused, then interrogated, "Who are you? What can I do for you?"

For an instant, I thought I recognized the resonant voice. It rang familiarly, but maybe not. Still, he was about a half foot taller and much heavier than I was. Meeting two men of that size within hours on the same night was not likely. I filed the observation for future deliberation. Another matter had priority this predawn hour.

I introduced myself and gave him my business card as I explained,

"Norma was my friend for about ten years. Since I know she was estranged from her family, I'm concerned that an old friend might wind up in a pauper's grave if no one takes responsibility for her." Then I asked, "Where will they take Norma? When and how will I know if I need to make burial arrangements?"

After a moment's thought, Sgt. Grabowski outlined, "Well, Ms. Stevens, it's pretty straight forward in an incident like this. After a doctor, whether from the Coroner's Office or the nearest hospital, confirms the death, she goes to the County Morgue. The Medical Examiner completes a post mortem exam to determine cause of death. That usually takes a few days to a week, maybe longer. It depends on findings, need for additional tests, that sort of thing. When she's released for burial, they call whoever claimed the body."

I sighed deeply, "Thanks for the information."

As I turned to leave, he gently touched my arm to stay me. In a voice that conveyed more compassion in an official statement than Max ever mustered on purpose, Detective Sergeant Grabowski said, "By the way, we'll be in touch. You seem to know more about her than any of the other people here. Whatever you can remember about her between now and then will help a lot to find the truth."

"I'll be at home. My boss said I have to submit the story from my last assignment before I start vacation next week. Call anytime during the day. If I happen to be out, for groceries or something, just leave your message on the machine. I'll call back."

Once more, I walked to my car, but, this time, got in and drove home. Working for the past months on the nearly finished story, an investigation of prostitution in the dock area, accustomed me to irregular hours and arriving home late. Even so, I felt so very, very tired this morning. I wondered whether it was just ordinary fatigue felt after a long day, or the emotional let down after I witnessed the death of someone I knew so well and counted as a close friend?

I kicked off my shoes just inside the front door, and left a trail of coat and bag on the way through to the bedroom, detouring to start the kettle as I passed the kitchen on the way. Once in the bedroom, I undressed, then pulled on my robe.

Back in the kitchen, I turned a cup of instant coffee Irish with a large splash of whisky. Seated at kitchen table, now bathed in pale almost-dawn light, I raised the mug to my lips and toasted, "One for Norma, one for an old friend."

The mug descended only halfway to the table when a flash of suspicion, first cousin to paranoia, raised a specter. "Did I really hear what Norma told me?" I mused, "Norma was a good detective for many years. In all our personal and professional dealings, she was always a straight shooter."

Despite her appearance and choice of the Blue Onion as the place we met, I couldn't believe that Norma turned tricks for a living after what she told me. What if she were on the docks on an undercover assignment? She said the information in the envelope could be lethal. Was she murdered rather than died an accidental death?

If Norma's report, and the overheard conversation between two detectives tied together with my main story, I might make that hit list too. The danger would be real and imminent if anybody suspected, let alone knew, what I had been told and heard. But right now, I still didn't know what that was. Maybe I can figure it out, piece together the puzzle before I bed down on the morgue slab next to Norma.

I also suffered anguish. I returned from an assignment in Spain six months ago, but had not made the time to see Norma. I allowed the press of work to take priority. My only excuse was that I never expected either of us wouldn't live another twenty years. Norma's untimely death just showed how wrong I can be.

I finished my drink and washed the cup. Then I washed my face, and dragged into bed for a short nap. I'd finish the main story later today. After I turned it in as Max wanted, I'd be free to start on this story I assigned myself.

Paranoia Whispered in My Ear

DETECTIVE SERGEANT CHESTER, 'CHET', GRABOWSKI ROUSED himself from his nap. He shaved, dressed, and drove to his office. He had another case. As of this morning, he would work the eight-hours-on and four-hours-off rotation that he endured whenever he had a big case, even though it drove his Captain crazy. During the drive, he realized this one clawed at him like no other case on his desk now, not any he had in the past. He hoped he would never have another one like it again.

He knew he would fight to regain and maintain professional detachment, but it would be hard. Norma Winslow was a friend, and now she was dead. She died under suspicious circumstances only hours after she phoned. The message didn't detail her suspicions, yet hinted at her theory about a serious ongoing criminal activity, a heinous conspiracy.

Chester knew that he could not afford self-recrimination, or second guessing that she might be alive if he had met with her last night. Instead, his reparation to her would be to find her killer, and see that person convicted and executed.

When he reached his office, even before he poured a cup of coffee, he called the last person to talk to Norma last night, the scandal sheet reporter, Mickie Stevens. Maybe she knew more than she realized and could shed a little light if questioned again. He would ask her some additional questions.

* * * *

The jarring bell invaded my sleep, terminated my dream before it ended. Half awake, I ruled out the alarm clock. That would clang steadily. This din was intermittent, but longer than the doorbell, and it came from the wrong place. Now fully awake, I answered the phone before the machine did, "Hello?"

"Michelle . . er … Mickie Stevens?" the tentative voice inquired.

"Yes."

Now confident, almost bold, the voice continued, "Hey, Mickie, long time no see, doll! This is Sid, Sid Koenig, to save you time guessing. Okay if I drop by at noon?"

"Business or social call, Sid? If your visit is about business, noon is okay, but this evening will be better if for pleasure. I'm finishing a story this afternoon."

More sedately than usual, Sid accepted, "It's always a pleasure to see you, Babe, but this is business, some stuff for the story you're on. I'll be there at noon. See you then."

"Then see you at noon, Sid." I hung up, checked the night stand clock, and threw back the covers. I had little more than an hour before he arrived to shower, dress, straighten the place a little, and make a large pot of coffee to compensate for only four hours sleep. There was a lot to do, so I could allow no moping despite a heavy heart.

The coffee maker gurgled happily as I stepped from the shower. I inhaled the appealing aroma wafting from the kitchen as I toweled off, then selected an outfit. Work-at-home clothes, sweatshirt and jeans, would do today. "Sid has seen me dressed this way before. It won't break his eyes if he sees me this way again, especially if the air is filled with smell of freshly brewed java."

While gathering the trail of clothes jettisoned between front door and bedroom on my way to sleep earlier this morning, I reviewed the known facts. The where and when of Norma's death seemed answered already, but other questions needed answers before I, or anyone else, solved the puzzle.

Already this morning. more questions arose. Sid hadn't called for months, not since that night he cried into his beer about the pending "divorce" from his girlfriend. I wondered why he called to offer information about my current story? How did he even know about it? Did he pick up some talk on the streets? Or did he call Max to find out where I was? What will he tell me? Is it important, really be relevant to this article? Or does the new information relate to Norma's demise?

The phone rang to interrupt my thoughts once more. After so many months of silence, except for those irritating phone solicitors, it rang twice in a few minutes. Who called now? I wouldn't find out if I didn't answer, so picked up. "Hello?"

"Ms. Stevens, Detective Sergeant Grabowski here. We met early this morning at the Blue Onion where Norma Winslow died. I have a few more questions. Would you prefer I drop by your place, or would you like to come to the station?"

"Sergeant, a friend said he'd visit at noon, and I really have to finish a story today. Please, could you come here?" I confirmed the address as he read from his notes. We agreed to meet around 3:00. That ended the exchange, but, maybe, I needed to choose a different outfit. Now, a sweater and slacks were in order. Sid wouldn't mind, no matter what I wore, but the sergeant expected a professional reporter. I decided that I should dress the part.

* * * *

The appointment made, Sgt. Grabowski opened the folder on his desk. He read the preliminary autopsy report before he finished his first cup of black coffee. It hinted that Norma's death had been more sinister than an accident. Dr. Samson, one of the best pathologists in the country, found and reported in all capital letters that Norma had a small injection wound in her hip.

Dr. Samson opined that Norma could not have given herself a shot in that spot unless she were a contortionist. Because his team played hers in a recent charity softball game, Chester knew personally that she was lithe, flexible, somewhat athletic for her age, their ages, but he also knew she was not a human pretzel.

Because of its limited budget, the lab only operated Monday through Friday. The toxicology test results wouldn't be ready until next Monday afternoon. Without them, Dr. Samson could only note a wound that was the site of some injection, and the other injuries were not a likely cause of death standing alone. Something else contributed to the death, or had been the actual cause of it.

That conclusion troubled Chet. He wanted something more concrete to work with right now!

At least the fingerprints in and on Norma's purse would yield information sooner. In fact, they should be on his desk before noon.

The autopsy also reported something that left him puzzled, bewildered. The fact clearly was extraneous to the case he investigated, but it bothered him nonetheless. He never suspected it.

Detective James Philips approached, placed two fingerprint record cards on his partner's desk. "Take a look at this one." He pointed to the one placed to the right.

Chester looked, did a double take. "She used to be a cop in this department? Get her records!"

Det. Philips smiled, "Thought you'd want to see them. Called Records already. They're sending them over this morning.".

A lone stranger stopped at the first desk, then walked toward them. Jim Philips guessed, "That might be them now." The records clerk brought them a thick folder. The purple border on the file tab indicated an officer retired for medical reasons as a result of wounds received in the line of duty. Ordinary retirees had a red border there.

Det. Philips noticed the distinguishing mark and commented, "If she tells us she was a cop, I guess she's what she says."

"We'll have the chance to ask her in about an hour." Chet told his partner about the appointment arranged earlier.

* * * *

I changed clothes quickly, finished just as the knock came. Composing myself, I crossed to the front door window, and peered through. The car parked at the curb was familiar. So was the face in that small window.

When I opened the door for him, Sid blew through it like a cold draft. He glanced over his shoulder as he ducked inside, took cover against the wall beside the doorframe. Twice before, but years ago, Sid acted like this, like a scared cat coming home with all its hair puffed out.

Those previous times, he offered no reason, no explanation. He just told me not to worry then, and did the same this time. As on those earlier occasions, I tried to ignore it this time too, but reflexively took a second wary look outside. I saw no threat before I closed the door, but that may have been only because I didn't know for what or whom I searched.

"Sid, give me your coat and have a seat." I offered the hospitality of the house. "Would you like a drink, a beer, or a cup of coffee? The coffee is only a half hour old and still hot."

As Sid handed over his coat, he ordered his usual, "Coffee - black!" At least that was a constant in all the turbulence and change in our lives since last we met. While we phoned each other regularly, that visit was some years ago, when he explained that his then-new live-in girlfriend objected to our close friendship even though it was, is, probably always will be, strictly platonic.

Still handsome, erect, athletic, a fraction shorter than six feet, Sid now showed a bit more age. Since his last visit, gray hair tinged his temples, more wrinkles lined the chiseled features of his face, and bifocals rested on his nose. While he supported a little more weight through the torso, he wasn't fat by any measure. He was just heavier, now more like a football player rather than the distance runner he had been in college. From the kitchen where I poured coffee, I inquired, "So what prompted this visit? And how do you know what you plan to tell me relates to the story I'm writing?"

Sid answered just loudly enough that I heard clearly, "A friend called early this morning, told me that Norma was dead. I knew you two were close friends, so I called your office this morning. You weren't there, obviously, but Max spoke to me. He said you were at home to finish a story. A couple questions later, he let it slip that you planned a working vacation to investigate Norma's death after you turned in your current story."

I returned to the living room. From his seat on the sofa, Sid still eyed the street. His anxious vigilance was infectious, made me a little more than nervous, too. As I handed him the mug of coffee, I tried to lighten the mood, "Boogeyman on your trail, Sid?"

Sid faced me abruptly. He tried to answer lightly, glibly, but failed. Apprehension showed in his steel gray eyes, resonated through his answer. He spoke quietly, "I can handle a boogeyman by sleeping with the lights on." He admitted, "It's worse than that, Mickie. One of my snitches said somebody real, with a reputation for making people suddenly real dead, is out there with a contract to kill me."

He sipped at his coffee, then resumed, "He's good enough at his work to worry me. I almost expect him to jump out of the woodwork any minute." Sid craned his neck to monitor farther up and down the street. Massaging his temples, Sid concluded, "It wasn't too bad when I knew where he was during the four days he spent on my tail, but he dropped out of sight late yesterday. I think he killed Norma this morning." Sid returned to his vigil.

I really wasn't ready for his answer. As Sid's revelation sank in, it hit me like a baseball bat on the side of the head. I sat back against the chair heavily, and tried to regroup. I protested, "But I was right next to Norma when she fell off the barstool. It couldn't have been a hit!" My denial drew his raised-eyebrow glance.

He only remarked, "Think back."

I voiced suspicions awakened, "Could it have been an assassination?"

I recalled the scene. Had the drunken sailor knocked Norma off her stool by accident or with intent? If he did so on purpose, how could he be sure she would die from the fall? Had he done something I didn't notice after Norma lay on the floor? Or did someone else in the crowd take advantage of a chance happening to commit murder? Nearly everyone there crowded around after she fell. In that confusion, any of them could have injected a lethal dose of something, or applied a sleeper hold for a few seconds too long.

The question flashed into my thoughts. Hey! Why did Sid connect the guy who followed him with Norma's death? I probed, "Were you and Norma working on something together?"

Sid swivelled to face me, studied me for a long minute. After thinking about it, he nodded, "Yes." then resumed his vigil over the street outside.

As I recalled the long parley with Norma last night, two plus two suddenly equaled four letters that spelled big trouble - UH OH! I exhaled suddenly, as if punched in the stomach. "Damn, Sid! Is that why you think a hit man killed Norma? The same one that's after you?"

Sid deliberated, clearly calculating how much he would tell me. When he spoke, he stipulated, "It's the case we're on. What I tell you is off the record, completely and unequivocally, until the case is solved. Understand?"

Alerted, I considered the constraint imposed. Sid seemed headed into a storm. I was involved because I saw Norma last night. The story, no matter how important, was subordinate to survival right now. I knew I couldn't write the story if dead, so agreed. "Okay. I'll sit on the story until you say it's over. But tell me why you two independents were working together."

Sid revealed, "OK! Here's the Reader's Digest version. You know Norma had a hard time of it after that con man took her to the cleaners. Some of her long term clients quit her, hired other agencies. She couldn't find enough new clients to keep her agency going. Well, I decided she was too good a detective to be forced out of the business. While the paperwork says I bought her out, really, she and I merged our agencies two … no, nearly three years ago now. It was while you were on that story in Spain. It was a good move for both of us. She dried out, and I got a hell of a good detective as a partner."

Sid sipped his coffee, then proceeded, "A month ago, we accepted a missing person case. Our clients' daughter, a journalism major at State College, never made it home after she came to town. Her roommate said she came to interview for a campus reporter job on a local paper starting the next semester. There's a problem with that lead, though. None of the papers in town interviewed any job applicants at any time near when the girl disappeared."

"But how did that take you and Norma into the dock area, Sid?" I asked.

Sid related, "We tracked the missing girl's movements from her dorm on campus until her trail faded out downtown. A little later, a usually reliable source called. That tip took us dockside. As you probably found out while you were down there, it's a tight-lipped community. We didn't get anywhere looking for the girl as outsiders, so Norma went undercover. She took on the role of just another girl working the bars because her life had gone to hell."

The revelation was small comfort, but, small as it was, it was still consolation. I thought, "Well, that's more like the Norma Winslow I knew." I asked, "So what Norma told me about drugs, drinking, and prostitution was about the girl you want to find?"

Sid confirmed, "Maybe it fits the missing coed, maybe not. But it sounds like she told you what we uncovered so far about a lot of the girls working down there."

Shame pounced upon me. I instantly knew I had betrayed a friend, believed the worst about that friend too quickly, swayed by a stranger's unsupported report. I should have known it was untrue. Soft tears welled up in my eyes. I fought back an incipient sob, admitted, "But I thought it was her story. After the bartender set me up, it sounded so ... so ... possible!"

Noting my tears, Sid consoled, "Don't flog yourself. You were supposed to believe it." I dabbed at my eyes while he explained, "Gwen has tended the Blue Onion bar for a long time. First as an employee, now as a part owner. She's been one of my snitches for nearly as many years. She was the caller who relayed rumors about a new girl in the neighborhood, but she didn't know whether it was the girl we tracked. After another week checking leads, we realized we were getting nowhere."

He glanced through the window, up and down the street. Satisfied no danger approached, Sid continued, "That was when Norma went undercover. Her cover story explained how she got there. Gwen agreed to help us. If anybody asked about Norma, Gwen told the story you heard to plant the idea. Then she fertilized and watered it with a few drinks. We intended that people, even Norma's friends, would buy the lie by the time Gwen finished with them."

Unblinking, I sat stunned as Sid added, "Anyway, a couple of my guys took turns acting as her Johns to have an excuse to be alone with her. Last night, she called to arrange a meeting. She left a message on my answering machine that said she had really big news, but couldn't talk on the phone because there were too many ears too close. When I arrived, she was fighting off two attackers."

One for an Old Friend

"After it was over, we got the hell out of there. She didn't notice she lost her purse until we were at the hospital. She insisted I go back for it, and outlined her theory. Now, she's dead, and I can't find the notes or her purse."

I told Sid, "It's a relief to know she was still a good detective, even if the honest work got her killed." Behind the words, I weighed the chance that Norma had been murdered because she neared solution of that case. Concurrently, I surmised that if the killer thought we talked about it, then, even if he never suspected how much, or how little, I actually knew, I, too, would be in the middle of it now.

As an outsider, I asked, "Sid, do you want me to claim her body? Make the arrangements? I already asked the detective in charge about how to claim her body as a friend who doesn't want her buried in Potters' Field."

Sid concurred, "That's a stroke of luck, Mickie. If you did that, it keeps me in the background. That way, I can send somebody else into the neighborhood to follow the trail from where Norma left off. Would you do that? Unless … hmmm?" He paused briefly, obviously to concoct an alternative, then added, "If her cover was shot, it won't hurt if I claim her body. Instead, how would you like to go in to finish up this job she started?"

I objected, "I'd consider it, Sid, but I spent a lot of time down there during the last few weeks on assignment. Surely somebody, maybe one of the crooks, will recognize me."

Sid countered, "Norma asked a lot of questions down there before she went undercover. She changed her hairdo, showed some cleavage and leg, and nobody knew her as the Private Investigator who was there the week before. I saw you down there, dressed like a reporter. Wear the clothes of the pros, and nobody will connect you to the questions you asked yesterday, let alone a week ago."

"Max expects the article I'm writing on his desk by Friday noon. Give me until then to think, and I'll give you my answer after I turn in the story." I bought time to think. Undercover work was not the kind of thing done on a whim. It might cost my life to do it, as it cost Norma. I shouldn't try it just because of ego, particularly if I would get in the way. Just as surely, I knew it would cost my self-respect to dodge this duty if I thought I really could help. The inkling of decision made first peeked from behind the veil.

"That sounds fair, Mickie." Sid allowed. "I know it's a damned if you do, damned if you don't choice. I wouldn't even ask except I think you can pull it off better than anyone else I know. You're a tough cookie that won't crumble under pressure." Then, as he rose to leave, Sid grinned, teased with a chuckle, "Just think about wearing those low-cut blouses, tight short skirts, and high heels to show off your charms for a good cause."

"Sid, that almost tipped the scales in your favor." I wouldn't commit myself to the scheme yet. I wanted to think it over a while longer, but already felt more than half-sure I'd do it. I wanted to be sure his flattery did not sway me. I would submerge myself in the plan only because I believed I could help. "But don't try to rush me. Call Friday afternoon for my answer."

After Sid left, I collected and washed cups, then hung them on their hooks to dry, all well before my next caller was due. In the time remaining, I freshened my face and combed my hair to make a good impression on the handsome sergeant during his visit.

As I prepared, I also entertained the disquieting thought that each conversation introduced yet more players to this intrigue. Already, even without counting the unknown persons I yet would meet or discover, I needed a program, as ballpark hawkers advised, to tell the players apart.

The serious business was made more dangerous because I still didn't know who among them were on my side and who played for the other side. The flight of fancy was simple enough. It would be so much easier if a tattoo on the forehead showed whether the person was friend or foe. As quickly as I made the wish, I answered myself. Well, that won't happen in the real world. I just need to be cautious around those I don't know well enough to trust completely.

After I finished cosmetic preparations, I organized notes from the now nearly finished assignment, and outlined the conclusion for the report. That kept me busy until Det. Sgt. Grabowski arrived. As I sifted through notes of the finished story, I concluded that the threads of truth were twisted into many yarns, but all were woven into the tapestry of this new story. Someone caused Norma's death. The only real question was whether Norma died by chance or design.

Through office window open to admit the warm Indian Summer afternoon breeze, I heard a car door slam. Heavy footsteps approached along the front walk, caught my attention. I listened intently. Is it one man? No, it's two, but they're almost in step. The barely audible, murmured conversation announced their approach, confirmed the count. A quick, furtive peek affirmed that the detectives were here on time.

Paranoia whispered in my ear, "Better to be safe, rather than sorry." I squirreled story notes away in the desk's cubbyhole, locked it and hid the key. Until finding which team these detectives played on, I decided to hold my cards close to the chest, guard against careless remarks that said too much too soon.

When I opened the door, Detective Sergeant Chester Grabowski smiled. He showed ID and badge while he explained "It was dark when we met earlier this morning, thought you might not recognize me without this. Don't want you to think we're just door-to-door missionaries or encyclopedia salesmen."

The remark caught me off guard, brought a smile. From my past, the refrain from a song echoed through my mind as I gazed up at the tall, muscular, brown haired, brown eyed, handsome man who had a sense of humor. Instinctively, I liked him. Bruno already claimed first place in my affections, but, if things didn't work out with Bruno, this detective easily could move up from second place without any need for me to work at it.

Great size aside, he was athletically graceful as a prowling tiger, a consummate predator. When invited in, he eased into the room like warm syrup poured over hot pancakes smoothly flowed to a plate's edge. Detective Jim Philips unobtrusively shadowed his larger senior partner, despite his less assured and more self-conscious, almost clumsy, demeanor. I almost didn't notice him.

As I offered coffee, I hoped they were among the good guys. I preferred when the police could be trusted, but had known one cop who couldn't be trusted. If these detectives were good guys, a short delay before I told them everything known or suspected wouldn't hurt. If these were bad guys, telling everything I knew could prove quite terminal. I had to remain wary.

Essentially, this was the game played with Sid or Max when either asked my honest opinion about something personal. I always told the truth, but carefully said it as kindly as possible. This time, though, there was a real difference. These new players were much calmer, slicker and smoother than either Sid or Max. Listening skills used to ferret out hidden information had been honed through countless hours on their jobs. I needed to be really careful that nothing slipped out.

Well, let's see what the police want. Girded for the battle of wits, I returned to the living room, and handed each a mug of fresh coffee. After another round trip to refill my own cup, I sat in the chair facing them. "So, Sergeant, Detective, what would you like to know?"

Sgt. Grabowski started gently enough, "I take it that Norma Winslow was your friend. How long did you know her?"

"I met her during my first important assignment, about ten years ago. Soon after the interview, she solved the Limburg Art Collection fraud for the insurance company. That helped police arrest the culprit, Art Limburg. She was a really good sport about talking to the new kid struggling with a first big assignment." I paused as he jotted notes.

When he stopped writing, I concluded, "I needed a follow-up report, some information about the investigative techniques she used. We saw each other a few more times after that and our friendship blossomed. We were close friends for most of those years. Lost contact when I went overseas for a lengthy assignment, but, even though we didn't get together, we started to talk on the phone after my recent return. Late yesterday evening, she called, asked me to meet at that dive near the docks, the Blue Onion. Next thing I knew, she was dead."

Detective Philips queried, "Did you look through her purse?"

The question was too easy to answer honestly without saying much. I knew they wouldn't ask unless they found my fingerprints on the gun and nearly everything else in Norma's bag. I replied, "Yes, I did. I found a purse in the gangway next to the Blue Onion. After years as a paid snoop, it must have been a curiosity reflex. I looked through it for a possible lead to a story. That's how and when I discovered it was Norma's. Since we were supposed to meet there, I took it inside. And, before you ask, yes, I was worried about her, but she joined me not long after I went inside. She said somebody jumped her, but a friend came along and got her away. She never explained why anyone would attack her, just thanked me for finding her purse and keeping it safe for her."

Sgt. Grabowski asked, "Do you know why anyone would want to attack her? Could that be tied to her murder?"

Learned while playing cards for a story on casino gambling, I knew I lacked a poker face. My emotions showed plainly. This time, I felt emotion and surprise were in full flower. It's one thing to wonder whether a friend who died violently has been murdered. It's entirely different when police confirm it, thus convert self-diagnosed paranoia into legitimate concern.

From his next comment, my concern showed plainly enough for Sgt. Grabowski to notice. He explained, "You should know the preliminary autopsy report says the fall off the barstool only knocked her out. The concussion may have put her in the hospital for a time, and she might have had headaches for a while after she got out, but it's not the probable cause of death." He paused to let the news sink in, then continued, "That means we have to examine whether she may have been killed after her fall. Did anyone touch her while she was on the floor?"

"Your second question first, Detective. I think the drunken sailor who bumped into her touched her after she fell, and maybe one or two others. A crowd gathered around, and some seemed to know first aid. They looked like they were helping, so I didn't think much about it." I tried to remember more, but drew a blank. "I'm sorry, Sergeant. I can't think of anyone else."

I paused for effect before continuing, "As far as who or why anybody would want to attack her, or whether the attack was connected to Norma's death, I haven't the foggiest notion." Again, I told the truth, as far as it went. I had no face, name, or motive for the shadow who killed Norma.

Oh, to be sure, I already developed several preliminary postulates. One might even be correct, but the best of them was still a bit fuzzy. Too, none of them connected all of the few pieces to the puzzle I had right now, and, certainly, there were more pieces still to find. Thus, speculations were nothing I wanted to share, especially if they might lead the police in the wrong direction. The detectives had to arrive at the same answer I finally reached to arrest the culprit, but I was free of other cases. I could afford a few wrong turns as I tracked down the perpetrator. They didn't have that luxury.

Detective Philips then queried, "Some of the other witnesses said you two talked a long time. What did you talk about?"

I related a blend of truth and cover story thought safe, "Mostly about how she got there. The bartender said Norma sold her business, then lost that money to a fraud, and was working the bars to make ends meet. I wanted to hear the story from my friend before I believed it. When we spoke, she joked that talk cost as much an hour as at my shrink. Then she told me a story that explained how she arrived in her present state. She never admitted that she was hooking, but never denied it either."

Sgt. Grabowski asked, "Could she have been working a case, pretending to be a working girl as a cover?"

I hesitated to simulate that I considered the question, then said, "Well, anything is possible, Sergeant, as I found out a long time ago. But if she was on a case rather than down on her luck, she didn't say." While Norma hinted at it when she passed the envelope, I only knew it as fact from what Sid told me. Technically, I still hadn't lied, so gave myself a well-deserved mental pat on the back for the performance to this point.

Then Det. Philips posed the question expected since he hinted that they checked fingerprints, the question I hoped they wouldn't ask. Talking about it always brought back unpleasant memories. "You say you're a reporter for the *National Rag*, but the records check says you're a retired detective. What's the story on you?"

"Long or short version?" I asked.

"Short," he snapped back.

As calmly as possible, despite the emotional baggage I still carried from the incident, I recounted, "I once trusted a cop, my partner. I shouldn't have. Seven years ago, he sold out and sent me into an ambush. I was shot twice, nearly killed. I lost a lobe of my liver and a piece of one lung. The only reason I'm alive is that Norma dragged me behind cover before the triggerman could finish me."

The deep breath before I continued couldn't mask my anguish as I reported, "The review board decided my wounds were serious enough to retire me for medical reasons. When I found that I wouldn't go back to a job that I liked, that defined my life and self-image, well, I got the blues, big time."

Involuntarily, I sighed at the painful memory, then pressed on, "Others, even the surgeon who repaired me, noticed my depression. She recommended a psychiatrist, so I went. As a close friend who witnessed my doldrums close up, I asked Norma to go with me to help her cope with my problem."

Det. Philips demanded, "Then you know the fingerprints show Michelle Stevens, you, used to be Steven Michaels?"

"Of course I do, Detective. I told you that we were close friends. We went to joint sessions to help her deal with me while I was depressed. During the therapy, the psychiatrist, Norma, and I determined that I also struggled with 'Gender Dysphoria'. In my case, I was a woman born inside a man's body."

The detectives were silent. Having gone this far, I concluded, "Midway through four years of therapy, I made the full change, and, after the surgery, got my name and birth certificate changed in court. I've been a woman since about four years ago. Actually, Norma saved my life for the second time by sticking with me while I wrote about my change. That story got me my job on the *National Rag*."

The two were motionless, speechless, unblinking statues on the sofa across from me. During their silence, I wondered whether the detectives were ready for the disclosure they just heard. After all, both were macho, worked at a macho job. Their blank faces said, more plainly than words, that they believed gender was bipolar. People were either male or female, a he or a she. With that philosophy, they didn't, and would never, understand that some people have bodies that don't match their hearts and minds. If they never contemplated possible cases between the two poles, they didn't care how many men acted masculine, or how many women acted feminine, just to satisfy expectations of families and friends based on a check mark on the birth certificate.

I remembered the session when the psychiatrist explained how fortunate I had been. She told us that few T's ever figured out why they're confused, conflicted by the roles they're forced to play, and fewer still ever made the change. Most people think the Steves and Michelles of the world are some kind of perverts, but we are human beings with a defined medical condition. Our difference was easier to bear when we accepted ourselves and undertook the profound transition to life in our psychological gender.

Sgt. Grabowski at last asked, "OK, Ms. Stevens, can you remember anything else about your friend's death? Did anybody stand out from the crowd?"

"Only a one-eyed sailor, Bruno, but that's just because he was so big, had a patch over his left eye, and bought me a beer." The part-truth slipped through my lips as easily as rain runs off a freshly waxed car. As I described him to the detectives, I hoped that wouldn't get him into trouble. I noticed when they glanced at each other, as if both recognized his description.

Something triggered recall of a detail judged insignificant last night. "Oh, and the tattoo! I just remembered that the drunk who bumped her when she came in also pushed me aside to give first aid to Norma. Thinking back, I realize that his hands were pale for anyone who worked outdoors, looked too soft for a manual laborer. He had a tattoo, a string of numbers, across his left wrist, under one of those POW/MIA bracelets."

"Can you remember what the numbers were?" Detective Philips questioned, "Or anything else about him?"

"I was worried about Norma, and didn't pay attention to much else. The only clear impressions, besides too-soft, pale hands, tattoo, and bracelet, are that he was strong enough to push me aside without much effort, and he seemed to know what he was doing. He didn't seem much taller than I am, but I wore pumps with four inch heels last night."

After a pause while they jotted notes, I volunteered, "If I remember anything else about him, I'll let you know." Their questions aroused suspicion which became voiced thesis, "Norma died while he checked her. In the confusion, maybe he applied a lethal sleeper hold disguised as checking her carotid pulse, and none of us noticed it."

"That's not a bad guess, but it's not likely. Her neck wasn't bruised. Any hold strong enough to choke her would leave bruises." Detective Sergeant Grabowski pursued another line, "Was your friend killed because she was with a transsexual?"

"I don't think so. I know six prostitutes were murdered in the past three months, only one of them was transsexual, but I really don't think that is it. The papers reported the others were killed in hotel rooms, possibly by the John or maybe their pimp found out something he didn't like. Norma was killed in the bar. Strikes me the killer needed a different motive to commit murder in such a public place."

Finally, the detectives glanced at each other, then flipped their notebooks shut to signal an end to the interview. I didn't know whether they did so with a wink of disdain for amateur sleuths, even one with credentials equal to theirs, or because they learned enough that they wanted to leave.

Det. Philips mumbled, "That's it for now. Thanks for your time."

Sgt. Grabowski added, "Here's my card. If you remember anything else, call. And we'll call you if we need to ask more questions later."

I assured them, "Sure thing, Sergeant, Detective. Norma was my friend, and I'm eager to do what I can to help." Cutting off the cliched instruction, I added, "I plan to take a little vacation time after I turn in the story I'm working on, so I might be out of the house, but I'll be in town. I have no plans to leave for anywhere else. I've got an answering machine. Just leave a message, and I'll call back as soon as I get it."

As the detectives drove away, I gathered and washed cups again, then switched on the computer and wrote the close for the story that took me to the dock area in the first place. Max insisted that I have the manuscript on his desk by Friday. Once delivered, I'd be free to pursue Norma's killer. If confirmed by autopsy findings, I witnessed my friend's murder, not an accidental death. Finding the murderer wasn't something I could let others do for me while I sat still.

Inspiration caused a pause to thought. Why do I think of just one killer? Maybe only one person committed the murder, but, with the little I know right now, I can't rule out that more were involved. It's too easy to miss the important clues if I put on mental blinders before I have all the facts.

Prodded by the need to start the new story, I wrote until, finally, I keyed the last period for the day. As the file copied to disk, I called Max, "The story will be on your desk tomorrow by midmorning."

Max offered, "How would you like to cover a story in Paris? Give you a chance to rub shoulders with expatriate artists and writers. It's a plum assignment compared to grubbing around on the docks with the blue jackets. If you want it, the paper will pay all your expenses and give you a nice advance."

I begged off. "Thanks for the offer, Max, but I'll take some vacation time. We agreed last night. This is something I have to do."

Max listened. He chided, "What's the matter? You against making some easy money?"

I sighed, "Got nothing against the concept, Max. It's just that I've never been that good at putting it into practice. That's why I still work."

After laughing at my small joke, he confirmed the quest with a "Go get 'em, Tiger!" and hung up.

When I finally closed the office window and curtains, it was fully dark outside, well past time for dinner. The microwave would fix something more palatable than yet another peanut butter and jelly on whole wheat toast sandwich. The evening stretched ahead promising boring routine.

Still, something during the last day birthed a deep, nagging, subliminal uneasiness. I didn't know whether it was the story just finished, something overheard or was told, Norma's death, or Sid's actions and jitters during his visit. I knew only that I was more skittish than ever.

While the frozen dinner heated, I ran a second copy of the files onto a separate disk, then shut down for the night. Early in my writing career, a story disappeared from my computer. I never found whether the loss was intentional or accidental, but, on that day, I learned to make a backup copy of whatever I wrote. And too, there were always simple vagaries of fate: a virus, power surge, or broken hardware that could wipe out my work with neither human agent nor malicious intent.

As I secured the backup copy in the fireproof document safe hidden in my closet, the faint 'ding' from the kitchen announced that supper was ready. Once I ate and cleaned up, an inventory of that closet was in order.

If I go undercover to help Sid, I needed to look the part. The prospect of adventure seasoned my dinner. At least I spent enough time on this last story near the docks to know how the pro's dressed.

The closet surrendered one outfit that just might do. I hoped it would still fit as I held it before me and assessed the look in the mirror. I felt a wry smile grow on my lips as the memory became clearer. I wore this the last Halloween before I had my sex reassignment surgery. I tried it on. It still fit.

Now, the image in the mirror was more flesh than cloth. I recalled that Norma teased, "I wonder how your neighbors will take it when you put a red bulb in your porch light? You might as well, you know, if you insist on wearing just a wide belt." Then she had laughed tenderly.

I smiled wider at thoughts of my friend, then forced myself to return to the purpose. But, one outfit , nor even two, won't be enough. I didn't know how long I'd need to skulk around the dives. It didn't take a lot of thought even a little bit more about it. I'd shop for a few more outfits with the hooker look on the way home tomorrow, after delivering the story. After all, I still had some space on the plastic, and know precisely which shop, if they weren't closed, where I'd likely find what I needed.

Studying my reflection, I considered my prospects. At 5 feet 10 inches, and 160 pounds, I'm no petite little thing. But, I stay in good enough shape to wear a size 14 without stretching it. Recent conversations with the prostitutes met while doing the story eased nagging concerns about my size and age. Some of those girls were bigger, some older, and many were plainer.

Under a streetlight, or in one of the dimly lit dives, makeup should hide how old I look. And I already knew that I could look very good to some of the Johns who frequented the area, even well covered in working reporter garb. Dressed for the part, I'll be all right.

There was even a target specialty clientele. Some guys down there looked for bigger women. I know I won't be the pick of the litter, but I can get by. Besides I only have to pretend to take a guy upstairs when I report to Sid or one of his detectives. It isn't like I really have to do anything more than look the part. I felt good about my plan.

All of that done, decided, I made another Irish coffee, and clicked the TV to a movie channel. It didn't matter what played. It was on only for background noise, to assuage the nagging loneliness and deepening blues. Still, I needed to reminisce some before I slept tonight.

Norma was my close friend for nearly ten years. Except for Sid, that was longer than anyone outside my immediate family had been part of my life. Above and beyond the call of that friendship, Norma saved my life twice. Partly to repay that debt, partly to support a dear friend, I stood by her after she made her transition from cop to private detective, when even some of her blood kin disowned her.

We met again shortly after my divorce became final. As a patrol officer recently promoted to detective, I investigated the arson fire which killed the night watchman and destroyed the Limburg Art Collection. The insurance company hired Norma to investigate the same case. She turned up at the same places I went, questioned the same people. Because I didn't believe that was coincidental, I interviewed her.

We got along well, so pooled our facts, then presented the evidence to the District Attorney who got the conviction. I collected the physical evidence used at trial, but Norma earned my respect because she found the motive which tied all the clues together. That led to the guilty person, and the guilty verdict.

After she noticed a painting listed as destroyed in another collector's home, Norma determined that Art Limburg, the museum's owner, displayed copies after he sold the original works to other collectors. Then Art set the museum afire for the insurance settlement based on appraised value of the long-gone originals. Limburg planned to pocket the settlement and what he got when he sold the originals, then flee to any country that didn't have an extradition treaty with the United States.

We found no evidence of conspiracy, concluded the buyers acted in good faith, as far as we could tell, so only Art went to prison. He escaped the death penalty because the jury held reasonable doubt. It decided the watchman's death had been an accident rather than deliberate. Even with that decision, Limburg faced a long stretch in the slammer for his crimes.

Later, as we discussed how she unraveled the clues, solved the case, I fell in love with Norma, or maybe, at first, she merely filled my loneliness. For a period, she was my live-in significant other. Then I was wounded seriously. During therapy, I made the unsettling discovery and changed.

While Norma and I went to each other's therapy sessions, we became uncomfortable as lovers, so became friends. We were good friends these last years, and talked frequently, not counting the time I was in Spain on an assignment. If anyone pushed for an answer, I would concede that Norma was my best friend.

We shared big and small secrets, talked about life, love, hopes, dreams. We shopped together and cried at the same sad movies. We giggled, at dinner or in a bar, when any guys tried to pick us up. Norma feigned indignation if they approached me first, and I reciprocated if they hit on Norma first. And we had a good laugh that I indeed had looked at love from both sides.

Easily, Norma was closer than Maureen, estranged sister who no longer spoke to me. That relationship was not able to weather the storm. It happened during a cocktail party Maureen held for her candidate, the one she slept with when he wasn't at home with his wife.

Indeed, Maureen tried to stop my climb onto the dais in front of everyone who just heard his speech about government officials' responsibilities to the citizens. She fainted when I read him his Miranda rights and arrested him. He was charged with building his fortune with protection money from the mob and kickbacks from firms awarded city construction contracts. Maureen never forgave me for disclosing that he was a criminal, even though the jury determined beyond reasonable doubt that he had committed the crimes. Her judgment clouded by emotion, Maureen wouldn't accept that he went to jail for real crimes rather than jealousy, and severed relations from that time.

By comparison, Norma risked her life to save mine, then surrendered her privacy to give me a new start in a new job. Sobbing a last time for this night, I judged myself lucky to have known Norma, and summed up that acceptance. So what if she had an unusual problem. We all have some deep trouble we learn to live with.

Like flower petals strewn on a casket, used tissues piled beside my chair, and around the waste basket I missed too often. The damp little flags evidenced how deeply I sensed great loss.

Sometimes, small details take a while to sink in, percolate through even the sharpest wit. As I sat alone tonight, one thing finally became clear. I felt better as the fog lifted. Norma carried spare pantihose in her purse, not stockings worn with a garter belt or lace topped thigh-highs. While Norma was prepared to maintain the look of a hooker, pantihose aren't very handy for the job if she actually worked that trade. I hoped Norma's spirit would accept my apology for ever thinking, even briefly, that she had turned to prostitution rather than staying a detective.

* * * *

Bruno strutted through the alley door into the Blue Onion. He claimed a stool at the back, the one he sat in when he met the woman. When Gwen approached, he dealt a $10 bill from his small roll onto the bar and declared, "Schooner of your best dark draft, please, Gwen." He was thinking about her, Norma's friend, again. Even though they spoke only briefly, she had gotten under his thick hide and into his heart and mind.

Bringing himself back to the present, he looked up. Gwen put the beer before him, but, instead of moving away, now hovered nearby. Bruno asked, "Did you get her name?"

"Slowing down with old age, huh, Bruno? You didn't think to ask her yourself before things went crazy, did you?" Gwen razzed gently. She let him dangle in uncertainty for long seconds, then added, "Yes, I got her name."

Toying with him, she maneuvered to the middle of the bar to dust and straighten the liquor bottles shelved behind it. Concern and nurturing fondness for the squirming boy-in-a-man's-body nudged her to return to the end where he sat before he burst. Gwen announced, "Norma's friend is Michelle Stevens. Her friends call her Mickie." She watched his features lighten with the small news. She asked, "You like her, don't you?"

Bruno thought about it through his waking hours over the last day, so already had his answer. He didn't hesitate, "Yes, Gwen, I do. I felt really comfortable talking to her, almost like we've known each other for years."

"I believe you do, Bruno. Just don't forget to tell her too." Gwen suggested.

"Do you think she'll be back?" he pumped.

"Don't worry, Bruno. She'll be back, but maybe not right away. We talked about it a little after you took your walk." She considered him, studied his face. Bruno had enough sorrow in his life. Gwen guessed, rightly, that so did Mickie. If she could help them find even part of the happiness she and Harvey shared, the effort would be worth it.

Gwen would take up the role of matchmaker for these two if she must. If Mickie knew Norma, maybe Sid could find her and steer her back this way for another tete-a-tete with Bruno. Gwen smiled wryly, like the Mona Lisa, as she thought to herself, "Of course, the road to Hell is paved with good intentions. I hope it works out for them. I hope I'm doing the right thing."

...*Before Deadline, Even*

SOMETIME BETWEEN MIDNIGHT AND MORNING, I went to bed. Even asleep, going by the dreams I had, I remembered someone special in my life, and special memories of good times and hard times shared. I slept, but slept fitfully, awoke with the blanket and sheet knotted around me from tossing and turning.

During the night, the tentative initial reaction to join forces when Sid suggested that I could help became resolve. Even though I had made a deadly dangerous decision, I saw no other course. I considered, then discarded, all alternatives to going back to the docks and dives. For my friend, I'd find Norma's last client's missing daughter. At the same time, with a little luck, I'd find, or help the police find, Norma's killer or killers. I hoped to do both without getting myself killed.

Untangling from covers wound around, I left the safety of my bed for the kitchen to brew a pot of coffee. While the machine gurgled, I showered and dressed for the day's tasks which lie ahead.

With a fresh cup of coffee in hand, I went to the computer, brought up the word processing program. Once it was running, I made a final check for necessary revisions to the story I would turn in today.

Max would be happy enough with the story to keep him smiling while I took a working vacation. During our talk last evening, he indicated in his obtuse way that he really didn't want me on this one. I knew Max worried about me as a friend, dismissed it in the face of my need to act. Well, fine, let him worry, but I have to do this - come hell or high water!

By the time I finished the half-pot of coffee brewed for breakfast, the last revision to the story was finished and saved to both copies, and I also outlined my plan. Sid would call tomorrow for the already made decision. I had another day to refine and flesh out my plan, to prepare to carry it out.

Yet, deep inside, behind a bravado mask I'd show the world, I was as afraid as I had been only once before, that day I nearly died. I searched deeply into my heart for the courage to follow the plan. I found it in something Dad told me before he died. "Only fools deny fear when real danger threatens, but only cowards allow that fear to immobilize them."

It was time to face the fear, then move on. After all, I lived through that earlier attack and found a new life after I healed. I forced myself to believe that this adventure will end well, too. Second thought sprang to mind. It won't have a happy end if I neglect the five 'p's' - Prior Planning Prevents Poor Performance. I smiled - that was the polite version of the old adage Dad used around children. He added another 'P" after we were grown.

Whether five or six 'p's', I knew that anticipating threats and taking appropriate precautions would help get me through this. I retrieved the Officer's Model pistol from the back corner of the night stand drawer. After completing the other errands, I planned a stop at the range for some target practice on the way home tonight. During training at the academy, a firearm's instructor put it simply, "God created people, but Samuel Colt made them equal." If I could hit the target, I didn't need to be as big or strong as some assailant in Bruno's weight class.

As I stowed everything needed today in my bag, I mused through the doubts about the mission. Norma always had been much better at cloak-and-dagger missions than I, but was dead. Would I fare better? That daunting thought was quite sobering when the script was not yet written, let alone read and studied.

While dressing, I reflected on more doubts. Did long-ago training as a detective and recent masquerades for covert assignments as a scandal sheet reporter properly prepare me for the job ahead? Was my resolve to find what happened to a friend strong enough to see me through to the conclusion? I prayed the eventual answers to both questions would be yes, and that I'd be here to answer them.

Morning traffic thinned by the time I started for the paper's office, and repairs on the main road were finished until next spring. As a result, I walked into *National Rag* headquarters only thirty minutes later. An easy drive on a beautiful fall day put me in a good mood despite those earlier qualms.

The only known obstacle to a great day loomed ahead. As editor's secretary and self-appointed gatekeeper, Emma restricted access to Max's suite more zealously than St. Peter did heaven's streets. I breathed deeply once or twice, marched up, then cooed as pleasantly as I could manage, "Good Morning, Emma. Does he have time to see me now?"

Behind forced smile, I thought, "Besides blocking my path, Emma, you are a despicable little toad of a person." It wasn't that Emma had that many warts - the only one visible erupted at the left corner of her mouth. It wasn't that she wore her bottle-blonde hair, tinged green by the office flourescent lights, tight against her skull, and wore no makeup to disguise jaundiced olive-yellow skin. It wasn't the great, thick, round glasses which magnified lifeless eyes to reptilian proportion, even though her glasses perched on a nose barely a bump in her puffy round face. It wasn't that she had no neck to support a head that rested directly on her shoulders, or the roundness of 200 pounds carried on a five-foot tall frame which gave her body a toady shape, with arms and legs far too short in proportion to her girth. And it wasn't even that, today, she wore an olive brown-green sweater and leggings stretched around her to complete the lizard-skin look.

It was the way she made people feel that they were bugs, lower creatures in the food chain. Emma watched, nestled behind her desk, as toads watch from a pond's-edge rock. In time, if anyone hovered too near too long, she would suddenly send forth a great sticky tongue from her inertness, lightning like, to strike them down. Then she would devour their spirit.

Emma snapped her eyes from the article in the magazine resting on her lap to glare at Mickie. She croaked, "Oh, it's just you. I don't know why they keep you around. You're just a mediocre reporter. Why don't you quit to take a job as a whore? Even you could handle that." Emma repaid my low opinion of her, doubled it with open loathing.

I wanted to see Max this morning, so choked off the stinging retort that pride demanded. Instead, I wheedled, "Aw, Emma, don't be so mean. You know I'm just the staff 'token disabled ex-cop'. They keep me around just to fill some kind of quota or something. Please let me see Max. I have a story he wants for next week's issue."

Emma gloated smugly. She scored it as the easy victory of real secretary over pseudo-journalist. Her toady little finger pushed the intercom button.

Max growled, "What is it this time, Emma?" His voice notified one and all that he was higher up the food chain, much higher, than any of the rest of us. Even Emma recognized that.

Emma politely croaked, "Mickie is here, Max. She wants to turn in a story."

Earsplitting quiet settled over this outer office for a few seconds. The jovial greeting, "Come in, Michelle!", shattered that silence. It came, not over the intercom, but from now open door into the editor's lair. Then Max came out to meet me.

I never knew whether he made that uncommon gesture as a sincere personal welcome, or just to establish that, on this paper while he was in charge, a secretary occupied a lower rung than a reporter. Which reason prompted his action didn't matter to me. I just enjoyed the squelch he applied on my behalf, if only because it forced Emma's meek return to her patient vigil for her next victim.

Once in Max's office with the door closed, I thanked him for rescue. I grinned as I handed over the hard copy of the story, and the companion disk. "Down to business, Max. Here it is, and before deadline, even."

Max first scanned, then read the article. He was satisfied with the story just delivered, so pleased he even gave the all-too-rare "Well done." I would have been cheered by the usual "Not bad." grunted into his coffee, so was quite elated.

After we discussed the story in hand, conversation turned to

Norma's death, and events since. I recounted the questioning by police yesterday afternoon. Max considered the news, and made my day when he advanced part of my vacation pay a week early.

That gave me money for the needed wardrobe, and a bit more on which to start my prying vacation. He also authorized the payroll department to deposit the rest of the checks directly into my bank account. That saved coming in to get the checks in person.

With his now customary "Go get 'em, Tiger!" Max sent me out to get the story so very important to me, the story I would start tomorrow. I wouldn't jeopardize the good spirits, so said nothing directly to Emma-the-Toad as I left, but neither did I breathe freely until once more safely in the hall.

Outside the building, I met a pretty young woman, probably college age, who asked directions to the office. As I gave them, I hoped the girl would survive better at Emma's desk than I had.

In the back of my mind, I knew I wouldn't want to be that young again, looking for a first job, and run up against Emma. I didn't really like feeling as old as I did some mornings, notably when a loved one, family or friend, awaited burial, but, at least, age brought the experience to cope. I thought, "The girl better be tough enough, or Emma will drive her away in tears."

Driving to the mall, I opened the windows to breathe the fresh Fall air deeply, to let the wind blow away cares. All in all, despite that hurtful skirmish with Emma, hate embodied, my morning went well enough. Max pronounced the very rare well-done for the story submitted, so, I decided to give myself a small reward. I parked near the doors which led to the mall food court and stopped for a light lunch at the restaurant where Norma and I enjoyed other meals in earlier, happier times.

"After all," I rationalized, "an afternoon shopping for new clothes and getting a new hairdo will take more energy than I got from the two cups of coffee I drank for breakfast." Too, I planned that stop at the range for practice on the way home. I wanted to reassure myself that I could do better than merely hitting the broad side of a barn. Without something for lunch during this full day, I knew my stomach would growl embarrassingly loudly before I made it home again.

The best restaurant tuna salad isn't ever as good as that made at home, but this place served some that is quite tasty. Sometimes, almost good food near and now beats out more tasty fare over there much later. This was one of those times. Happily, I settled for food available here and now, and planned to savor the treat sweetened because I won't have to wash dishes after the meal.

At first, I enjoyed the sandwich, the pleasant surroundings, and fond memories. Even under the cloud of my friend's death, I reminisced about happy times we shared in earlier outings.

Slowly, though, I began to feel that something was out of place. At first, I downplayed the anxiety. Perhaps Sid's rushed entry and undisguised vigilance during his visit unnerved me more than I wanted to admit. Maybe I just felt a lingering doubt or fear raised when Sgt. Grabowski reported that Norma had been murdered.

Failing to quell concern, I attempted to isolate, to examine, to identify the feeling. At first, I couldn't decide just what it was. Slowly, it came to me. Somebody watched.

Now I recognized a more concrete dread carried by the feeling, the certainty. This wasn't the casual if lingering glance of someone who eyed a room over the rim of their coffee cup to see who else was there. This wasn't just a lonely old man ogling a lone woman. This was being watched, observed, inspected closely, by someone in the surrounding crowd.

During the early stages of my transition, I became well acquainted with that feeling. Everyone we met reacted one way or another. Too few were genuinely friendly. Most were neutral, tolerant, albeit uneasy with the guy in a dress. Others, like Emma, were overtly hostile. All of them shared one commonality. They all watched to one degree or other.

I felt my hackles rise. This time, intuition whispered, whoever stared also held sinister intent. That raised goose bumps as a spontaneous shiver coursed through me. While I experienced this feeling before, the unwelcome nagging subliminal fear felt now spoiled lunch as it never had the times before.

I hurriedly finished the sandwich, paid the tip and bill, then left the restaurant. As I walked away, though, I was keenly aware of those behind and around me, much more so than I had been on the way in.

At my next stop, I expected few other customers. Anyone who followed me inside would be more visible than in any other place I could go. If no one followed, I could extend the visit so long that only a dedicated tail would still be outside when I left.

A short, brisk stroll later, I arrived at the small shop. Norma called this the Pro Shop, and didn't mean they sold golf equipment. Some women, when being catty, called it the Bimbo Shop. While not really a hooker's boutique, it would do until and unless such a thing ever opened. In here, shoppers for this style fulfilled their fantasies.

From the entry, a bright rainbow greeted the eye, punctuated by basic black and gleaming white examples of the displayed items. On the right side, two-tiered racks of exquisite blouses, sewn from jewel-bright colored or satiny black or white cloth cut on the bias to magnify even small busts, beckoned.

Arrayed along the middle aisle, similar racks were filled with short skirts tailored to hug, accentuate lower curves of hip and thigh with fine gauge knit or woven fabrics or supple leathers. Jackets to flaunt or disguise a figure, as the buyer required, hung along the far wall.

Toward the back, lingerie of lace and satin, designed by a man who liked sexy women, especially those willing to sacrifice comfort to titillate, tempted shoppers to spend. Displayed against the back wall, shoes and boots had heels not made for walking, but for looking sexy, and hosiery of every style to accentuate the wearers' legs.

Browsing the racks, I found three must-have outfits, then tried them on. I knew I had the look when, gazing in the mirror, I felt completely, wickedly sexy, almost naked even though fully clothed. While marked as my size, the clothes were a tad snug. Still, that tightness was part of the look, and I could zip or button them without strain. Remarkably, all of the styles wanted came in sizes that I could wear.

Undoubtedly, my efforts to find appropriate clothes succeeded because the manufacturers tried to meet the needs and wants of the younger market segment. I read a recent article which reported that girls are bigger, taller, heavier now. It must have been right, because several girls who looked like they played in the women's professional basketball league shared the salesgirls' time while I shopped. Self-conscious because of my size, I was pleasantly surprised. They made me feel smaller.

Stepping with my bundle from the shop into the main hall, I recognized some people seen in the restaurant. Most of them had new bags filled with purchases from neighboring stores, so it was unlikely any of them was the watcher. Of the rest, I wondered which one followed me, and who just meandered in the same direction by chance. Well, a stop at the salon will thin those ranks even more.

Another brisk hike through the main hall brought me to the beauty parlor at the far end of the mall. There, I explained the emergency nature of the visit without an appointment, and what I needed.

Consuella, skilled artisan and my regular hairdresser, listened, smiled, then fit me into the afternoon appointments. Resulting new hairdo and color, stylish worn with business suits, would scream that this is a woman-of-the-evening when worn with the new outfits. Both of us giggled, pleased with the profound change. As final step of the make-over, we selected cosmetics better suited to the planned subterfuge.

That part of advance vacation pay allocated for clothing nearly expended, I sauntered through the mall toward the car. Along the way, I dawdled several times to check store windows, but not to view the wares displayed. The crowd scene seen in them changed, except one figure who became all too familiar in the reflections. Dark haired, clean shaven, thin, taller than average, he wore a newer trench coat, and a brand-new black eye. At first impression, he might be a business man who was also a mugging victim, except that he toted no briefcase, and looked accustomed to fighting.

He had been on the fringe of the crowd since I first detected him at lunch. Now, he was obvious. No man I knew spent four or five hours merely wandering about in a mall without buying something - an hour maybe, but not more. He must have followed, and waited while I got the new hair style and makeup to be behind me still.

Who and what was he? I considered whether he was an independent agent. If so, was he a run-of-the-mall stalker, or a hit man? If he were a team player, which team did he play for? Was he one of Sid's guys, or the guy who made Sid nervous? Was he a police detective tailing me for some reason?

This wasn't the place or time to find out. At end of the corridor, I darted through the doors, crossed the parking lot at a brisk pace calculated to lose him or to force my tail into the open. I saw that he still jogged toward the other end of the line as I neared my nimble little sedan.

It lacked enough horsepower to outrun a pursuer on straight road, but could zip through corners at fairly high speed. Pursuit driving was the one course I passed with highest rank in my class at the Academy. Given these factors, I'd take the most winding roads in the area. I was confident that I could outrun him if I followed a scenic detour to my next destination. Still, the next time I buy a car, I'll get one with plenty of horsepower under the hood even if it burns a little more gas.

Ten steps away, I clicked the gizmo to unlock the door. Reaching my car, I grabbed the handle, swung it open, threw parcels into the back seat, jumped in and started toward my next stop with small squeal of protest voiced by the tires. Speed and violent maneuvers would confirm whether the trench coat truly followed, or merely traveled a parallel course by chance.

Headlights on bright exposed that he followed openly now. They glared in my rearview mirror, made it impossible to see who drove the car, difficult even to identify the make or color of the chasing vehicle. I turned from the parking lot onto the main road, filling a minimal gap in traffic. His car followed to the tune of angry horns and squealing brakes.

Heavy, end-of-the-evening-rush-hour traffic minimized chances that the tail would try anything drastic immediately. So many cars provided a surfeit of potential witnesses. He couldn't assume that all would claim, like the fabled monkeys, to have neither seen nor heard nor spoken evil.

Nevertheless, I was unnerved, and becoming upset. It had been a long time since anyone followed me, and, that time, I asked him to make sure I got home safely from the party. This uninvited escort provided an unpleasant experience. I wove through other cars, put more distance between us when I just made a light that stopped the pursuer. Often an aggravation, that traffic signal assuaged my anxiety. If the tail intended immediate harm, a red light would not have stopped him.

A quarter-mile farther, I turned abruptly onto Hill Road. Seven bending, curving miles beyond, I pulled in at the gun shop which offered an indoor shooting range. My tension eased as the short line of following cars drove past, but rebounded when I spotted the tall man in the trench coat in the driver's seat of the last car. I prayed the curve around the outcrop hid my turn in here, and the shadows hid me from his view well enough. I repositioned the car for a fast getaway if he came back.

Fifteen white-knuckled minutes that didn't help my nerves at all passed. He didn't come back. I relaxed again, but this close encounter of the unpleasant kind was all the excuse I needed to buy an extra box of ammunition to take home with me after I shot at some targets in serious practice.

Critiquing my own performance, scores on the bulls-eye targets were adequate, considering the extended interlude since the most recent previous practice session. Satisfied for now, I returned the rented hearing protection, then visited with Jerry, duty manager tonight.

If the fellow who followed today, or someone else on the other side, posed real danger rather than imagined threat, I would need to shoot well in a far more stressful milieu than a practice range. That meant practice to remind muscle memory what needed to be done should an overload of adrenaline and fear shut down my brain. I arranged to have Jerry coach a refresher session on the combat range out back during daylight tomorrow morning.

As we discussed my needs, Jerry commented, "Your old rucksack holds a lot, but too much stuff gets in the way. Let me show you some of the latest for ladies who need to carry."

Maybe Jerry didn't flaunt official credentials, but he won a gunfight with two would-be robbers in a real world attack when the opponents truly tried to kill. I counted myself lucky to have him as coach, rather than just somebody who could beat the clock in a contest where the cardboard and paper targets didn't shoot back. If he suggested something, the least I could do was to listen, and listen well.

"They're over here." He indicated the direction, and migrated toward a surprisingly impressive display of purses designed for concealed carry of a firearm, as well as transporting the usual contents in style. These were the fruits of our less polite, more violent society, in which many women now go forth as well armed as did the men of the old west.

With a sweeping arm gesture, Jerry started his pitch, "Now, any of these will hold everything you have in your old rucksack, but the compartments keep it all better organized than if loose in one big pocket. They'll keep your pistol separate and accessible so you can draw more quickly when you need it."

Jerry took a medium size, black leather bag that resembled Norma's purse from the rack and opened it to show off cavernous twin main compartments. His spiel continued, "Like this one. This is the edge over your rucksack." He slid an open hand into a slot, easily opened the back compartment to demonstrate built-in holster, pockets for two extra magazines, and a third, small flat pocket for the concealed carry permit needed to meet legal requirements. "And my girlfriend says it looks right whether you wear blue jeans or a dress." Jerry easily closed the sale.

As I considered the serious risks faced while on the trail of Norma's killer, this purse struck me as a practical, essential addition to my wardrobe. In fact, I paid for this tiny bit of reassurance with my own money. I planned to keep it after this case ended, and didn't want to argue with the paper's auditors over who really owned it.

As Jerry made change, he asked if I wanted the bag wrapped. I just shook my head and appropriated the end of the counter for work space to transfer the contents of old rucksack to new holster-disguised-as-a-purse before I left.

During the move, the forgotten envelope that Norma gave me last night came to the top of the pile. In light of the tail, and everything else, I knew it couldn't be just my writer's imagination. Whatever the envelope held was important enough to get a friend killed.

Clearly, I must give it to Sid when I see him tomorrow. Meanwhile, when alone, I'd have to open it, read it, try to figure out what it told. Curiosity allowed no other course.

Despite concern that I was tailed, uncertainty whether the person who followed was friend or foe, I reached the safety of my cottage without another incident. Passing through the living room toward the bedroom to drop my burden, I saw the answering machine message-waiting light blink.

I changed into something more comfortable, the sweatshirt and jeans so much better suited to a little quiet misery than anything else in my closet, and made a cup of cocoa. When I curled on the sofa, an hour and a half still remained before the late news. I just knew an important message waited in the queue if I merely ignored the waiting messages until morning, and was resigned to the immutable fact that they wouldn't go away by themselves. I had to listen to them sooner or later. It may as well be now. I sighed and pushed the play-messages button.

First up was Sid's short request to call the number he left as soon as I got home. He sounded insistent rather than anxious.

Second was a null message. The kind left when a phone solicitor's computer dials, gets an answering machine and thinks the resident picked up. The caller hangs up when they realize that no human is speaking. If no one is home, they can't raise any money for their candidate, cause, or charity by talking to a machine, so go on to bother the next person on the list. But, I knew I couldn't merely skip the message. A real caller might just start to speak after a delay.

Another dial tone message had the third spot. Tonight must have been a busy night for the fund raisers. I fumed silently, then cursed them, "A pox upon them all. If I want to give them my money, I'll call them." These calls are just electronic junk mail, and not as useful as real letters. Those, at least, could kindle a warming fireplace blaze when winter arrived.

A sip of cocoa calmed, yet, even allowing for the tension felt after being chased, I questioned my near tantrum. Why do these guys get under my skin so badly? Someday, when I have time, I'll try to figure that out.

Sgt. Grabowski asked for a return call as soon as possible in the fourth. I prioritized, "Well, Sid called before you did, Sergeant, so I'll talk to him first, but I will call you."

The fifth message surprised. This wasn't Mom's usual night, so I wondered why she called. Nothing important, she said, just wanted to chat. I'd take her word on that, and would phone her after the two who claimed some urgency. If I called before the news started, the time zone difference would let us talk before Mom's bedtime. I checked the clock. I didn't want to wake her-who-growled-even-at-me if awakened after she turned in, but I had enough time.

I dialed, and spoke after the machine finished its little speech, "Sid? This is Mickie. If you're there, pick up the phone. I don't want to play phone tag tonight." He came on the line with the excuse he was in the shower. Without chiding or teasing, I got to the point. "So, what did you want?"

Sid answered with his own question, "Wondered if you've decided yet. Will you go undercover?"

There was no purpose making him dangle in the wind, so told him, "I've got until tomorrow to answer that, but, I've already decided. Yes, I will. I have to do something tomorrow morning, but come over about noon. I should be home by then. We can talk over what I need to know."

"Thanks, babe. It means a lot to me to have your help."

I stopped him before he embarrassed us both. "Sid, quit that. I want to find Norma's killer as much as you do. If that helps you find the missing girl, that's okay with me. Just be here on time. Bring pictures of my contacts, plans for my backup, and anything else you think we need to talk over. Don't forget the little details, like who do I trust down there."

Sid complimented in his left-handed way, "See, I knew you were a tough enough cookie for this job. Until we meet tomorrow, take care. The Boogeyman is still loose. Bye!"

Any self-delusions of calmness disappeared as the thinly disguised warning sank in. The night could feel too long if I dwelled on the threat of a professional killer in the picture.

I called Sgt. Grabowski as the first step in combating that dread, although I only left a voice mail for him. After confirming his message, I reported that I would be out of the house during the morning, but asked that he call around noon tomorrow.

Mom answered after only two rings. She explained that she heard about Norma's death. I had no idea how she heard, and she didn't say. I guessed either Max or Sid called her, then thanked her for the moral support offered. She wise-cracked that it was just part of a mother's job description to care what happened to her children. Both of us laughed at that, one of Mom's standard lines, then said goodnight until our regular talk Sunday night.

I felt a little better. Crippling dread downgraded to mere caution, quite reasonable under the circumstances.

All the bookkeeping done for the night, I put my purse on the coffee table and took out the envelope. Once more, conscience argued weakly that I should turn it over to Sid still sealed, but curiosity demanded far more strongly that it was time to see what the envelope held. Curiosity won.

The envelope held a notebook written in Norma's flowing hand. Serving as bookmark to the last entry, a photograph showed a tall, thin man that looked very much like the man who followed me at the mall. He held the wrist of a pretty blonde girl that he led up the front stairs into a house.

The entry noted the address of the house, 1313 Calabash, a side street in the dock area. Norma's log indicated that, from where she watched this scene, he seemed to pull the girl up the stairs against resistance, to make her go somewhere she didn't want to be. A chill settled over me as I read the last line, "If we're lucky, this is only Case # 5!"

I flipped back to page one and read the investigation notes in sequence. An early entry revealed that, during initial inquiries about the subject of her search, Norma quizzed a source on the local police force. After reviewing files, that source reported requests for information and assistance from three other departments. Comparing those other requests with his department's records for the local case showed some similarities, but other details differed enough that no one would connect the cases unless they expected a link for some other reason.

Page 2 summarized the reports. Officially, four girls were listed as missing persons, not kidnap victims, because their parents had not reported any demands for ransom. Four jurisdictions examined separate cases, so each case was assigned to a different detective. Norma believed that normal snafues and interdepartmental rivalries thwarted communication and coordination between the departments involved.

Without effective liaison, they wouldn't see any but the most blatant connection.

Somehow, perhaps because she was an outsider without turf to defend, Norma connected her case and the three other recent cases of missing girls. Police traced the four girls from their schools to the downtown area. The clues led them no farther, even though these girls would have been obvious if working those streets. Norma had another piece of the picture they lacked. For the price of a tumbler of good Scotch, Weasel reported he saw some young girls near the docks. He noticed because that's a place where they had absolutely no reason to go, and several very good reasons to avoid.

Staggered by the information, I wondered what made Norma seek that tenuous thread in the first place. It gave me yet another thing more to ponder in the quiet of some later night. For tonight, I turned another page and continued reading.

The next entry noted the girls shared similar physical descriptions. Norma's notes coupled the two facts, stated her conclusion that the disappearances were connected.

Norma evaluated motives sufficient for someone to abduct the girls without asking for ransom. In a section headed "WHAT IF?", while not usually considered a contemporary problem, she listed 'kidnap into white slavery' among alternative reasons why four girls disappeared, seemingly without trace.

In the outline of this thesis, Norma speculated that some men with money and power desired young girls enough to pay somebody to procure one, or more, for their pleasures. She estimated that an infinitesimal percentage of the world population as customers, say one per two million, and an even smaller number willing to supply the girls despite laws against it, could support that trade.

Under Norma's premise, a white slaver gang committed all four abductions. Overseas destinations explained neatly why clues to the girls' whereabouts led to the docks, then ended there.

But, by itself, that could not explain why the clues ended there if anyone searched diligently. Norma felt the police investigations were frustrated by two more factors. The kidnappers took careful efforts to obliterate their trail. They were abetted by someone who knew about the investigations and was in a position to throw red herrings across the path whenever the investigators reached a certain point.

She noted an earlier case when a detective turned a bribe-blinded eye toward the evidence. Just one investigator had to be dirty, and only had to suppress any vague connections between the cases, to thwart the police efforts.

I closed the book at the last entry. Norma died before she determined the truth, so that job fell to Sid and those who worked with him. Starting tomorrow, I would be one of them.

The late news played, but I heard only the lead-in sentence for each story. Constantly, I revisited the white slavery thesis. I could not accept it immediately, but neither could I refute it with the scanty information available. The possibility that it was the true answer remained.

Now drowsy after a long, busy day, I readied for sleep. Last thought before the sandman came was that I would trust Norma's hunch. This wasn't the first time Norma guided me to the end of a trail I didn't see, but, unfortunately, this would be for the last time.

* * * *

In his living room, Stretch pounded the chair arm as he watched the late news. "Damn stoplight! That's when I lost her." He swallowed another two fingers of whisky neat. Straight whisky was tough on his incipient ulcer, he knew, but 86 proof sour mash eased his frustration quicker without mix, undiluted.

He recalled the day. Toad called this morning, told him that he could pick up her trail at the paper's offices. He got there before she left, then followed her. Through the day, she was always just up ahead, not too far, but far enough that she would not likely spot him. He was satisfied that even his long vigil at the mall went unnoticed, although he had to jog to his car to stay with her.

After they left the mall, he stayed a few cars back but still close enough to see her car. Then he lost her when she made the light that stopped him cold. That traffic delay was the last thing he needed while he tailed that woman, the one who was speaking to Norma Winslow when Casper made the hit.

She got too far ahead before he caught up. He lost sight of her when she turned onto Hill Road. He tried to close the distance. He even passed in no passing zones trying to re-acquire his target, figuring he would spot her if she just stayed on this street for a few miles more.

Stretch poured and swallowed another bourbon. He wondered why she headed away from town, not that it mattered. Earlier this evening, he figured it might have made it easier to catch up. Once past the last subdivision, there would be fewer cars to eyeball. Sooner or later, he'd get her, maybe where they would be alone, with no witnesses for miles around.

Stretch pushed, broke the speed limit, then realized that he was alone on the road, following only his own headlights. He checked the odometer. Stretch was twenty miles out into the country, at least seven miles since the four lane arterial street of city narrowed into two lane country road. That's when he admitted to himself that it hadn't gone well.

"Hadn't gone well? Hell! This was one of those days when the Fates poke you in the eye with a sharp stick, then let you hear them laughing at you." he thought. That's when he gave up the chase and came home. He would just have to try again.

A minor plot hatched through the warm cloud of the whisky. Maybe Toad could sneak a look at the files and find the woman's home address. An ambush was more certain. And a sure kill is what they needed, before she started to put things together. They - he, the boss, and even Toad and Nick - had too much riding on this caper to let it fail because some broads got nosey.

Stretch poured a last drink for the night. He noted the new quart bottle, bought on the way home, was only half-full. He shrugged, "Just like my life lately." Then he swallowed the whisky in the glass, turned off the TV and the lights, and joined his wife in bed.

Check the Flying Fish

JERRY WORKED ME HARD. HE YELLED constantly to build my stress level. He complained that I was too slow in his efforts to rattle me. Still, at session's end, he encouraged, "I'll bet on you to make it out alive if you ever have a gunfight, Mickie. And, I only bet on sure things."

Over a cup of coffee inside the shop, Jerry critiqued my performance. "Mickie, you need to use cover better. If you don't learn on the combat course, you won't get a chance to learn during combat."

He let the advice sink in, then continued, "On the plus side, you saw all the targets, even the ones hidden. You didn't shoot any friendlies, and scored solid disabling or lethal hits on all hostiles with few misses. You even cleared the malfunctions caused by inert cartridges mixed into the magazines without losing your self-control. You did well."

That helped my confidence more than anything else he said. I could face whatever lie ahead because I had the factor which prompted Jerry to make his bet. In Jerry's estimation, sang-froid, a cold-blooded self-control under stress, is the one thing needed to survive any confrontation. It's also the one thing that can't be taught, only developed. I thanked him for his time, paid up, and left.

As I eased out onto the street, I prayed I'd never need the skills and attitude relearned this morning. A mile closer to home, I determined, "But, if bad goes to worse, I want to remember the advice Jerry passed on this morning, 'Just keep your head when those around you are losing theirs.'"

If someone tailed me as I drove home for the noon meeting with Sid, they were damn good at it. I watched the rearview mirror carefully, but saw nothing suspicious. I knew better than to pat myself on the back prematurely, but tension eased with every block the rearview mirror showed that no one followed. Soon, all the butterflies settled.

It seemed to be going well, at least so far, a mere six hours into my new adventure. No, it's almost 18 hours since I spotted the tail in the mall. I can't guess how long he watched me before that. Well, whatever the clock, I am still all right.

Another minute, another thought contemplated. It's an interesting mix of emotion to be both hunter and hunted. I don't recommend it for the faint of heart.

Without recognized threat, mundane concerns overtook me instead. A small internal rumbling announced it was nearly time for lunch. Checking my watch, I figured I had time for a cold sandwich before Sid arrived.

Streets and stores became more familiar as I neared home. Sanctuary was just one more turn, a few blocks more, and the rearview mirror was still empty. As I neared my house, I checked cars parked along the curbs, recognized all as those which belonged to neighbors.

After parked and inside, breathing a little easier, I mused. Just three days ago, I blithely made a similar short trip. I wasn't concerned that anyone followed. Today, I expect sinister interest by person or persons unknown who murdered Norma. I felt a grin arrive with the next thought. At least I'll eat my lunch before the feces impacts the ventilator.

The grin faded as I built a sandwich meal. Despite efforts to keep an open mind, to consider facts without biases that blinded me to other possibilities, Norma's conspiracy notion had rooted deeply in my thoughts. Some additional detail might show another option, but, for now, it explained the data better than any other theory I tested against the known facts.

Shortly, I finished the sandwich and sipped the last of my coffee while waiting for Sid. The coffee pot stood just that one cup below full, ready to fuel the brainstorming session Norma's notes would ignite once he saw them.

At quarter to noon, the phone rang. Before the second ring, I remembered the voice-mail message left for Detective Sergeant Grabowski last night. He called a little early, but the sooner the better. I had a lot to finish before evening. "Good Morning."

"Ms. Stevens, glad you're home. This is Detective Sergeant Grabowski. I've got a few questions more, if that's all right."

"Sure, Sergeant. Ask away."

"You've had a little time to think. Have you remembered anyone who might have wanted Norma Winslow murdered badly enough to have hired a hit man, or who might even have killed her himself?" Chet queried.

"I told you about that first case that brought us together. I remembered more details later last night. Art Limburg made a few thinly veiled threats during the trial that sent him to prison, but I don't think he knew how to hire anybody to carry them out from his cell."

"You say Art Limburg? Was that the arson fire set to hide an art fraud? That also killed the watchman? Happened ten years ago?"

"Yes, that's the case, Sergeant."

"I'll check on him. Ten years is long enough that he might have taken Revenge 101 at Gray Stone U. He might even have made some contacts to help him follow through on the threats."

It seemed time to tell him a bit more. "And since we talked, I found out that Norma was working a case. She wasn't hooking to support herself, just using it as a cover."

"Who told you that?"

"Sid Koenig. He knew that Norma and I were close friends. He stopped by to console me a little when he heard she died. I carried on about the shame that Norma turned to prostitution, and he said she didn't. Then he explained that they were working on a case." That was enough to ease him into the same line of inquiry without dragging him too far down the trail I followed. I didn't want him to follow that trail too far in case that path turned into a dead end. I cut off further questions along those lines, "Before you ask, I don't think I'm at liberty to say which case, or give any details before I talk to Sid. But you can call him directly if you want to ask him."

"Thanks, Ms. Stevens," Detective Sergeant Grabowski said, "Your answers will help me check a few things. I may call if I have more questions later, but that's it for now."

"You're welcome, Sergeant. I should mention that I think I'll be busy for a while myself. You can leave a message on my machine, and I'll return your call as soon as I get home. But, if it's something really important, call Sid Koenig. He'll know how to reach me fast if I'm not here. And you can call me Mickie."

The phone call ended just before noon. At noon, a car pulled to the curb behind my car. Once parked, Sid carried a briefcase up the walk at a brisk pace, slowed only by the time I took to open the door for him. As a leaf before a gale, he made another explosive entry, punctuated only by a momentary pause to look back over his shoulder before he entered the living room.

Pleasantries exchanged, he dropped his coat across a chair, and took a seat on the sofa. That perch allowed use of the coffee table as makeshift workbench, and offered a vantage point for intermittent observation of the street outside. As I poured his coffee and warmed up my own cup, Sid stacked folders taken from his satchel in the corner of the table. He then selected one and spread out the snapshots it held.

I handed over his coffee, commented, "We have a lot of pictures to look at. I have one more you need to see." His quizzical look begged for explanation.

I breathed deeply, and apologized, "I'm sorry Sid, but, during your first visit, I forgot about the envelope Norma asked me to deliver. I found it when moving my things into a new purse. My curiosity got the better of me. I looked inside, read the notebook, and studied the included photo."

Instead of anger, relief sounded in his exclamation, "So that's where it went. I worried it got impounded in the evidence locker with her purse, we lost it, or the other guys got it." He gathered the photos before him into a neat pile as he instructed, "Get the notebook and picture. Let's look at them first. These will wait."

While I fetched the requested items, Sid asked, "You read her notes? What did you make of her theory that white slavers snatched these girls?"

"I don't know that I buy it all the way, Sid, but I can't think of a real argument against it… Just because the girls lived in different towns and went to different schools doesn't mean the kidnappers aren't the same people. One common thread is that all four trails led to the docks before they faded."

Placing notebook and snapshot before him, I concluded, "It may be coincidence or conspiracy. Either way, four girls are missing. I wouldn't overlook the possibility that they were all snatched by the same people just because we don't have a concrete physical link yet, but I wouldn't hang my hat on it, not before we have that tangible connection."

Sid responded, "I know what you mean. When Norma first told me, I wrote it off. Figured it was just her fondness for conspiracy theories getting the better of her. The more I thought about it, though, the less sure I was that she was only grasping for straws." He paused, sipped at the java, resumed, "It sure would be easier to answer some of the questions if it's true."

I opened the notebook to the last entry, and let Sid study the photo. "Sid, this tall thin man followed me at the mall. He's wearing a fresh black eye now."

Sid related, "An informant said this man passed an envelope to the triggerman who tailed me."

That confirmed connection between the two, hired gun and thin man, warned we were already in the middle of something. I filled in another blank, "Just before she died, Norma warned this is big enough to get us all killed. I hope that she was wrong."

Sid detected my concerns, and eased them when he reopened the first folder to spread some photos around the table. He stated, "You wanted to know who to trust and who would be your back up on this job. Here they are." Pointing to the top picture, he identified, "Gwen and Harvey told me you already met them. They're good people. You can trust them with your life."

"I hope it won't come to that, Sid, but it's good to know they're on our side. I liked them."

Sid grinned, "But don't trust Harvey with your good liquor. He's got a weakness for the hootch. He doesn't talk, but he's a little too slow to help when he gets tight. That's why Gwen keeps him on the beer. He doesn't like it enough to drink too much."

A brief flashback to that night prompted my next question, "Sid, what do you know about the big retired sailor, Bruno? He was there that night, too."

"Don't know for sure. Gwen says he's all right, but admits that he's been a customer for only a couple months. While she's right a lot of the time, she has been wrong, too. Bruno could be in the middle, or on either side, as far as we know. Be careful around him until you get him pegged." Sid advised.

I wanted an answer that would let me trust Bruno, but if this was all that Sid knew, I'd have to be careful. Getting careless could get me dead. I didn't feel ready to shuffle off this mortal shell just yet, so that option lacked appeal. At least Bruno wasn't connected to the adversaries so clearly that I had been warned off.

"So, who else is on our side?" I asked.

"Huey, Dewey, and Louie." Sid chortled as he dealt three pictures from the stack. After the array was readied, he identified each in turn, "Bill Hughes, Al Dewey, and Martha Lewis will be your contacts. They'll pose as Johns. Take them upstairs to pass along anything you learn. Study these photos so you recognize them, even if they wear disguises."

Sid dealt the final pair of photos as he said, "You may see these other two, Teddi Ames and Felicia Gonzalez, down there also. Their assignment is surveillance and photography."

Sid concluded the picture show, "With the address in Norma's notebook, we have a discrete target to watch. We won't have to run around the whole neighborhood. If any of us see anything you need to know about, I'll get word to you. If it's a rush message, I'll send it through Gwen. Otherwise, we'll update you at the meetings upstairs."

Now was my time to come clean. "Sid, just before you got here, that detective, Sgt. Grabowski, called. I just had to tell him Norma was on a case rather than hooking. He might have gone the wrong direction if he thought she was a prostitute, or killed because she was with a transsexual and possibly one herself. We might find the missing girls, maybe even find Norma's killer, but we both know the District Attorney is more likely to prosecute if the police bring the case. I told him to talk to you about details… I also told him to call you if he needed to reach me quickly."

Sid didn't seem openly perturbed, but he clearly wasn't overjoyed either. We sat silently as he considered this complication. When he looked ready to continue, I asked, "So, what's the plan?"

"You know it's dangerous. This is your chance to back out if you're not committed to it completely." Sid counseled, offered me a graceful retreat if I had doubts.

"I should be committed for getting into this, Sid, but I want to go through with it. I owe Norma a lot, both personally and professionally. This is my chance to help square the books. I'm doing this one for an old friend." I affirmed enlistment in Sid's troop for the duration.

"I counted on that, Mickie. I figured you were tough enough to take the job." Sid lifted his hand, waved about, then put it back on the table to fumble with the photos.

It seemed to me that he resisted the impulse to rest his hand on my thigh as he spoke, even though he could get away with it without a black eye this time. I remembered our romance, and wondered whether a small ember still smoldered in his heart, although the fire cooled years ago. He did that himself. Before his government sponsored field trip to southwest Asia, he told me that I was like his sister. Too young, I didn't recognize what was a damn fool act of unselfishness. He freed me to find someone else because he didn't expect to come home. Now, I figured, two ex-wives and several former girlfriends since his return kept him from showing whether he still cared today.

I noted his restraint because, usually, he patted my shoulder when he encouraged me. This time, he was much more formal, didn't touch me at all. Was this some gesture of respect, or some signal he wanted to change the relationship but didn't know how? Whichever was a concern for later, after the case was solved.

As he put the pictures into their folders, Sid outlined, "If you're ready to start tonight, I'll call Gwen. We should meet with her before the bar gets busy. I think we both need a nap before the late night ahead. Get a couple hours sleep while I phone around to set some things in motion. I think we need to get to the Blue Onion about six tonight, so set your alarm for five. Wake me when you get up if I'm not up before you."

I acquiesced, obeyed the field commander, "You're in charge, Sid. Yes, I can start tonight. And I'll be ready to get to Gwen's by six."

Sid grunted acknowledgment, then dialed the first of his contacts as I retired to the bedroom. I don't usually nap in the afternoon, but knew I had to be fresh tonight to have a chance.

* * * *

Two blocks from the Blue Onion, Bruno paced the length and breadth of his small walkout apartment. Gwen telephoned about an hour ago. She swore him to secrecy because he wasn't supposed to know, but she trusted him. Gwen reported that Mickie would start at the bar tonight, working undercover to continue investigating the case that cost Norma her life.

Bruno agreed to pretend that Mickie was a long time fixture there, as long as she worked as a waitress, not a hooker. Gwen said she would take care of that. She herself thought Mickie was more the barmaid type, rather than a sportin' girl.

And, Bruno decided, during his fifty-seventh lap, that he would be Mickie's shadow to the extent she let him stay that close. That would be the best way to protect her, he figured. Six laps later, he admitted that he didn't know her well yet, but intended to overcome that little obstacle. He wanted to get to know her very much indeed, not just for a roll in the hay, but for a long term relationship.

Maybe that was the source of the nervous energy he expended by wearing a path in the carpet. Bruno didn't want to lose her before he got to know her, before he sorted out whether she was the one he wanted to spend the rest of his life with.

He snorted to himself. Why did he think about that so soon after he met her? Was it merely because she was pretty? No, he decided, while she was pretty, there had to be something else.

What drew him to her? Bruno wanted to know whether the fascination had just been too much beer and a late hour, or if the connection between them, between their souls, had been real. So many women brushed him off with a callous "Who cares?" She listened to him without showing boredom, helped fill his loneliness that could be cured only by sharing it with someone. He felt that she really cared. That, he reckoned, was the real spur to his interest. If only she feels drawn to him. He sighed.

Bruno set his alarm clock for 6:00 P.M., then forced himself to take a short nap in the reclining chair. He wanted to be fresh and rested during his watch this evening. The hour of sleep would help him fulfill his duties as protector of the possible future Mrs. Bruno Grabowski. He wouldn't lose her like his brother lost his girl, not without a fight, by God!

* * * *

Nagging foreboding of evil soon to be confronted woke me from my nap a half hour before the alarm sounded at five. I stared at the ceiling fan. If I try to get more sleep, I'll be groggy when the bell rings for the next round. Good thing I don't need a lot of sleep. I rose and started a pot of coffee. Checking, Sid was still asleep on the sofa, stretched out and oblivious to the world. I'd let him sleep a few minutes more. Meanwhile, to the tune of the coffee maker's happy music, I started to put on makeup, the official war-paint for my coming battles.

Between powder and blush, I paused. Scrutinizing image reflected by the mirror, I decided Adrenaline could offset lack of rest, at least for this one night. For the rest of this trip to the dark side of life, I'll be a night hunter. I'll need a few nights to adjust my biological clock to sleep through the days and prowl when it's dark. But, others did it. I could.

Applying tips and tricks Consuella showed me, I painted a face scarcely recognized in the mirror. New, transformed appearance engendered similar change to attitude. By the time I combed and brushed my hair, I almost became a working girl, ready for whoever and whatever the world threw at me, provided they paid very well for the privilege of my company.

New fuchsia silk blouse, open one button too low over push-up demi-bra to reveal cleavage, topped the short black leather skirt worn over thong panties and thigh-high stockings. Black four inch heel pumps were in disregard of my height. Gaudy jewelry iced the image. A line of movie dialog succinctly described the woman looking at me from the full length mirror, "I may be easy, but I ain't cheap!"

Just one minor glitch appeared. The clothes went on easily, but I struggled to don the new attitude, the new persona without reservations. A small, faint voice whispered objections from the back of my mind. I wasn't raised to be comfortable in this role. Contradicting conscious efforts to accept the guise and enjoy it, subconscious doubts surfaced. Could I overcome the taboos Mom spent all of my youth enforcing?

I had to try. I had to act my way through the doubts to maintain cover. My life, perhaps the lives of friends, might depend on my ability to convince others that I AM what I appeared to be.

The qualms only came in spurts. When busy with something else, I didn't feel self-conscious. Simple resolution promised cure. I have to stay busy, whatever it takes.

In the kitchen, I poured from the fresh pot of coffee. Glancing at the clock, it was time to wake Sid. Moving to his perch on the sofa, I ran fingers down his back, feather-gently at first, becoming ever so slightly more vigorous with each pass, until he roused to a firmly gentle touch. As he roused, Sid's eyes became wide with the realization of who I was and where he was. He sat up and lamented, "To think I slept out here! Damn, but you look good."

Through forced laugh, I retorted, "Thanks, Sid, I needed that, even though you're just saying it to make me feel good." I knew it was just some of Sid's applied psychology. That thought changed when I realized how openly his gaze fondled me. *So this is how it feels to be desired, not necessarily with affection, but just with outright lust.* I struggled with the unaccustomed feeling.

"Sid, there's fresh coffee in the kitchen. Help yourself while I pack my purse. Be with you shortly." While I already loaded the purse with everything needed tonight, I wanted a little time to compose myself after his unexpected reaction. It would never do if I became noticeably flustered by such attentions while on assignment at the bar. It's not the reaction the seasoned old salts expected from an experienced virgin, a pro, a soiled dove, a prostitute. The old taboos had triggered my reaction. I must learn to accept such blatant interest without becoming openly embarrassed.

After composing myself, I joined Sid at the kitchen table. "Better have Gwen pave the way with an explanation that I'm new to the trade. The way you reacted was unexpected. It really set me back, and that won't do if I'm approached as an experienced old timer, just if I'm inexperienced."

Sid comforted, "If you were shook, you never showed it. But you better be ready for a lot of interest. You look as fine and foxy as anyone I've ever seen."

This time, I felt much more comfortable as his stare brushed over me lightly, lingering on certain attributes. With a little difficulty, I ignored his interest to ask, "Should I follow you to the Blue Onion?"

Sid answered, "No, I've already garaged your car. You'll ride with me, then use Norma's Corvette until this is over. It fits the image better than your old sedan." He swallowed the rest of his coffee, "It's time to head out. I need the time to brief you on the plan as we ride over. Gwen expects us there by six. Get your coat and purse. Let's go."

Sid had only two speeds, full stop or flat out. He had the pedal to the metal now, and wouldn't slow down until we caught the murderer. I would be running to keep up for however long that took.

"Okay, let's go!" I experienced mixed enthusiasm and dread. Nothing is so daunting as a headlong rush into the unknown, a dash into danger from a place of safety, nor no quicker way to get the adrenaline flowing at flood. Fueled by that hormone, we swooped toward the car.

A thought struck from ambush as I scurried forth. Damn, I've been a spy for less than a day, and I'm already starting to get used to the uncertainty, the ambiguity. I wished my drama teacher could be here now to see how well I act this part. She said I couldn't act, gave me the only 'F' grade I ever got.

In a flurry, we were on the road, headed to the docks at maximum legal speed. Sid ignored the differences between green and yellow lights, stopping only for full red as he outlined the plan. Subject to adjustments as circumstances warranted, I'd spend nights at the bar of the Blue Onion until known in the neighborhood. When well enough known to be accepted as part of the regular crowd, if I were careful, I'd be able to snoop around without arousing undue suspicions.

While I played my part, Sid and his agents would seek intelligence from other sources in other milieus. Jointly, our efforts should uncover enough to find the culprits, or, at least, lead in their direction. Once we collected enough facts, we'd turn the data over to police to make the actual arrests.

After Sid finished, I quipped, "That sounds like a plan. I just hope it works." I had to believe it would, no matter how hard the sell, or should never start this masquerade.

Sid grinned broadly, "Nothing to it, Mickie. With my looks and your brains, we can't fail."

Sid's explanation used almost the whole trip. I recognized landmarks from the interviews for the story submitted yesterday. He turned a block short of where I expected he'd go, then made another turn into a paved lot behind a row of buildings. As he shut down, he announced, "Here we are. Yellow Corvette there is your ride until you quit this case. Come on. Gwen's waiting for us."

Sid was out of the car and headed across the lot by the time I merely gathered myself for the task ahead. Quickly, I followed him toward the only lighted door. The single-bulb fixture illuminated the faded rendering of a blue onion which identified our destination. Arriving first, he waited with hand on the doorknob. I caught up to him, then checked my face in the compact mirror. After quickly touching up powder and lipstick, I took a deep breath, then nodded.

At the signal, Sid encouraged under his breath, "It's opening night and you're on, Mata Hari. Knock 'em dead." Touching my arm, Sid whispered, "Head toward the bar. If Gwen wants to talk about this play, she'll meet us part way." Then Sid swung open the door with enthusiasm befitting a coachman opening the carriage door for a monarch newly crowned.

I noted the flourish, "No matter what else people say, you have a flair for the dramatic." Sid grinned, hung back just a little as my entrance turned all heads toward me.

Following the instructions, but wondering whether Sid hung back to watch over, or merely to watch, I headed for the bar. The sway of my hips was unplanned, but natural, unavoidable in the high heels I wore. Besides, deep down, I knew that it was in character for my role in this drama. I was pleased. Finally, the boys at the bar paid attention, after I had been overlooked as too plain for so many years.

Well, as long as my admirers remain polite, I could get used to having men interested in more than just my mind. Immediately, as if self-administered antidote for a poisonous thought, I suspected I just coped with the silent infatuation of men who hadn't given a second look before, at least not this decade. I dropped both thoughts. I had a job to do. It was just the uniform for that job which brought the almost embarrassing stares of strangers.

Movement caught my eye. Harvey took the bartender's post behind the bar while Gwen came out. She met us part way, and directed us to a quiet booth in a back corner to discuss the plans.

After we sat, Gwen's first questions assured me that I might just really pull this off. She asked, "So who's the new doll, Sid?" Without waiting for the answer, she probed, "And, when does Mickie get here? It's Friday night. We'll get busy pretty soon."

"It's me, Gwen. Do you think I'll do all right?"

"Good God, girl! Is it really you? You sure fixed up really nice, not at all like that plain girl who came in here two nights ago. Bruno will shit when he sees you!" Gwen exclaimed. "Oh! Speaking of Bruno, I think we need to change the plan a bit."

Sid, with an edge to his voice, asked, "Change it how, Gwen?"

Gwen continued, "After we talked earlier, I thought about how Mickie and Bruno hit it off. I like Bruno, and so does Harvey. We don't want to hurt him, even through an honest misunderstanding. None of my barmaids hook, at least not during their shift. Maybe Mickie should be a barmaid instead."

After a pause to let the idea sink in, Gwen reasoned, "That keeps her mixing with the crowd. She gets known by the regulars sooner, but she doesn't risk her cover if she refuses to go upstairs with a John. Besides, moving around the tables, she should hear something quicker than if she waits for somebody to slip up and spill the beans during pillow talk. Really important stuff is rarely mentioned, so depending on pillow talk is something you can count on only in books or the movies. Hearing something discussed while you wait tables is a lot surer way to find out what you want. Even that's iffy."

A thirtieth of a second later, I concurred. "That's a great idea, Gwen. Sid flustered me when he said I looked good. Shook me up enough that I don't think I'd be comfortable presenting as a pro when I hardly even date."

Sid interrupted, "But how do we get Mickie alone to pass along what we learn and find out what she's heard?"

"Figured I'd have her work from the waitress station at the bright end of the bar. Nobody sits there unless we're really crowded. It's almost as private as one of the rooms upstairs. Those walls are awfully thin, Sid, and some of them have ears." Gwen offered.

Quiet reigned for a brief interval as we considered this alternative. Sid broke the silence, "Okay, then that's the way we'll go, at least for now. We'll see how it works. I'll tell the others about the change. But I've got bad news for you, Mickie."

"Now what, Sid?"

"Give me the keys to the 'Vette. No barmaid would have the money to drive one unless she won the lottery, and then she probably wouldn't still work as a barmaid. I'll get my stuff out of my car, then I'll be back in to leave the keys. I'll pick it up at your place tomorrow, and you can use your car for the rest of the time." Sid pronounced.

As I dug the keys from my purse, I tried to extract the chance to drive it. "At least promise that I can drive it once after this is over, Okay, Sid? Here are the keys." I was surprised by the whine in my voice. Until that realization, I hadn't really appreciated how badly I wanted to drive a Corvette for a few weeks. Oh well, maybe I'll get a chance to drive it later.

Sid snatched the keys from my fingers and headed out. Despite the disappointment, I was rid of a big problem. This revised plan erased misgivings that I would not have done well in the intricate role of a prostitute, despite every effort made to convince myself that I could have done it. The ride here had not taken long, but it had been a long enough ride for misgivings to bloom anew.

Taboos for good girls and boys, learned across Mom's lap and reinforced by vigorous applications of the flat side of her hairbrush, had risen in revolt. They overwhelmed and eroded the tenuous initial flush of confidence felt when I first dressed for the role I thought I would play this night.

Gwen interrupted my private thoughts with new instructions, "While he's doing that, I'll show you where to put your things while you're working. He can be your first customer when he gets back." She led the way to the waitress station, bounded by the usual chromed rails, next to the end of the bar. Quizzical eyebrows framed her face as she voiced the next question, "You ever waited tables in a bar before?"

"It's been a few years, Gwen, but I did it for a story once. At least I'm sure that I can pull off being a barmaid better than I could act a whore. I kept having second thoughts about it on the way over. I kept trying to think of another way. Thanks." The confession brought a wan smile to Gwen's lips.

Gwen consoled, "Not every girl is cut out for the sportin' life, Mickie, and I don't think you are. You seem to be a one-man woman." Then, sighing, she pointed to the top shelf under the bar, "Put your bag here, and you'll be able to watch it. I guess you're carrying, but if you can't reach your purse and need help or back up, I've got a gun at the register. Harvey may be an old geezer, but he's a pretty good street fighter to boot, should it come to that. Hang your coat on the rack, and I'll get the other girls over here to meet you. The Friday night crowd should keep us too busy for introductions later."

I ensured I left nothing in the pockets, slipped the coat onto a hanger, and left it on the rack. By the time I finished that brief chore, the others were gathered around my station. I tried to relax, then joined them.

Gwen introduced Harvey officially, then Sharon and Kim. Sharon was about my age, thin, quite attractive, and as tall. Kim was quite a bit younger, a bit shorter, but pleasant, pretty in her own way. My costume was appropriate for the job. The other girls wore similar outfits.

Then Gwen assigned work stations for the night. "Sharon, work the front end near the door. Kim, take the middle. Mickie, you have the back end, last three booths and five tables, from the tail of the swordfish to the back wall."

"Thanks, Gwen." I croaked the answer with rising nervousness. I fought it off and relaxed.

After the others returned to their posts, Gwen advised, "You shouldn't be too busy, but, if anybody hatches a plot in here, they do it in back. Listen and you'll learn a lot. Just don't blush too red at some of the crap you'll hear." She smiled harshly, added, "Oh, almost forgot. Tell me if any of the drinks are for working girls. I mix theirs a lot weaker than I do for the guys. Get a little perverse pleasure watching a guy get so drunk he can't walk while the girl is still sober, even if she matches the guy drink for drink."

"Sure, Gwen. I can do that... Here comes Sid."

Sid clambered onto the stool next to my station. "I'll have a mug of draft, please, Gwen." He laid a five dollar bill folded to conceal a set of keys onto the bar.

Gwen snatched the money with a flip of the wrist that propelled the keys onto the rubber mat behind the bar. I reached behind the bar, retrieved the keys and deposited them in my purse as I grabbed the pack of cigarettes with the thought, "Pretty smooth moves for a new team."

Sid quietly confirmed the conclusion as he offered to light my smoke, "I see you have a talent for this sort of thing. You did that as well as some of the old pro's." He paused to sip his beer, then asked, "Mickie, ever think about doing this for a living rather than working for that paper?"

"Is that a job offer, Sid?" Remembering his reaction to the way I was dressed at the house, I teased, "Or a proposition because your girlfriend left you, and I'm dressed this way?"

Sid grinned wryly, "As a matter of fact, yes. Talk to me about it later, provided we get out of this in one piece." He returned his focus to the beer in hand.

A half dozen merchant seamen entered in a rush, then swaggered to the largest back table. Duty called before I could decide which question Sid answered. Either was an unexpected offer, but it would be a while before I could find whether Sid were serious about the job, or solicited a changed relationship because he just suffered from the Friday-Night-Alone-Blues. I smiled as I approached the incipient mob scene, "What will you boys have?"

The gray-bearded one at the far end spoke, "Schooners all around, missy."

As I served their beers, the self-appointed chief of table unfurled a pick-up line so old that it had false teeth, "Hey, if I told you that you had a great body, would you hold it against me?"

"Sorry, that's not in my job description. I just serve your drinks." I was a bit surprised that I said it. In fact, I didn't know where it came from, but it must have been from a corner of myself rarely if ever explored. I smiled warmly to take the edge off the cold, cutting reply.

Silence descended like a falling wall. Then young sailors laughed raucously at the old timer's expense. I almost felt sorry for graybeard, occasionally having been the butt of others' jokes. Before I apologized, I saw him flash a large roll of green. Hell, he doesn't need my sympathy. He'll find company easily before night's end, especially if he waves that around.

Graybeard unfolded the thick wad of bills to pay the tab. He cooly flaunted it to signal that he intended to have a good time regardless of cost. If this barmaid didn't want it, there were a number of fallen angels at the bar quite willing to help relieve him of his tensions for a small part of his bankroll.

"Six schooners at $3.00 each, that's $18, please." I stated flatly.

The graybeard dropped a fifty on the tray with his own rejoinder, "Stone-hearted Lady, bring another round. I need balm for the deep cut you just gave me. And keep the change if you tell one of the girls who does have it in her job description to get over here. This is our last night in port, and we won't be back this way for a while."

The young sailors around the table laughed again, and I felt a lot less sorry for him. He could hold his own in a match of wits. Old scars and long-healed broken nose showed too that he wasn't afraid to fight when he felt the urge, or the necessity, to enforce his will, at least try to do so.

As I conveyed the re-order, I asked Gwen, "Is it always like this?"

Gwen assured, "Usually, but the sailors quiet down when Wanda and her apprentices join them. Those girls will take their minds off hitting on you in short order."

I only half-heard what Gwen said. Another worry surfaced just now. Where has Sid gone? I'd be more at ease with a friend at my back in case of trouble. And, I expected trouble, as quickly as the table of boisterous potential drunks finished that first round. Already, even before Gwen finished drawing the second round, I needed to take away their emptied glasses from the first. They'd keep me busy.

That thought was no unmitigated joy. I had been on my feet for only a half hour, but already knew that four inch heels were a mistake. I"ll wear two inch heels tomorrow night.

The graybeard shouted above the din that all the other patrons made, "Hey, Bruno! You old salt, join us for a beer!"

I half-turned to face the back door, and watch the hulk of ample-protection-in-tough-times enter boldly. He left no doubts that he was A top dog if not THE top dog in this or any other joint where his travels might take him. I hoped he'd be on my side if needed.

Bruno strode directly to the noisy table. He greeted Graybeard, "Manny, you're not in port for dry dock, not the way you're drinking. Just get in or shipping out soon?"

"Sailing on the morning tide." Manny replied as he pulled a chair from the adjacent table. He slid it toward Bruno, "Here's a chair. Come on, take the load off your pins. Anchor in this slip at least long enough for a draft with me and the boys from my deck crew."

Manny and Bruno claimed one end of the table for their reunion, forcing the younger ones to shift perceptibly down toward the other end. I loaded seven freshly filled schooners on the tray, and, with a deep breath, headed to their table.

Bruno got his beer first, then Manny, who paid for this round, then the rest of the table. On the second turn around the table, I picked up empty glasses. In the background, Manny goaded Bruno about getting priority service, getting a beer without even having to order it, then quietly announced, "They're here."

Glancing toward the front, I spotted a squad of Cupid's paid retainers file through the door. From Gwen's earlier statements, I guessed that Wanda was at the head of the column, followed by her crew. Their flamboyant entry allowed no doubt they wanted to be noticed by all the mere mortals. Only the blind, or the blind drunk, could have missed them.

Wanda halted the march to visit with Gwen. It seemed Gwen gave

Wanda her targets for the night, because she started straight back for Manny. Her girls followed in trace, to meet the other sailors at the back table, to separate the eager youths from their pay.

And, I realized how much more I could observe as part of the staff than if I had been fighting off one of Manny's boys instead of waiting tables. Gwen had a really good idea to station me at the back of the bar.

Manny saw them coming, quickly added his seven and their six, then ordered, "Thirteen at a table is bad luck. Boys, spread out, have a good time." He turned to the next-senior rating next to him. Without mocking fidelity, he instructed, "Jeff, since you're saving yourself for your wife, take charge of this detail. Stay sober enough to get these guys back to the ship by 04:00 if I don't make it." As he put his arm around Wanda's waist, once she was near enough, Manny spoke to Bruno, "Come on. We've got a lot to catch up on before I take this winsome lass some place more private."

With that, Manny moved his beer to the back corner booth still in my section. Wanda and Bruno followed him. Two other sailors moved to an empty table, trailed by two of the girls, while the first table still held six.

The new arrivals might need a drink, so I started around again. My feet hurt, and it seemed I'd get no rest soon. I wondered if I'd ever hear anything other than tired old pick-up lines if this kept up. The writers don't ever write about the drudgery of covert operations, just the exciting parts.

As I neared their booth, I heard Bruno ask Manny, "Still on that same old tub?"

It looked like a fight just before fists fly. Manny leaned forward, wagged a fist under Bruno's nose, asserted angrily, "The *S.S. Flying Fish* is no tub." His eyes flashed, belied by the broadening smile. Then he leaned back to laugh, "She may be a tramp and a rust bucket, but she's not a tub! Yeah, I'm still sailing on her."

Bruno laughed with his friend, two who shared some inside joke. He sipped his beer, then asked, "So, you sail with the morning tide. Where to? And when will you get back here?"

"Mediterranean cruise this time, spend the winter trading warm waters. Scheduled to dock at Bordeaux first. Got a load of something or other the French want. Then we'll take on what they have that somebody else wants." Manny paused, wistfully sighed at a stray thought. "At least it's not the Murmansk run my Dad made… Remember the Bogart movie about merchant ship convoys to Russia during World War Two? My Dad said, on the best trips, the North Atlantic was at least as bad as they showed, and often worse." The table went quiet with private reminiscences.

After a decent interval, I butted in. "Another round, guys? What about you, Wanda?" Gwen must have passed the word, or Wanda had it happen before, for Wanda didn't act surprised that this new waitress knew her name though they never met before. She just ordered and returned to the conversation interrupted.

I took their orders and empty glasses back to the bar. While waiting for Gwen, I wondered what they talked about now.

I delivered two beers for the sailors, and one mostly colored soda water for Wanda, while the three spoke of people and times gone but not forgotten. While their greetings made it obvious that Bruno and Manny knew each other, it seemed Manny and Wanda had a history too, spent together whenever he was in port. Briefly, I speculated how many more Wanda's around the world shared a past and present, but no future, with Manny. I knew it was stereotyping, but asked myself anyway, "Do any of them have even the slimmest chance at a future with the old rogue?"

No matter that their yarns aroused reporter's instincts and human curiosity, I couldn't neglect my other customers without compromising my cover. Yet, more than my feet hurt when I turned to that task. My heart ached. When Norma died, I lost a friend with whom I shared such closeness, even after I changed. Maybe Bruno, or someone else, could share a bit of life with me later. Reluctantly, I admitted that Sid wasn't the only one who suffered from the Friday-Night-Alone Weeps.

The Blue Onion offered rooms upstairs. Officially, those rooms were where a patron could sleep it off after that last one too many rather than report for duty still hammered. Unofficially, Gwen and Harvey never asked whether for single or double occupancy. Soon, Manny got a key, and went upstairs to 'nap'. Wanda followed Manny upstairs. Their nap would be quite short, if they slept at all. A few others from that boisterous crew also took advantage of the rooms.

As suddenly as it had swelled, the crowd in my section thinned. I gathered emptied glasses left behind. I would have a chance to sit down for a little while, after I delivered used glasses to the bar to be washed and readied for the next wave.

I scanned the crowd. Bruno didn't go upstairs, but sat at the bar next to my station. When I returned with the last tray full of dirty glasses, he said, "Gwen says you started working here tonight, but I'm supposed to act like you've been here a while." His gaze swept over me, caressed me. He murmured, "Damn, Mickie, you look good." Even at my age, I fought the blush rising to my cheeks. Didn't work. I blushed. Only the dimness kept it our secret.

"Thanks, Bruno. You look well, too... Have a good talk with your friend?"

Bruno answered, and said more than he knew. "Old Manny? Sure did. I've always liked his stories, but, this time, his blue eyes are about as brown as they can get. He expected me to believe that, while he checked the cargo hold hatches last night, he saw the Captain of his ship take a passenger on board. That old tramp steamer hasn't taken passengers for years, especially not young, good-looking blondes traveling alone. He's just been at sea too long or something." After sipping at his beer, he continued, "But I've never known him to lie. Sometimes he doesn't see what he thinks he did, but he doesn't lie."

I touched his arm. "Bruno, maybe he just saw the Captain take some company aboard. Even Captains get lonely. Don't they?"

"Sure they do. But Manny said she never left the ship. The two guys who brought her aboard left after just a few minutes. Even a new Captain knows better than take his woman along." During following lull, Bruno turned to people watch.

Jeff sat alone. Abandoned, deserted at the big table, he nursed a coffee. The little bimbo who would have listened for a fee found a more generous companion. Bruno commented, "Guess he didn't want to spend $100 an hour just to talk. Wonder if he'll pop $3.50 for a beer to have somebody listen?"

I realized that not all sailors have a girl or two in every port, and recognized a fellow sufferer of the blues. I didn't object when Bruno joined Jeff, tried to cheer him out of the loneliness brought about by separation from his wife and family. Besides, customers already seated and more just entering would need a drink. That would keep me too busy to talk, even if that was what I really wanted to do.

I made the rounds of the customers still in my section. For the thirsty ones, I delivered another round of drinks. For the ones already gill-full, I brought coffee. The routine was now clear despite the first night jitters felt earlier.

* * * *

Stretch cringed as he listened to the grating voice. "You know that I took a hell of a risk to get you this address? They could fire me for poking about in the personnel files." Toad scolded Stretch because she had to cover for him again. "Can you handle it this time?"

Stretch decided that, if Toad weren't so useful, she'd be totally repulsive. He responded, "Yeah, I can handle her."

Toad ragged on, "If you didn't know all the ships we can use, I'll bet the boss would have fed you to the fish by now."

Stretch winced inwardly at the thought that she might be right. His stomach churned against his ulcer, did a double back flip. His brain hurt just to think it. After all, he headed the export function only because the boss had, in fact, fed his first partner to the fish after a minor dispute. His latest screw-ups were worse than the one that got Smokey killed.

Stretch decided that he needed to watch his own tail. The boss might be ready to replace him, already searching for another with his connections to step into his shoes. His thoughts leaped forward. If it didn't work this time, he better have a letter on file with his lawyer. At least he could take the son-of-a-bitch down from the grave. The thought of vengeance from the grave made him shudder visibly. He was grateful that this was a phone conversation, so Toad couldn't see him.

"You're awfully quiet, Stretch. Did that hit home, you incompetent weasel?" Toad challenged.

Stretch wanted to retort, "Just remember, when they're hungry enough, weasels will eat toads, Toad!" but Stretch bit his tongue. Instead, he let his silence confirm that the idea he could be replaced disquieted him. He breathed deeply, then gave her a safe answer. "Yes, the idea bothers me, but I can do this right. I just need the chance to pick the right time."

"Okay, Stretch, I won't say anything to the boss until next Friday. If you haven't been successful by then, you better hope you can swim with cement boots." Toad didn't say good-bye. She just slammed the receiver down.

Stretch wondered what Toad held over the boss. She wasn't pretty enough to actually be his girl friend. Hell, in Stretch's book, she wasn't even plain, but flat out ugly, two-bag ugly. And, unlike many of the heavy set women he knew, she didn't have a pleasant personality either. It was more like concentrated sulphuric acid.

Stretch decided it was more than enough to deliberate a next attempt on the woman's life without worrying about the boss or Toad. And, he decided, he'd do that thinking after supper with his family. He smiled at the blessing the fates gave him. Yvonne, his wife, was a good cook, and pretty. And she loved him as much as he loved her.

The phone jangled again. This time it was Nick, good old Nick. "Hey, Stretch, what's going on?"

Stretch answered, "Supper. Just a minute." He didn't cover the mouthpiece, just lowered the phone as he yelled into the kitchen, "Hey, Vonny, is there enough to ask Nick over?"

"Tell him to get his butt over here before it gets cold, or burns while I keep it warm." The affirmative from the kitchen was loud enough that Stretch didn't have to ask. Nick heard and accepted the gracious, if you knew either Stretch or Yvonne, invitation.

Nick had been laid up with aches and bruises from the beating taken a couple days ago. Stretch supposed, because Nick would share supper, that he had healed enough to take part again. Likely, Nick would still move a little slowly, but in a few more days, he would be back in top form.

Stretch weighed waiting yet another day until Nick could help with the next hit attempt. Nick wasn't a good shot, but he was a damn fine wheel man, the best Stretch ever rode with. Stretch could do the shooting if Nick did the driving. They'd make their plans after supper.

* * * *

While Bruno and Jeff talked, Gwen quizzed, in tones used by an employer to new hire, "How's it going? Feet tired yet?"

"They're killing me! I must have been at that desk job too long, Gwen. I never used to feel this tired after only a few hours." I answered, then asked my own question, "Can you call Sid tonight?" Gwen nodded yes.

As an agent reports to her contact, I reported to Gwen. "Tell him to check out the *S.S. Flying Fish* before it sails on the morning tide. Manny said they have a passenger onboard, an attractive, young blonde girl. Bruno says that's unusual for that tramp steamer. Might be a lead."

"Sure thing, Mickie, I'll pass that along." Gwen responded. Then she alerted, "Second wave is due soon. Sit a bit longer, but don't let your customers get thirsty."

Not one to ignore an unsubtle hint, I puffed once more, then stubbed out half-smoked cigarette in the ashtray. As I made the rounds to check the customers, Gwen made a call. I presumed it was the call to Sid.

Two newcomers in the first booth in my section ordered a first round. Jeff needed a refill for his coffee, and Bruno wanted another schooner. Two sailors at another table said nothing, preoccupied with topping each other's tales of past voyages to the brink of disaster, but signaled they'd take another round.

When I returned to stand between the chromed rails of the waitress station, Gwen was mixing drinks at mid-bar. After she arrayed the glasses on Kim's tray, she approached to take the orders. I noted that she still had a spring in her step that belied her age and time on her feet. "How do you do it, Gwen?"

She responded, "Been doing it a long time now, kind of used to it. Makes a little difference, a little easier to stand, that this is my business, and I want to turn a profit. Can't do that in a little place like this if I had a hired bartender in every night." She paused, then warned, "Just remember to stay alert even if your feet hurt."

I felt left behind at the gate. Maybe the pain in my feet slowed my mind, or I had not practiced enough for the speed at which everything seemed to happen. Gwen was gone, back to mixing drinks at the middle of the bar, before I figured out what she meant.

In fact, I almost turned away after delivering drinks to the first booth. Images from the photos Sid showed her came back to me. "So, what else, Huey?"

Huey smiled, "Wondered if you'd recognize us or we'd have to introduce ourselves." Then he turned to his companion, "You owe me a buck, Dewey. She figured it out by herself."

"Will Louie be here tonight?" I used the question to screen. The answer would tell, confirm this meeting wasn't coincidence.

"Martha stayed home tonight." Dewey quipped. It was the answer needed to confirm the tenuous identification from photos not studied long enough. I confided, passed along the information about the possible female passenger on the *S.S. Flying Fish*.

Al Dewey grunted into his beer, "That shoots our night off." He looked up, "Guess we better check it out, Bill."

"By the way, I asked Gwen to tell Sid. Confirm that he got the message, okay? You guys stay safe." Both grunted, unhappy about their short night off. I resumed my rounds, Bruno's table next.

"Here you go, Jeff, coffee black, and your schooner of best dark draft, Bruno. Would you like anything else?" I wanted to bite my tongue as Bruno looked up with sly, roguish smile.

He suggested with wanton leer across his lips and in his eye, "Mickie, we'll talk about that later." Then he shrugged, sighed, "For now, this will do." With that, Bruno turned back to Jeff and talk of ships, their captains, ports-of-call and such. While he may accept his life as it is, clearly, he still missed the sea.

The third table paid for their beers without interrupting their yarns. Before going back to the bar, I collected the dirty glasses. Bill and Al had finished and gone in that brief span. The other table was empty now also. I had time for a cigarette and a short sit-down with the momentarily small crowd. It hadn't seemed so long, but the clock now showed 1:00 A.M. as it chimed twice.

Wanda descended the stairs, followed closely by Manny. They signaled for service as they rejoined Jeff and Bruno. So much for my rest. Shortly, the rest of the men came downstairs, followed closely by their companions for but an hour or two. The resulting mob once again filled my section.

I hustled to and fro with drinks and empties. At least moving made the time pass more quickly. Unexpectedly soon, the back-bar clock chimed four bells.

Manny and his crew downed the last of their drinks. They gathered themselves, then flew out the door as suddenly as they had blown in some hours earlier. They sallied forth in search of their last land breakfast for several days. Most other patrons already made similar exits.

I gathered last of the emptied glasses and took them to my station. As Gwen moved the glasses to the sink, she offered, "We ought be quiet the rest of the night. Only a little while until we close, anyway. Don't want to overwork you your first night. Why don't you head home? See you tonight at 6:00."

Disregarding the subtle dig contained somewhere in that offer, I accepted. "Thanks, Gwen, but I just want to sit a minute first." I took my purse from its resting spot, and sat at the bar. Bruno joined me, sat on the next stool as I lit a smoke.

"Done for the night?" he asked.

Exhaling, I answered, "Done, and nearly done-in. Didn't remember waiting tables was this tough until a little while ago." After a second puff, I quizzed, "Did you have a good visit with your friends? Did Manny have any more tales too tall to believe?"

"Yep, I did." Bruno sighed, "Just that sometimes, when I talk to guys shipping out, I miss the sea, and wish I could work another cruise ... " His voice trailed off, speaking eloquently of his yearning. "But Gwen will kick us out of here pretty soon. As long as I'm a shore-bound man of leisure, what do we do with the rest of the night?" He probed for an invitation.

Without my usual caution, I took the chance that he would be an understanding gentleman. "Well, if you promise to behave yourself, you can come to my place. I haven't had supper yet. While it's late for that, maybe I could cook you an early breakfast. I'd enjoy the company."

"Separate bunks after, I presume?" Bruno verified.

I nodded, "Yes, that's the arrangement tonight."

"Well, Mickie, I would like a little breakfast, and the chance to talk to you without interruptions."

He paused to consider, although I felt I safely could bet a week's pay that he was just playing the game according to the rules as he understood them. I knew he'd say yes before I asked him to come over. And, I guessed that he knew I would ask. Inexplicably, we connected far more deeply than our short meetings might suggest.

"Okay, I accept, limits and all, but next time, you come to my place. I may not be a great cook, but I can make an edible breakfast." Bruno grinned his mischievous little boy grin, not at all like the leer I saw earlier.

I called to Gwen, "I'll be back tonight." I went to the rack, retrieved and donned my coat. Taking purse from the bar, I placed my arm in the crook of his arm. Bruno led the way out the back door to the parking lot. Once inside Sid's car, we headed to my place in light late night, early morning traffic.

* * * *

Not yet used to the aloneness since his girlfriend left him, Sid left the bar early. He had been ready for sleep, but two phone calls brought news, pumped that fresh energy of an adrenaline rush through him. First, Gwen called. Not half an hour later, Bill and Al called.

Mickie thought an old sailor's implausible tale was important enough to pass along through two separate messengers. The young woman passenger on the *S.S. Flying Fish* might be the missing girl. That made it crucial enough for Sid to act immediately.

He checked the mirror, and approved of his seaman's garb, even with the small bulge where the coat fit too tightly over the shoulder-holstered pistol. Sid felt sure he would look like just another wharf rat while they watched the ship. And, like the wharf rats, they would hide among the piles of cargo stacked along the quay, watch without being seen. Even if spotted, they would look like they belonged there. They could be seen without being noticed, invisible in plain sight.

Sid made coffee, filled his stainless steel quart vacuum jug, and drove to the docks. On the way, he brooded about many things, but one thought returned most frequently. "Blending with the background is the secret to effective surveillance. You can't wear a suit and tie, and just sit in a late model sedan with pizza boxes and coffee cups piled on the dashboard. Sometimes they showed it that way in the movies, but that is the wrong way."

Sid knew he had to become such an integral part of the scene that the subject didn't notice even if looking right at him. While he occasionally got cold and wet doing it this way, he saw more, sometimes even heard things, that helped solve a case. Even if he just trailed a cheating spouse for a divorce, the client deserved his best effort. This case was a lot more serious than a divorce, and called forth resolve that Sid didn't know he still had in him.

A half-hour later, Sid met Al and Bill outside the Port Authority Office, open even at this hour because there were ships in port. Inside, they applied for passes to drive within the fence erected long ago to prevent wartime sabotage. Now, without patrols of armed sentries, it barely reduced thefts of cargo. The obliging clerk on the overnight watch chatted while he issued the tags still required by the old rules.

Misled by the ruse that they wanted to visit a friend before he sailed, the clerk provided the map given to new delivery drivers. He marked their direct route through the warehouses to Pier 2 and noted that jetty was long enough to dock four medium sized ships. Once he started talking, the clerk divulged that the *S.S. Flying Fish* was berthed to starboard. He cautioned them to watch out for heavy machinery because a second ship, berthed port side, took cargo aboard even at this hour. Sid ranked that as a good thing. Bustle better cloaked an observer or two, even if they had to dodge stevedores, front-end loaders, and cranes.

As instructed, they parked in visitor spaces near the shore-end warehouse servicing Pier 2. They faced a long walk to a post from which they could watch the ship, but walking was part of blending into a nondescript background rather than standing out as a threatening foreground detail. Only bigwigs or cops drove a car onto a pier where right-of-way belonged to longshoremen shifting mountains of cargo.

Sid mentally measured distance from his car to the selected vantage point, not in yards, but in the time it would take to come back without giving away their disguises. The survey prompted a change to the initial plan. One of them would stay with the cars to follow any interesting traffic that might visit.

After he opened the car trunk, Sid leaned in, hunted through the tools-of-the-trade stored there. In seconds, he emerged with three sets of compact headphone walkie-talkies. Compared to top-end units shown in the trade journal and specialty equipment catalogs, these were merely cheap toys. They had short usable range, and couldn't encrypt messages, but, Sid figured, serious smugglers would never suspect he still used radios which transmit in the clear. Those guys often had the latest gadgets. It had been so long since anyone, on either side of the fence, used ordinary Citizens Band radios that his simple spoken codes usually worked well enough.

Besides, these were cheap. Sid made a point of telling his agents that these were reasonably inexpensive so his agents could use them when at physical risk without fear of bankruptcy if they lost or broke one. That gave them one less distraction that might get them killed. The radios were replaceable. His people weren't.

Sid turned to his sidekicks, detailed his plan as he doled out radios and fresh batteries. "We'll flip for it. Odd man stays here. The other two amble onto the dock, find a good spot to watch the ship. If anyone leaves on foot, one stays to keep watch, the other follows. If the target catches a ride here, or if somebody drives up to the ship, the one who stayed back takes a car and tails the visitor to destination, if possible. We'll keep in touch on these radios. Keep the chatter to a minimum. These things transmit in the clear on an open channel. Okay? "

Al and Bill nodded to signal that they grasped the simple plan as they dug coins from dungaree pockets. Three coins glinted in the night air as they acted out the coin-toss ritual. Al showed 'heads' on his quarter when they compared results. He would stay with the cars, so wished his friends good luck.

As if they belonged, Sid and Bill swaggered down the quay. They disappeared into shadows of pier pilings and stacked boxes, far enough out of the way that moving machinery would not threaten accidental injury. From there, they could watch the entire length of the ship, but weren't exposed to casual observation. They settled in for a long watch which would end only after the ship sailed from port.

Pro Bono Publico

NOISES FROM THE KITCHEN WOKE ME with a start. The bedside clock showed only 9:00 A.M., yet somebody unfamiliar with the kitchen rifled cupboards, searched drawers, drew water from the tap. Initial goose bumps shrank as the coffee maker began to gurgle. A friendly elf made the racket. Shoot! Bruno was making coffee. He behaved well, quite gentlemanly, last night, and I almost forgot he was here during slumber.

Aroma of brewing coffee greeted me as I pulled on a robe to join him. Bruno wore his tee shirt, revealing scars on his arms, but he still cut a fine, muscular, athletic figure in his dungarees. Gwen was right. Even with the patched eye, he could make a girl's heart flutter, and he didn't do so badly with we who had lived a few years beyond girlhood. "Good morning, Bruno. You're up early. Sleep well?"

"Well enough, allowing I'm at least one size bigger than the sofa where you billeted me." he teased. "Figured I could at least make the coffee this morning. After, I'd appreciate a ride home."

"That's fair enough. Let me get dressed while the coffee brews." Blessed by his smile, I returned to the bedroom. Whatever emerged from the closet, it certainly would be something I could wear with my favorite walking shoes. The long night in heels made me really appreciate their padded comfort.

In honor of my guest, I selected blouse and slacks. They were nicer than I usually wore this early in the day, but still casual, comfortable, just the thing for running errands with a handsome man riding alongside.

When I rejoined him, he had put on his shirt, poured the coffee, and served some toaster pastries. Small talk, time later for serious conversation, accompanied the brew, and made strong counterpoint to the aloneness I often felt in the morning.

Aloneness, yes, that's the word. Most of the time, I wasn't lonely. After all, I was on quite friendly terms with myself, but there were days when I so wanted someone to share the little pleasures. Walks in the park, some quiet music, that sort of thing always seemed so much more fun when someone I liked came along. And, yes, there were those days when my aloneness downgraded to outright loneliness.

Bruno broke into the reverie, "You look far away."

"Just thinking about something."

Bruno roared with mirth. "I know a little bit about that from personal experience. Got to watch out for that thinking stuff. It can be dangerous!" His good eye focused on me, but the look was gentle, as he added, "Especially some of the thinking I've been doing lately."

Daylight, filtered through the kitchen window curtains, lighted his face. He was much gentler looking today than that first night when I thought he was so fierce, so dangerous, a modern day pirate.

"You have a philosopher's soul, Bruno." We laughed. I felt we had become more at ease with each other. I mulled a sudden question and answer. What's that term some of the other women use? Soul-mate, that was it. While I'm not sure that I use the word the same way they do, I know I feel a closeness to this large man which cannot be explained, given the short time since we met. I just hope that we aren't star-crossed lovers, destined for an unhappy end.

I broke the comfortable silence that friends share, "I have to make a call, arrange to return the borrowed car to the guy who loaned it to me. Then I'll get you home. Will I see you at the Blue Onion tonight?" I blurted the last question without thinking, then hoped I didn't sound too anxious.

Bruno confirmed the plan, "Sure, to all three parts." Wide smile beamed from his face, "Especially the last part."

"Imagine, having such a case of the warm fuzzies at my age!" The admission came with a smile. I rose, and as I passed on the way to the phone, bent down and kissed his cheek lightly. The old salt actually blushed!

Bruno recovered by my return. I asked, "Are you ready?"

"That wasn't a very long call. Guess I don't have to be jealous." he teased.

"Just told him, well, actually his machine since he didn't answer, that he could have his car back, pick it up, anytime. And no, you don't have to be jealous. He's the friend of a girlfriend." I was getting the hang of telling the truth without saying anything.

Of course, Sid had been friends with Norma. They couldn't work together successfully if they weren't friends, at least friendly, and shared a mutual respect for each other's professional prowess. But Bruno did not need to know that I meant the friend who died Wednesday, or the friend with whom I worked to find the killer, not yet anyway.

We got our jackets and headed out. The trip to his apartment took only a short time, filled with pleasant banter.

I was halfway back to my house before I noticed the tailing car. Damn, where did he come from? Hackles on my neck prickled, goose flesh erupted with the question. Knuckles whitened on the steering wheel while I struggled for self control. If I examined the situation calmly, logically, a far higher probability was somebody merely headed the same way without actually following me. The city holds too many people to expect sole occupancy of the road wherever I drove. Still, caution could too easily turn into paranoia, especially since the day I was shot.

The car stayed back far enough that I only saw outlines of figures in the car, both a driver and a passenger. The image of a driver and shooter from the movies haunted me, upset me.

Norma's quiet warning now shouted from memory, "This is big enough to get us all killed." I felt the adrenaline flood my system. I just hoped the cavalry would arrive in time if the tail were related to the case rather than just someone on the same route by chance.

This turn from the major artery onto quiet secondary streets of my residential neighborhood would tell whether I were followed, or just shared the road. I watched the rearview mirror carefully, as intently as

I could and still pay adequate attention to the road ahead. Oh, Damn! They are following!

Home, and a phone to summon reinforcements, was just a block farther. If they remained as far back, didn't speed up, I had a chance to make it inside before they closed the distance.

I turned into the driveway and parked next to Sid's car. That it was still here said he hadn't been by yet. Maybe he'd arrive soon, the cavalry that I hoped could keep me from being scalped. "At least get here before I join Norma at the Morgue." I broadcast the thought as I reached inside my purse. The small pistol gave me the chance to make them pay dearly if they attacked.

I bailed out as the engine stopped, and briskly strode to the door of sanctuary. As I reached the top step, the trailing car slowed, then parked in a spot across the street. Darkly tinted windows hid the identities of the two inside. Those windows look nice, but now I knew why the police don't like them. I couldn't see whether foe or friend, threat or solace, resided within.

I fumbled with the lock as the visitor's passenger door opened quickly. A figure alighted. Peacoat and dungarees indicated a sailor, but, as he turned to come around the car, I recognized Sid. The adrenaline ebbed. I felt so very tired. "Sid, you scared the daylights out of me. I thought I was being followed by that trench coat, or one of his cronies, again."

"Sorry about that, but there wasn't any way to let you know it was us." Sid explained as he neared. "Still, it's good to know you can spot a tail. You're damn good at this stuff, you know. You could do it for a living."

Temper flared, "Cut the crap, Sid. I could do it for a dying just as easily." Then, vented, anger subsided, although so short lived that I wasn't sure whether I was angry with myself for being frightened so easily, or at Sid for scaring me.

Once anger dwindled fully, I almost laughed aloud as I thought what the neighbors might think. A man who obviously spent the night left only a little while earlier. Now two more, dressed like sailors, arrived. My reputation, at least with the old biddy who lived next door, was shot.

Oh well, that wasn't a great loss. We hadn't ever been friendly, just civil to each other. Once again calm, hospitality displaced hostility. "Would you two like a cup of coffee?"

Sid waved, and Bill joined us. I opened the door, and we went inside. Two sat in the living room as I went through to the kitchen to start fresh coffee. An advantage of my just-big-enough house is that dialogue between occupants of different rooms is possible without shouting, just by speaking a little louder. As I dumped leftover coffee from the first pot, then scurried between cupboard, sink, and coffee brewer, I asked, "So, what's the report from the *S.S. Flying Fish*?"

Sid spoke. "That tall thin man, the one who keeps popping up in this case, took a girl aboard just before they sailed. Since it looked like she was fighting him, we passed the word to Chet Grabowski. He's the detective in charge of the missing person cases, including our clients' daughter. He said he'd alert Interpol. They'll be watched when the ship docks at Bordeaux, just in case."

"I thought Grabowski was with Homicide, Sid. How did he get assigned to investigate the missing girl cases too?" I wondered aloud.

Sid scowled, "They give Chet the missing person cases too. Often, he finds a body at the end of the track, especially of young girls when there's no ransom demand. He's good at his job. If there's any scent at all, he'll trail them and find them," Sid paused, added unabashedly, "especially with our help."

Serving fresh hot Java, I challenged the pair sitting in the living room, "So! What do we do in the meanwhile? Just sit on our butts?"

"No, we keep at it. The girl taken aboard today wasn't the girl we're looking for." Sid explained. Then he asked, "Gwen told me that you said a sailor talked about a girl taken aboard two nights earlier?"

"One of Bruno's old chums talked about it at the bar last night. Bruno called him Manny, but I never heard his last name." I recounted, "He said they brought a passenger onboard the night before, an attractive blonde girl. Bruno thought that was strange, maybe curious is the better word, because Manny also said that ship hasn't carried passengers for quite a few years."

"If we didn't see the same girl taken aboard twice, there are two on board. Bill, call Grabowski, tell him this new piece." While Bill dialed,

Sid continued, "By the way, we checked on your friend Bruno. He's the genuine article, as near as we can tell, and he's Chester Grabowski's older brother."

"I thought they looked a lot alike from that first night I met them. But how did they wind up … ? Oh, never mind! If Bruno is one of us, a good guy, I'll have time to talk later." Too many thoughts crowded my mind, fought for priority. I needed a minute to sort them, but didn't get it.

Sid kept speaking, working through an idea aloud, bringing the others along the same path, dragging them along if either balked or tarried. He did the sorting for all of us, and brought me back to focus on the larger problem. I could almost hear gears whirring and grinding as Sid thought. I just couldn't tell which brain, his or mine, made all that racket. Maybe it was both of us, for we reached the same thought closely together.

Sid proposed a working hypothesis that fit the known facts, "The girls would draw attention, suspicion, if they traveled by air or on a regular cruise ship, especially if they tried to land without passports or visas at any place customs is set up to handle visitors. If they were ever detained at one of those places, it would be all over." Sid sipped his coffee, then continued, "But if they send the girls out of the country by tramp steamer, that might explain how they get away with it. Those old tramps haven't carried passengers for years, just crew and cargo. They might just slip somebody through the cracks if they traveled that way. A hat big enough to hide her hair, a jacket, and a pair of dungarees are all the disguise they'd need to get a girl ashore as a crew member going on liberty."

"Sid, we should check whether the *Flying Fish*, or any other tramp, was in port around the time those other girls disappeared." Bill contributed, just a half step behind the power curve, but catching up fast.

Sid answered so quickly, obviously he already had the thought. "I'd bet we won't find many of the old tramp steamers still afloat. A friend at the Port Authority can check that on her computer. Grabowski can get us dates for other missing person reports. That will show whether there's any possible connection."

Sid paused, added with sudden concern, "We better find out if any girls went missing at other ports visited by that old scow or her sisters. We know four local girls went missing recently. Norma logged a possible fifth case in her notes. Then we saw a girl taken aboard ship this morning. I wonder. How many more there have been over the years?"

"If this is international, maybe that's what Norma meant when she warned about the danger, that we could get killed if we found out too much." The realization stunned me, even as I spoke it. "I always thought it was bad enough when the crooks spoke poor English. Be a real can of worms if they speak Russian, or German, or French, any of the other languages."

"That's a no shitter, Mickie!" Sid added, "When my friend checks dates when the *Flying Fish* was in port, I'll have her check the registry, find out what flag the ship sails under."

"Is this for real, or a red herring, Sid? I don't want to track a false trail."

"Mickie, we'll know that only after we check it out." he answered.

Another car pulled in front. Sid recognized Al as he came up the walk. Allowed in, Al waved the manilla envelope he carried. "Hey, Sid, Bill, Mickie. Wait until you see these!"

Sid interrogated, "See what, Al?"

"These photos we got yesterday from the surveillance on that house Norma found. Real interesting stuff! And the picture of the girl taken aboard the *S.S. Flying Fish* this morning came out." Al shot back as he spread the prints across the coffee table.

In the first photo, the tall thin man, who seemed to be everywhere this case took us, stood in the open door of a house. It looked like the same house shown in the snapshot Norma passed along the night of her death. He spoke to a squat woman who stood on the porch with her back to the camera.

Surveillance notes indicated the caller passed a thick envelope to the occupant. It was just barely visible between the two on close inspection of the second picture.

The third picture chilled me. The woman faced the camera to descend the stairs. I recognized her immediately, "That's Emma, my editor's secretary. Well, she certainly has the attitude to do this kind of thing to innocent girls... Then again, to her, no one is an innocent."

"Then this only helps us." Sid noted, "If she's asked directly, she can explain that she just bought a manuscript. Nothing we know would refute the claim. It would be our word against hers, and we're just talking theory, not facts. That's not enough evidence to get her arrested."

"Shit, Sid. Emma is in this to her eyeballs. If she isn't in charge now, she's not very far from whoever is, and already plots to take over soon. I wish her to hell if Norma died at her order."

Sid's eyebrows almost raised off his forehead at my unexpected outburst. As he learned more about Emma, he speculated the position on the paper gained her access to details somebody just walking in off the street would never learn. A clever interviewer could learn bits and pieces during a conversation that later assembled into an accurate sketch. Grudgingly, I admitted that Emma was a good interviewer.

Sid asked, "As the editor's secretary, could Emma arrange bogus appointments with coeds looking for work?"

I answered, "Yes, she could. It wouldn't be difficult to pretend to interview while she sized up a potential victim. And she wouldn't keep any official record that the girls ever visited. The trail would end downtown while one of the other gangsters took the girl to the docks."

Almost all pieces were in place. The last surveillance photograph of the house at 1313 Calabash showed the thin man talking to another man while they stood on the porch. Both Sid and I recognized Detective James Philips. A close look showed a thick manila envelope. The notes with the pictures specified that the envelope passed from the tall thin man to the detective.

I wondered aloud, "Is that a cash payoff so Detective Philips turns a blind eye? If it is, are both partners bad, or just the one in the photo?"

Sid mulled over the prospect. "Maybe we should go slow on what we tell Chet." He thought briefly longer, then professed his conclusion, "No, I've known Grabowski a long time. I trust him. My bet is that Philips is bad all on his own. One thing, Philips is in a position to stymy any probe once it reached the docks. Or give a warning because others were getting too close."

Al brought out the last picture, enlarged to show detail, "Here's the picture we took at the docks."

Taking a look, my stomach churned. "I can't be sure, Sid, but I think that's the girl I met in front of the paper. We didn't talk longer than I needed to give directions to the office, but ..."

With each additional piece of the puzzle, Norma's theory grew stronger. A gang of thugs shanghaied girls for white slavery and sent the girls to foreign ports. That also presented a serious obstacle. Members of that gang would be unlikely to spill enough during any interrogation by legal means to ever find those four - no, six - poor souls.

And, that was only the number we knew about. We might find the most recent victim, but the others disappeared long before. They were probably gone, shipped to God knows where, lost to their families forever. That sad thought haunted me, as it would haunt their parents when told their daughters' fates.

My emotions had no balance, no center, right now. I swung from extreme anger to extreme sorrow with each new thought. I fought to control them, eventually won, and resolved that I would stay in control until this case was over. Then would be my chance to cry.

Overriding sorrow, I fumed, "I'm pissed - excuse my French - angry. I feel like evil barged into my home with these photos and notes. That violated my sanctuary. The only way I know to exorcize it is to find enough information to have the kidnappers convicted of their crimes at trial and executed. And, we're not getting anywhere nearly fast enough to suit me!" I took a breath.

During that pause, Sid remarked, "Excuse my cynicism, but when we catch them, they probably won't even do life. Too many criminals are scarcely punished for capital crimes. They get a slap on the wrist negotiated through a plea bargain."

Sid's comment bothered me. I suspected the courts might prove inadequate for the job. The crooks might get a lenient sentence even if the District Attorney presented an ironclad case sealed with voluntary confessions made while their lawyers were present. Just to vent frustration, I fantasized that I could torture the perpetrators to extract confessions from them.

That was the best I could hope, that is, unless they attacked me and I could kill them in a fair fight. Presuming the girls were lost forever anyway, the criminals' deaths would put a permanent crimp in the distribution system. For me, that would provide surer closure than wishing some too-often-too-lenient judge had the stomach to jail them forever if they escaped the death penalty.

Mute, grim faces and slumped shoulders showed the others held similar, albeit unvoiced, thoughts. In the silence, I knew it wasn't civilized, not politically correct, but this case seemed to cry for a little vigilante justice, like in the old western movies I used to watch with Dad. These thugs deserved to swing from a tall tree by a short rope until the buzzards picked their bones clean, and the coyotes dragged the bones away.

I reminded myself, "But I'm civilized. Dissatisfaction with wimpy judges is my right as a citizen. My duty as a citizen is to live by the law."

Sid finally spoke again, "There is no guarantee the conflict between what we want and what is will ever be resolved. There never has been, and probably never will be. It's part of life to cope with that dichotomy. Even the Constitution only guarantees the right to pursue happiness without any promises that you'll find it."

I gave final voice to my hopes. "And maybe, just maybe, the judge will be an old-school hanging judge this time. One who reads corrected translations of the Old Testament where the commandment prohibits murder, not justifiable killing, and that the punishment for murder is being put to death by someone from the community where the murder took place. That would give the bad guys what they deserved, and ulcers to the anti-capital punishment crowd. At least I can hope so."

Al contributed, "These bums deserve it, but a lot of people say the death penalty doesn't keep anybody from committing a serious crime."

Bill concurred, "Yeah, I've heard that argument myself. Okay, so maybe the death penalty won't stop a murder or kidnap. One thing sure, an executed murderer won't kill again. That can't be all bad."

Our quartet pondered deep, dark thoughts in silence for quite a while. Finally, Sid broke the spell, "These photos give us a starting point. The house is a headquarters or gathering point for the gang. We have pictures of a few bad guys, and maybe figured how they transport the girls. I'll put everybody I can spare from lower priority cases to work on this one until we have enough to turn it over to Grabowski and his team. And I'll show the Philips photo to Grabowski so he doesn't let his partner in on anything that might blow the case."

Through Norma's efforts, Sid found a big bone while looking for a little one. Like the optimistic dog, he wouldn't quit now until he dug up the rest of the dinosaur that had to be somewhere nearby. He didn't mind calling in the rest of the pack because, when they found this dinosaur, there would be plenty of bones to go around. He could even share these bones with the dog packs at Police Headquarters, the District Attorney, and even the Feds and Interpol.

"Bill, Al, pass the word to the rest. I'll cover wages and expenses, but it looks like this one will be *pro bono publico*, for the public good. Nobody is going to pay us enough if we do the job right. Watch the overtime and expenses, but don't be afraid to spend the time or money you need to crack this." Sid barked the marching orders for his little army's campaign.

I knew of one previous time, in a similar situation when a seemingly simple, routine investigation uncovered a larger crime, when Sid committed his agency without regard to who would pay him, or even whether he could afford to expend his agency's resources to find the guilty. The business finance classes taught him well that the primary task of any business, like any animal, is to survive.

Only thinking animals, sentient beings, dare all, even life itself, for another person, an ideal, a principle, or a cause. Sid made the cut this time. Sid just risked his business to find Norma's killer, now presumed to be part of the white slaver gang, or working for them. Bill and Al, too, recognized the level of commitment Sid authorized. Their faces showed it.

"You don't mind if I put in a little of my own time gratis, do you Sid?" Bill offered.

"Count me in, too!" Al chorused.

"Thanks, guys." Sid accepted the volunteered help. After briefest pause, he commanded, "Well, don't just sit there. Meet me at the office. I'll be a few minutes behind you, after I talk to Mickie."

Al and Bill reacted like the old war movie RAF fighter pilots scrambled to defend hearth and home from Nazi bombers overhead. Al quipped, "Tally Ho!", while Bill chimed in, "Aye, aye, Sir!" They chugged the last of their coffee, now cooled enough to permit it. They grabbed their jackets and the photos, then bee-lined for the door and their cars beyond at a fast walk.

Watching them depart, I turned to Sid, "So? What do you want to say."

"About last night... "

I cut him off, "No need to apologize, Sid. We've been friends too long for an ill-timed proposition to come between us now."

Sid grinned sheepishly, "Hell, I almost forgot about that! I meant it about the job, though. Think about it and let me know. We've got desk space for you if you ever want to sit at it." He sighed, "Write off the other part as a stupid remark. I must have had a bad case of the lonelies is all."

"Then what did you want to say?"

Sid got serious, "I want to say well done. You kept your ears open and picked up on a chance remark that may have broken the case open. If you can, hang in there for another week, see how much more you can learn."

"I can do that, Sid. I want to see this through until the bas ... bad guys are in jail." It was the truest thing I said in a long time, but not only that, now. Staying on the case would let me keep the cover job where I would be close to Bruno. "And thanks. Nice to know I've got a job waiting, other than being a bar maid down at the Blue Onion, if I want it."

Sid made his pitch to convince me, "You've got a talent for this kind of work. I'd be a fool, too stupid to run a competitive business, if I didn't recognize potential assets when I saw them, whether people or equipment." He looked at his watch, "Got to roll. Weekend crew needs instructions, a pep talk. You know what I mean. Until later, Mickie."

While Sid pulled on his jacket, he showed friendly concern as he instructed, "And check in tomorrow! You've got my number?"

"Unless you changed them, I've got both your office and home. Which one is better?"

Hand on doorknob, he paused to face me. "I've still got the same numbers. Before noon or after six, call me at the house. Noon to six, try the office first." The afterthought came as he started to turn the knob, "The crooks are still loose, so watch your back tonight. Don't want to lose you before you even get on the payroll."

With nearly audible whoosh, Sid exited as explosively as he usually made an entrance. Had I blinked, I would have missed it. Closing the door, I watched through the window as he sprinted across the front yard, got into his car and drove off to battle the forces of evil. It struck me that sometimes, I picked my battles. At other times, like this time, they picked me. But, I counted myself lucky to get into this one with good friends at my side.

I always regarded Sid as a prototype for the real heroes in my life, not like those tin ones in the movies. While he sometimes backed an unpopular cause, or took a politically incorrect stance, he did what he believed was right, and did it with enthusiasm and determination. I never knew him to backdown once he decided, even if sometimes his side lost.

I analyzed the situation, and concluded that, if Sid had his way, the bad guys were goners. They might be buried or merely jailed. Even if they got away, they'd know they had been in a fight.

Returning to the kitchen, I collected dirty cups and saucers left by the visitors. This time, I loaded the dishwasher rather than doing them by hand. A train of thought arrived at my station, and it needed immediate attention. I closed the dishwasher door and poured the last cup of coffee for myself. Seated at the kitchen table, I pondered the ponderable. Long ago, I learned to leave pondering the imponderable to the philosophers. That's what they get paid for.

I had my part to play tonight. It felt so very good to have a role, even if only as a supporting character, rather than just reporting what others did. That's why I joined the police in the first place, what now seemed a lifetime ago. If not invalided out because of wounds, I'd still be a cop.

Maybe that's the part of me that I needed to find again. Maybe Sid's job offer was the light needed to see things clearly in this dark hall of my life.

Soon, I would get ready for another shift at the Blue Onion. After this shift, I still had four weeks of vacation to think about it. That should be enough time to sort out the rest of my life, at least until the next time I must choose between sticking with the status quo or making some major change.

After all, this was only another of the many "Y" intersections in the road from birth to death. Even if I put in another week as barmaid without thinking about it at all, I had time to decide which trail to take. Of course, like everyone else, I presumed that nothing will attack from the shadows and I would live that long. That is far from a sure bet.

The bad guys might get me on purpose. They were, after all, trying to prevent any interference in their racket. Some random event, like being hit by a wheel falling off an airplane as it flies over, could stop me by accident. Or, I may just be called home, at any time. That's what Mom told me when Dad died, that he had been called home. The way she described that home, it should be a nice place to live, not just to visit. Admittedly, I'm in no rush to get there, but I'm not afraid of the move when the time comes. At least there won't be any bad guys in the neighborhood.

Subsequent thoughts turned to family. Thanks, Dad, for teaching me about God, duty, honor, country, and family. Thanks, Mom, for sharing your Eastern European fatalism. And thanks, both of you, for raising me with the spirit to try despite the odds and obstacles.

Too soon, for I hadn't finished thinking, the shadow of my house nearly touched the alley. Soon, the sun would set. I had about two hours before I reported to Gwen at the Blue Onion. Meditations ended. The clock moved while I made no progress. I already spent too much time thinking. Or, maybe, I had not spent enough time. I resolved nothing during the interlude between Sid's departure and now, except recognizing that question I must answer soon. How would I spend my life? That question nagged at me through preparations for the coming night, and for days more after.

But I didn't have time to think about that now. Practical considerations required prompt attention and scrambled to the front of the line of concerns. For one, I need to wear comfortable shoes tonight. Without them, my feet would kill me before anybody else got the chance. If I can't find that pair of comfortable-for-hours-on-my-feet mid-heel pumps quickly, I'll put on my face, dress, and stop at the shoe store on my way to work. I have no time to waste. That store closes in an hour, if they haven't changed hours. The clock became an irritating prod, a limiting factor on what I could do before work.

It was time to dress for work, and I still need to eat supper. I didn't have time to both dress and cook, but I wanted more than a cold sandwich. Whether I find or buy the shoes I'll wear tonight, a burger and fries at the Blue Onion will have to pass as supper tonight. The crowd at the local fast food stand won't be ready for me dressed this way, for sure not the regulars at the restaurant where I treat myself to the occasional meal out.

And, nagging worry lurked behind every thought, never quite left my mind. Some thugs wanted to stop us before we tipped over the rock that hid them, pests which carried a disease dangerous to society, and to people individually. I must guard against complacency, stay aware of their hidden threat, if I expected to live long enough for any decisions about my future to matter more than just as an exercise in logic. I had to balance that against the danger I could sink into debilitating paranoia again.

One thing went my way immediately. I wouldn't have to break-in new shoes tonight. The foot-friendly pumps hid unsuccessfully at the back of the closet. With a quick wipe to remove dust gathered since last time I wore them, they'd look as good as I would need tonight. Surprisingly, they passed with the outfit selected. They weren't as sexy as the high heels, but I would be on my feet almost all night. Those high heels worn last night almost demanded the interlude on my back that the projected image hinted was when I made some real money.

Putting on my makeup, I wondered how Wanda and those other girls did it, night in and night out, often with more than one guy.

Maybe they had the personality, or the upbringing, or some harsh financial need that allowed them to sell themselves that way. Yesterday, I looked over the edge, but a strict upbringing brought me up short of crossing into their profession despite an occasional fantasy about what it would be like.

No, aside from the sham of respectability offered by my current career, prostituting myself as a scandal sheet reporter was as far as I had gone. Likely, it was as far as I would ever go. I would feel no sorrow when, if ever, I left the *National Rag*. A bit of the decision came with that realization.

Dressing more hurriedly now, I marveled that I made a living by trading on the secrets and sorrows of the rich, famous, or unfortunate. My readers' lives must be empty if they needed to fill them with such gossip. If they ever realized how full their lives can be without the trash, the rags will all go out of business. Maybe even the networks will report real news rather than manufacture it as they do now, or cross into the *National Rag's* territory on a slow news day.

The evening was too short to agonize about that now. It was time to leave for work. The radio announced the weather forecast, cooler than last night, so the longer coat would offer warmth for tired legs on the drive home. At least there was a bright side to working around the lively crowd at the bar. I surely didn't have time to get so somber in their company, even if my feet hurt.

After checking the street, I left my fortress home and drove to the docks. The rearview mirror reflected no threat, and the trip passed without excitement.

Turned in and parked behind the Blue Onion. Pausing to scan the surroundings, I spotted no unexplained company in the rear view mirror, no apparent threats in the vicinity. Checking my watch, I noted that I had enough time for that burger before the shift started.

Gwen looked up, then nodded as I took the stool at the end of the bar. After she served the customers at the other end, she came over to chat during the slow period. Despite eyes dark with concern, her voice was cheerful, "Hi, Mickie. You're in early."

"Hi, Gwen. Yeah, I didn't have time to cook, so need to eat some supper. Thought I'd try one of the burgers before my shift started."

"Want everything on it? And do you want fries?" Gwen asked.

"Sure, that sounds good. Will I work the same section tonight?"

Gwen signaled Harvey, who did the cooking, then turned back. "Yes, you'll be at this end. Seemed to work all right for us last night. How did it go for you?"

I told Gwen, "Picked up sore feet, and a little information. Guess that's par for the course, so no complaints." Little did I suspect I would only gain tired feet tonight. There would be no dramatic revelations in any of the overheard conversations, unless I counted those of questionable taste. None were so putrid that I needed to spill the drink into the speaker's lap, but some left me with a felt flush of embarrassment at some of the suggestions and propositions.

Such overtures muted after Bruno arrived. Larger than most of my pseudo-suitors and, likely, holder of a reputation as a formidable brawler, none challenged his first claim when he sat beside my waitress station. Despite niggling uncertainties which plagued me since I didn't know him very well yet, I accepted his protection. I would have time to find whether our relationship was deeper than a passing infatuation only if I made it through tonight and the nights yet to come.

By midnight, it was quiet, so quiet that Gwen sent me home early. I wasn't scheduled for my next shift until Monday night. Arrivals and departures usually brought thirsty crews into the place. The neighborhood grapevine reported no ships docked today, and no ships planned to sail before Tuesday. Gwen concluded that I wouldn't be needed with just the few regulars who came in on Sundays, but business would be more brisk during the Monday night football game. The neighborhood regulars who came to watch would be joined by crews of two ships scheduled to leave on the next morning's tide.

Bruno invited me to his place, but didn't push the matter when I asked for a rain check. I needed time alone to rest, to think, and knew I wouldn't get either if I went there. I waved my good-byes, gathered coat and purse, then headed for the back door and home. Work as a barmaid assured late hours. Even with early release, I knew sleep was several hours away. I planned to use the leisure offered by this short shift and day off to rest, reorganize, shift my internal clock to the hours this mission required. Tonight, I would kick back, put my feet up, and remember Norma as a late movie played in the background. No doubts about it, I would likely think about Bruno, and Sid's job offer, too.

Personal reflection would not be my only company tonight, this early morning. Experience with prior investigations reminded me that the case would come to mind to interrupt the flow of pleasant thoughts, as it did now. Away from others and distractions, I would consider all that I knew, evaluate alternative explanations for the past week's incidents. Maybe there was another answer to why all this happened. Maybe something new would break in the situation next week. If anything happened before Monday, Sid would let me know about it.

I caught myself just before I pushed open the door and charged into the dark outside. Preoccupation with the future almost blinded me to potential present dangers. That would be reckless, given the little I knew about the adversaries. If I failed to watch in the present, I could be taken by surprise. It would be my own fault if I let something or somebody sneak up on me, but it wouldn't hurt less. I moved more carefully after that thought.

* * * *

Back in the office for yet another late evening, Detective Sergeant Grabowski drained a second cup of coffee as he tried to forge some chain of logic. For now, individual links of that chain were scattered across his desk. It was somewhere in these bits of paper - fingerprint cards, mug shots, reports from first responders and Coroner, even his own notes. He needed some unifying, ordering mechanism to turn the raw links into the chain that would bind the guilty.

Perhaps, he deliberated, he too readily accepted that this death was murder. He leaned toward that conclusion because he knew both Sid and Norma. Sid told him Norma related her theory that white slavers engineered all the disappearances of young women in the state, maybe even the region. She died soon after that. Yet, other conclusions were possible, considering that she fell from a barstool. Still, the autopsy report showed an injection site where she could not have done it to herself. Someone had to have given her something. Monday, test results would show what it was.

That's when the thoughts rushed from every dark corner of his mind and formed a jabbering mob. To clear his mind and start over, he rose and crossed the Saturday-Night-empty office to the coffee pot for a refill. Unnoticed in the clamor as they flashed before him, the mental files on three unsolved hits came and went as he covered the ten feet with empty cup.

Other thoughts dogged him as he poured number three. Why did he feel so driven, try so hard? There were enough active cases on his desk to keep any two capable detectives busy. Why did he feel that he had to solve every one of them himself? If he ever kept one of the appointments the Captain set up, would the psychologist retained by the department judge him obsessive-compulsive? Or would the verdict be that he was just a dedicated cop?

Jim Philips, his partner, worked only his regular shift. No one thought badly of him, or said that he shirked his duty to spend time with his wife and children.

Maybe, Chet thought to himself, he could have learned to work a normal day if Norma were still alive to take his mind off these cases, had not added this latest case when she died. But that thought was part of his turmoil, part of his personal distress as he slumped at his desk.

His mind now wandered far from any of the cases which demanded his attention. Sergeant Grabowski had been tolerant of them, keeping with department policy, but had never liked the guys on the force who were attracted to other guys. He wondered how it became his lot to like a woman who used to be a guy with other women, a woman with the guys she dated, if they paid enough. Without these other pressing concerns, that alone was enough to drive him crazy.

Maybe he should show up for the next appointment with the department's shrink, before this quandary distracted him when he needed concentration, needed to duck instead of getting killed himself. For now, these clues were just raw data. He had to comb them again, interpret them with all the experience, intelligence and instinct he possessed. He must convert them to information, then use the knowledge to solve the mysteries.

Chet shook off concerns about his mental and emotional state, disturbing self-doubts about his fitness to investigate this case where the victim was his friend through act of will. At least he felt justified putting this case at top priority. Besides the personal reasons, the affection they shared, his effort to solve Norma's death might also lead to the missing girls. He believed breaking this gang would prevent disappearance of other innocents. The youth would be safer, at least until some other low life found and resurrected the dastardly scheme just to make money at it.

Chet again bent to the task of sorting chaos into order. As he sifted through the reports once more, he found the while-you-were-out sticky-tag message. During the afternoon, the Warden of State Prison reported that Art Limburg had been a model prisoner after he recovered from the beating received during his first month there, and had been paroled early, almost four years ago. Chet recognized the possible key. If it actually fit the locks on this case, this could be a first glimmer in the fog.

One frustration about finding this information on Saturday Night was that the Parole Officer wouldn't be back in the office until Monday. There would be no way to discover the known associates of Mr. Limburg before then. And none of the clerks worked in Records over the weekend. Even if he could find the names of people associated with the suspect, Chet couldn't pull their records before Monday. The realization that one more thing waited for Monday was almost enough to send him to a bar for several stiff drinks.

Hell, it was enough to drive him over the edge, at least for tonight. He needed a break before his mind broke irreparably. Chet decided to visit the Blue Onion. Bruno hung out there. His brother always was a good sounding board for his troubles. Chet gathered the paper residue of the case. He stacked the bits and pieces of paper, folded them into a folder, and put the whole mess into his desk drawer. Symbolically, he substituted temporary solution for the actual resolution he needed.

* * * *

My focus and senses readied to discern any threats waiting. I scanned as I stepped out the door. The alley and parking lot were well lighted. I could spot danger before the demons of the night jumped from the shadows, but there were none lying in ambush.

Half way to the car, I decided that no threats lurked in ambush tonight. Just as certainly, I knew I had to remain alert. Just because nothing with fang and claw waited this time, there might be a time not too far in the future when fears would take form, become real dangers.

Anxiety occupied the passenger seat during the drive home, then shadowed me inside. Even turning on the lights, I couldn't shake it until I patrolled the perimeter. Dead-bolts slid home to double lock the exterior doors and all the window latches tested true and secure.

Before apprehension dozed, he reminded me that physical security measures would not stop a determined assault against my little fortress. I knew locked doors and windows couldn't prevent forced entry, but that wasn't their purpose. I only asked that they slowed entry by the uninvited, gave me time to react, to ready an unpleasant welcome for the interlopers. Recalling a sign I saw once brought an inward smile. Like that other occupant, I could hang the sign, "Don't worry about the dog. Beware of Owner!" on my own door.

Trepidation finally curled in the corner and yawned. At last asleep, snoring in his corner, he left me alone for the night. I saw no reason to rouse him. A stiff drink, a little pleasant television, and my thoughts were more than enough company for this night. Somehow, the Sandman infiltrated my defenses, probably invited by fatigue.

* * * *

I jumped awake. The icy drink held as I dozed into fitful nap had spilled into my lap. I mopped up the mess while recalling the vision.

Given the concerns that napped with me, the dream began benignly enough. Alerted by noises in my office, I grabbed a cast iron skillet hidden under my pillow and went to investigate. Whoever invaded my house was in trouble, deep trouble, now that I was ready to repel boarders, and that was even before the police arrived. When I looked up the hall toward the noise, I saw a black, horizontal slash of dark coat sleeve against the white-painted walls. It seemed to end with a metallic glimmer.

Without time to determine whether the glint came from watch, knife or gun, I aimed and threw the pot. It thudded rather than clanged, and the black shadow disappeared. The hall light came on and Bruno came from the kitchen. Because dreams and nightmares proceed at their own pace, it took a long time to find the intruder down in the middle of the room, separated from his gun by more than an arm's length. Even though still alive, he wasn't likely to make any sudden moves. Bruno trussed the intruder with manacles and irons taken from his pockets. It seemed strange, even in my dream, that this burglar wore a frog outfit and swim fins rather than shoes.

Then weird dream turned into nightmare. Emma and her helpers, led by the tall thin man, pulled down the wall to rescue their comrade. Their entire crew boarded a schooner that sailed down the street under a flapping Jolly Roger ensign. Bruno and I followed in the only craft available, a small dinghy. As we rowed in the pirates' wake, thugs snatched young women from bus stops along the way, using fishing nets hung over the yardarms. After a police cruiser joined the chase, Emma ordered her crew to jettison their contraband cargo of young women, one by one, into a sea full of sharks. Forced by that action, pursuit converted to attempted rescues. Each time Bruno and I neared one of the women, a shark swam up and snatched her from our grasp.

When we neared the last woman thrown overboard, I recognized Norma. As she stretched her arm toward us, a great shadow engulfed her, and she was gone. The shadow transformed into a great shark wearing a tan trench coat. He turned to attack the dinghy. A toad wearing glasses sat on his head, directed the onslaught. Huge jaws crashed down on the small boat. The jaws crushed the craft, narrowly missed us, but left us to swim to shore or await rescue by the police cruiser. Either way, the pirate ship escaped across the dark sea.

I shuddered at the end of the dream, and finished mopping up the mess, then went to bed after another tour around the perimeter. Hopes for rest evaporated as the spilled drink dried. After that dream, only uneasy sleep came even though the night passed quietly.

* * * *

Chester Grabowski left badge and title in the glove compartment when he parked his car. He entered the Blue Onion through the back door as a private citizen who needed respite from turmoil. As he started for the bar, the booming voice from behind him instantly raised his spirits, before any spirits passed his lips.

"Hey, Chester! Hobble over here and join me." Then Bruno ordered for his younger sibling, "Gwen, get him a beer, a schooner of your best dark. Put it on my tab."

Chet faced about. His gaze found the source of the fraternal greeting seated alone at the farthest-back corner table. It was past time for a long talk between them. And, it would be safe to spill his guts about his problems. Besides the bond of blood, Bruno intuitively knew when something was a For-Your-Eyes-Only-Top-Secret, the kind of secret, Bruno used to joke, that he'd have to kill you if he told you. Chet marched over and stood at attention alongside the table. "Reporting as ordered, Aye, aye, Sir!" Both brothers broke into gales of hearty laughter that resounded through the nearly empty bar. Even Harvey and Gwen joined the mirth.

The brothers finished several beers and swapped several lies, even traded some true stories. Finally, Gwen declared last call. Chet bought a bottle of Canadian whiskey, compromise between his preferred Bourbon, and Bruno's taste for Scotch, to take out.

As Harvey locked the door behind them, they adjourned the meeting to Bruno's nearby apartment. In this privacy, they talked like they had when they were boys camped out in the backyard tent. Shared pleasures, sorrows, and secrets from their past bound them together closer than mere accident of birth to the same parents. During their talk, Chet confessed his confusion over his feelings for Norma. Bruno admitted his growing affection for the recently met Mickie. Each consoled the other, then buoyed the other's spirits. When Chet left at dawn, both brothers felt renewed closeness to the other.

In fact, Chester beamed that Bruno bestowed on him the weighty duty as best man if ever the opportunity arose. And, he felt far better about loving Norma after Bruno advanced the concept that his brother experienced affection for the soul of the person despite activities in which the body partook. As a mildly disfigured person, Bruno presented the idea with forceful conviction that washed away all confusion or guilt that Chester perceived in that relationship.

Despite lack of sleep, Chester experienced renewal, felt strangely rested. He needed only a short nap, for his body's sake, before he went back to work. And, he had enlisted his brother as additional eye and ears in this neighborhood. Bruno was situated perfectly to observe covertly. The blood-bond worked in the diamond trade. Why not give it a chance in the more dangerous venue of solving crimes?

* * * *

Nick left Stretch's home, located mere blocks, but a world away, from the blue-collar district where Bruno lived. In the white-collar territory of mid-level managers of stores, banks, and, yes, even of gangs, their conversation had been less than lofty. Stretch's perceived position as peer of lawful citizens, and his good reputation as generous member of the prestigious local church and Chamber of Commerce were not armor against selfish interest. They condemned their opposition to death at the earliest possible moment, plotted the attack in this household built on income earned through wickedness.

Neither Nick nor Stretch recognized the irony. In fact, Nick wasn't sure he understood the plan. It hadn't been devised until after the sixth Canadian Mist and soda. He was confused by something else Stretch said, too. While listing alternatives, Stretch suggested the Imperial Guard stage a preemptive palace revolt. Nick always slept through history classes, so couldn't understand what his friend and host intended. However, he grasped that his ass was grass, and the boss, or somebody the boss hired, would be the lawn mower if things continued to go badly for them, if the hit on the nosey reporter didn't work.

Stretch said that either the cops or the boss would get them if they screwed up again. Well, Nick thought, if that's the choice, Stretch is right. I'd rather face a hanging judge and stone-hearted jury while represented by an inept lawyer than wait around, let the boss feed them to the fish without a fight.

But such weighty concerns perplexed old Nick. During his efforts to figure out just exactly what Stretch intended, he got lost among the cul-de-sacs the architect built into the middle class development. His fatigue, reinforced by too much whisky, and those too many blows to the head during all his fights, prompted him to pull in and sleep. What could it hurt? At least they wouldn't read about him as the drunk who ran over the paper boy.

The flashlight beam played across his eyes, and woke Nick. The uniformed officer was polite, but insisted that he take the field sobriety screening tests. He explained that he hadn't been able to find his nose with fingertip since a fight in 1985, but it cut no mustard. Too, the breath analyzer indicated blood alcohol at 0.15, compared to an allowed 0.10. Nick was most definitely drunk by the legal standard. He would spend the rest of the night in the drunk tank, 24 hour guest of the city, under the new ordinance.

The part that hurt worst, besides the fine that would be levied, Nick had to pay towing and storage for his car. The next worst part was that he wouldn't be there to help Stretch.

Without We Fools

MORNING CAME NONE TOO QUICKLY, FOR its full light finally dispersed the lingering sense of dread the vision, the nightmare, left behind. Still, lacking restful sleep, I was cranky. I could almost kick a dog without remorse when I feel like this. Detecting my testiness, I chided myself. It's a good thing I live alone when I wake up like this.

I needed physical outlet, but remembered six weeks on crutches after I kicked a chair and broke my foot during an earlier tantrum. That moderated my outburst before I became self-destructive, but choking off a tantrum would play evil tricks with my disposition and digestion for the week. I did the only thing I could. I vented frustration on the eggs, beat my omelet into a froth. By the time I loaded breakfast dishes and started the dishwasher, I was calmer. In fact, I could laugh that I just ate the fluffiest omelet ever made, one that could pass for a skillet quiche. I needed another cup of coffee before I would be fit company for anyone, but made progress as I dressed for the day.

Suddenly, I felt a serious need to let the Deity know I thought of Him when I could. Maybe He would think of me when the press of the job, especially this job with its inherent dangers, distracted me.

Perhaps it was a reaction to the sordid side, the cesspool of life in which I had been swimming for several months. At first, I was working on the story for the paper. Now, I searched for kidnappers and killers. I needed the company of people who at least talked the game of morality on Sunday mornings.

If I hurried, I could make the last morning services at the

neighborhood church. They didn't espouse the religion in which I was raised, but it was the nearest church. That made it the nearest port in a storm, as the old adage advises. I didn't know any of the congregation well enough to judge whether they lived according to those rules during the week, but at least they talked the talk on Sundays. Laws of probability suggested some walked the walk, at least most times.

I tried to control the grin brought by realization this would be one scene deleted from the movie of my life. Hollywood seemed to have no religion but the dollar. Despite efforts to control it, the grin widened as I contemplated what the preacher would think if the pistol fell from my purse during the collection. The congregation surely would faint.

I considered leaving the gun behind, but decided I couldn't take the chance. The miscreants wouldn't care that I went to church, wouldn't respect the inviolability of the Maker's house. I believe He watches over us, but also believe the first age of direct intervention ended at the last page of the Old Testament, and the second age won't begin until the Second Coming. I live between the two.

He'd help me, but only if I prepared to help myself. Even with His help, it was likely that I'd have to take some actions because I couldn't count on a miraculous rescue. I might need a miracle, but knew I had to be prepared to do it on my own in case He had something really urgent to watch over, or let it play out the way the players set it up. That's the price we paid for having free will.

I locked the front door behind, then walked up the street until I reached the church. Members of the congregation straggled in before and behind. Soon, the pews filled. The designated hour arrived. A lively hymn signaled start of worship.

The sermon barely addressed the evils I witnessed, sometimes faced, but was calming through that very failure. The preacher extolled the family virtues and decried the lack of charity, one for the other. Clearly, the pastor lived in a more sheltered world than I knew, but believed the congregation could make a difference. More hymns and a blessing brought the services to a close.

I felt better, calmer, when I left, even though I knew I'd muddy my skirts again tomorrow. He hadn't spoken in a thunderous roar of certainty, but the usual whisper He used when speaking to mortals of the human persuasion. The thought reassured me.

It's my job, my calling, and I'm good at it. Without we fools who throw ourselves into the breach, bad guys would take over. Then where would that gentle soul who stood at the pulpit be? Where could she shelter from the storm that would be loosed if none of us stood between her and them?

The weather was quite pleasant, so I walked a block out of the way to buy fresh milk, a few doughnuts, and the Sunday paper at the local convenience store. By the time I wended my way home, I decided to join Sid's agency. With the decision, the job at the *National Rag* was now as much in my past as the time spent on the police force.

Detective work would drain me. I knew that from the short time spent on this case. For all its disadvantages, there was the undeniable certainty that I could make a real difference if I spent my energy pursuing the bad guys. Once again, I could be proud of my calling, not like when I chased gossip and rumor just to pander to the prurient interests of scandal sheet readers.

As I neared my door, some unseen force yanked the milk jug from my hand, and sent a geyser of milk skyward. While startled enough by that, I was sure the mild report of a handgun followed. Reflexively, I ducked the shower of milk, then fell to the lawn, and hoped the shooter thought I dropped because I'd been hit. With a little luck, the car parked in front of the neighbor's house offered cover from any additional shots he might take.

A car departed with squealing tires. I knew a partial license number and sketchy description of the car wouldn't ensure the police could find the attacker, but would be better than nothing. I rolled to open a line of sight in time to watch a maroon, two-year-old Chevy sedan speed into the distance. Somebody shot at me, and that somebody drove a car with M 15 as the first three characters of the license plate number. At least it looked like M 15 before it got too far away to read the rest.

At the main street two blocks down, the sedan turned left without obeying the stop sign. If it didn't turn again, I would bet a week's pay, it wouldn't stop before it got to the docks.

I gathered my soggy parcel, what was left of it, and made my way up the stairs on shaking legs to fumble the key into the lock with trembling fingers, the same ones which managed to dial 911 on only the second try. By the third ring, when the dispatcher answered, fear gave way to anger. I told him in certain terms, "Somebody just shot at me."

The dispatcher confirmed address shown on his computer screen, and assured me that a patrol car would respond promptly. He cautioned that even a prompt response took a few minutes.

While I waited, thoughts flooded my conscious. First, I really dislike getting shot at. Now, I'm drenched with milk and my new dress is ruined unless the cleaner can do some magic.

Finally, I reexamined my position on Divine Intervention. I shifted the milk suddenly to the left to use right hand for the house keys. The shot came at the precise moment the bottle of milk was directly on line between me and the parking space which I surmised had been the spot from which the ambusher fired. If the shot had been taken a fraction of a second sooner or later, the bullet would be somewhere inside me. And, rather than a full metal jacket or soft point bullet, the shooter used a hollow point which expended its energy causing the geyser of milk, spent before exiting the bottle. I took a second to thank the Creator for the extra chance just granted.

About a half hour after I spoke to the dispatcher, a squad car leisurely rolled into the parking spot vacated by the attacker. The patrolmen were condescending until shown the bullet captured by what had been a gallon jug of milk. They sobered instantly at the realization I wasn't some crackpot with a spurious request for help.

The senior man trotted to the car, and called in. What seemed only a minute later, though I knew it was longer, Sgt. Grabowski pulled into my drive. He looked genuinely concerned as I greeted, "I'm glad it's you investigating this. Sid said he knows and trusts you. That's good enough for me. I'm not hurt, buut …" I rattled the bullet in the milk bottle.

Chet gave a long, low whistle which confirmed my evaluation that I had been extremely lucky, or watched over by Somebody you didn't want to cross. He commented, "I've only seen something like that once. A guy wanted to check how a new bullet expanded. He set up a row of water-filled gallon milk jugs on a table, then shot into the front one from about ten feet. Knocked all the bottles off the table, but the first one held the bullet. Mushroomed just like that one." He sniffed the air, then inquired, "How long ago did this happen?"

The odor now was strong enough that even I noticed the new perfume. "Long enough ago that it's started to spoil. The officers over there took a while, nearly thirty minutes, to show up. The sooner you take my report, the sooner I can shower and change clothes."

Chet wore the same sheepish little grin I saw on his brother from time to time. My complaint must have hit home. We moved to the kitchen where the hard chairs would not absorb the smell of souring milk. I gave the best description of the car I could, and reported the partial license plate number. Chet dutifully entered the information onto a clean notebook page. As he prepared to leave, I asked, "Have you spoken to Sid since yesterday afternoon?"

"Not since yesterday morning, although he left a couple of messages." Chet replied.

"You need to see the picture of Jim Philips taking a fat envelope from a man we suspect is deeply involved in kidnap, possibly murder. Your partner may be dirty." The words spat forth with the venom once reserved for the former partner who sent me into a nearly fatal ambush. The statement staggered Sgt. Grabowski visibly.

I warned, "Be careful Philips doesn't send you into an ambush like my ex-partner did me. From what we can tell, an awful lot of money rides on their caper, enough to make them extremely dangerous if they feel threatened."

As I showed Chet to the door, the younger uniform rushed up the stairs, two at a time. He hollered, "Sarge, look what we found in the street!" A shiny new 9mm cartridge case dangled from the end of his pencil. He wore a large, confident smile which I thought incongruous for someone saved by Providence from finding a dead person on the street too.

Chet spoke, "Good job, Jacobs. Now bag it before you mess up any fingerprints or lose it. Take it to the lab with this." He handed over the plastic milk jug with the bullet still rattling around inside. Then he instructed, "Have the techs test them. I want the results as soon as they can get them to me, but not later than Tuesday. Tell them that. That's a good boy." His voice hinted a supervisor's pride that a subordinate had done his job well, but diluted by the expectation that it should have been done better.

"Right, Sarge. I'll get it right over there. And thanks for remembering my name." Patrolman Jacobs turned and descended the steps more gingerly, now reminded that evidence could be lost if he weren't careful.

After Jacobs was back at his car, I scolded lightly, "Chester Grabowski, that wasn't very nice. I could almost see my Dad petting Tar after he brought back a duck." Then I asked, "By the way, how did you know his name before you could see the name tag?"

"He was in a class I taught at the Academy. I talk to him that way because he knows a lot, but sometimes gets excited and forgets procedure. Give him a couple more years in a patrol car, then the detective's course, and I wouldn't mind having him for a partner, though." Sgt. Grabowski hesitated. "Will you be all right alone, or do you want a squad car out front?"

"I'll call in my own reinforcements, thanks. Just tell the dispatchers to get somebody over here pronto if I have to call again." After pausing, I asked, "Is it a smart move to ask Bruno to camp here for a few days?"

"Mickie, I met you as a witness in a current case, so I can only judge on first impressions and by your record when you were on the force. I've known my brother a lot longer." The familial little grin crossed Chet's lips as he spoke. "He likes you a lot. Enough that he asked the same question about you last night. Unless he's hiding something, the only trouble he's ever had were a couple bar fights that the other guys started. I'll tell you what I told him. I think it's not only a smart move, it might be the best move you make." He laughed, "Besides, I've always wanted to be best man at Bruno's wedding."

"Chester, you're a stinker!" I feigned anger. Still, Bruno and Chet would be a heck of a pair to count on in tough times. "Thanks for the advice. Be careful so you can be there."

"You too! Nobody has shot at me yet, not recently anyway. I'll talk to Sid as soon as I can." He turned and walked to his car. I watched as he radioed headquarters, then drove away. Left alone, I locked the doors and showered. Toweling off, I felt better, now that I didn't smell like an infant's nurse who forgot to put a towel over my shoulder before burping the kid. Once dressed, I phoned Sid to report the morning's excitement. Then I checked the phone book and dialed Bruno.

By the time Bruno arrived, I combed and brushed my hair into a semblance of the recent hairdo, fixed my face, and dressed. When let into my home, he gave me a gentle peck and a one-armed hug. It was the best he could manage because his other arm carried a sack that smelled of Chinese take-out and a small overnight bag. In contrast to the morning, the afternoon started quite well.

I directed him into the kitchen and took his duffel to the bedroom. When I rejoined him, he had set three places at the table.

"Do we expect company?" I asked.

"No. I always set an extra plate. It's a reminder of friends who won't ever join me for a meal again." Bruno explained, briefly solemn. Somber musing quickly gave way to good humor, "Or friends who arrive unexpectedly. I know a couple guys who can smell a free meal from across town."

He pulled a chair away from the table and indicated that I should sit while he did the honors. As he dished chicken chow mein from its white carton over fried noodles taken from their waxed-paper bag, Bruno joked that he had "cooked" a special meal to celebrate the invitation to be my house guest for a few days. The rumbling chuckle that accompanied the explanation was musical, magical. I relaxed, bathed in his cheerful company.

Quiet small talk seasoned the meal more interestingly than any spice or sauce could have done. A second pot of tea steeped as we reached the fortune cookie course. Bruno became one of the very few I knew who ate the cookie before reading the fortune. I admitted, "I'm the other way. I read the fortune first."

He chortled as he washed down the last bite with a sip of tea. Slowly, he unfolded the slip. He moved deliberately, triggered my curiosity until I probed, "So? What does it say?"

Bruno swallowed, then read, "Genius is 10% inspiration but 90% perspiration." A wry smile widened across his lips, "Wonder why I never find the one that gives me the winning lottery number?"

I laughed, "If your luck runs like mine, they'd be last week's numbers." In my turn, I cracked open a fortune cookie. "Mine says, 'Dark stranger enters your life, changes it many ways.' Oh, I hate it when I get this kind of ambiguous message!" I reached across the table and gently touched his hand, "If you're the dark stranger, I think I'll like the changes. But, if there's another dark stranger out there, I don't know."

Bruno thought for a minute. He turned his hand to hold mine, then said, "Whatever lies ahead, let's just enjoy the rest of the day. Life's too short to spend it all worrying."

I accepted his help clearing the table, but sent him into the living room with a cold beer while I put leftovers into the refrigerator and washed dishes. When I joined him, Bruno watched the second of the two football games broadcast today. He was settled into the far end of the sofa, so I sat at the near end.

At half time, I retrieved two fresh beers and some snacks. The bowl placed in the middle of the coffee table drew us closer as we nibbled toward the bottom of the chips. I could feel the warmth of his body so near, yet still far enough away that no one, not even Momma, could accuse him of being too forward. Gwen was right when she pegged him. He is a gentleman.

And I also decided that he was a gentle man unless pushed beyond reasonable limits. That's the way I deciphered Chet's report that the only trouble Bruno had were fights started by other guys. I speculated those fights ended with Bruno standing over the vanquished, but wouldn't ask. I wouldn't dig. I had enough of a fight facing me in the present without worrying about his history. Besides, Dad had a fight or two during his youth, Mom said. When he wanted me to know about them, Bruno would tell me, as Dad told Mom, or the reasons and results would stay buried.

The football game was not very exciting, except for the partially blocked punt run back for a touchdown. Unfortunately, the other team scored, not ours. When the game finally ended, Bruno surrendered the remote control, "Here. You find something."

"Any requests?"

Bruno snorted, "Something serious. But only serious compared to that game. The way those guys played today would have embarrassed the Three Stooges."

"A comedy? I've got a video tape of the Pink Panther." I suggested one of my favorites. That movie would be the ticket for the mood tonight.

Bruno assented, "Get it ready. I'll be right back."

I turned on the lights during his absence, and readied the VCR to play. Then it was my turn for an intermission. Just like Dad, he left the seat up. Well, that was not a capital offense, even if exasperating. When I rejoined him, unopened beers awaited. Quizzing glance directed toward Bruno brought most straightforward answer.

"You're nearly out. Figured we'd make a supply run before we finished the last two beers. They'll keep better if we don't open them until we get back. My car is out front, but you have to drive. I'm restricted to daylight only. Makes the powers-that-be nervous that I wear this patch."

"Okay, put the beer back in the fridge while I get my coat and purse."

On the way out, I locked only the one lock. We wouldn't be gone long. The grocery store was nearby, and it hosted only small numbers of shoppers on Sunday nights, others who needed a few things but not a full list. Bruno had already folded himself into the passenger seat as I went around to the driver's side. As he handed over the keys, he asked, "Is there space in the garage for my car when we get back?"

"I think so."

"Then let's roll. I'm hungry and thirsty. Sooner we get back, the sooner we can have supper." Bruno jovially commanded.

"Aye, aye, Cap'n." I teased. "Just as soon as I move the seat up so I can drive this thing."

We made the trip only a little slower than expected, so were back in the house in good time. Supper was a frozen pizza doctored with added slices of pepperoni and shredded cheese. We settled back and I pushed the play button. The movie just started, only a little way into the opening credits, when Bruno queried, "Are you expecting company?".

"No. Why do you ask?"

"Car just pulled to the curb in front. Looks like the one I saw drive past a couple times this afternoon."

The streetlight, located directly in front of the living room windows, often was just an annoyance, but I was glad it lit the scene tonight. Shadows prevented distinguishing who was in that car, so it was an even bet whether the occupants were friend or foe. I considered whether Sid or Chet sent someone as an over-watch, or the bushwhacker came back to find out whether he killed me those few short hours ago. Perhaps it was just someone looking for an address. Someone not involved in the plot at all. I didn't find out.

Before we became concerned, the car pulled away. While Bruno watched the movie, I evaluated the day's events. The rotten thing about paranoia turned into legitimate concern is that simple, small events convey warnings. Like that car at the curb. Given three of the four possibilities are benign, the still significant 25% chance that it included a shrouded threat can't be ignored. I'll sleep easier with the big guy in the house whichever case it turns out.

* * * *

As he drove away, Stretch grumbled to the Universe. How could the sure hit have gone wrong again? He had just checked the house, stopped along the curb to take a closer look. Yes, lights burned inside the house. At least one person moved about, casting a woman's shadow on the drapes.

Even though Nick got lost somewhere last night, and didn't drive while he did the shooting, Stretch was a good shot with just one hand and had a clear line of fire. After he shot, he watched her drop as if pole-axed. But she must be alive, and unhurt, at least not hurt badly. There was no likely alternative explanation to lights inside that house at this time of night. Somehow, he had missed earlier.

But this was the second time he failed since last Wednesday. The boss would not like the report of another failure in less than a week. He wouldn't like it at all, especially not after the premature report that she was dead.

Casper finished the job on that other woman, but cost too much to hire every time they needed to eliminate someone. The boss warned that he would deduct Casper's fee from Stretch's pay if Stretch couldn't do the job himself. He'd have to try again. The next time, he'd use the sawed-off 12 gauge shotgun with magnum buckshot loads. He couldn't let the boss call in Casper again.

Stretch didn't make enough to afford a drain on his budget that big, not with a wife and daughter to keep clothed, fed, and housed. Of course, their support was only a worry if he wasn't bumped off for missing these last two hits. And there wasn't any sense even thinking about quitting this gang for another one. The boss had a real poor sense of humor about that.

This whole thing had been Smokey's idea. He shared the idea with the boss because they shared a cell, and because the boss promised to finance the project start up costs. They worked out details during five years living together and walking together in the exercise yard.

Smokey organized the ring and ran the export department. The boss ran marketing and collections. Before prison, the boss dealt with some of those who were current customers when he traded in paintings and statues. Some deals had been legitimate brokerage, but others, more lucrative, moved stolen art work to other states, or even other countries.

That greed put the boss in jail, but was still a driving force in his life. And, clearly, the boss passed the postgraduate courses in revenge and ruthlessness before he even finished his first year. Greed and revenge proved quite dangerous to a few others since they started operations four years ago.

Before then even. The boss financed start up with money inherited from his parents' estate. They died in a car accident the day after a visit. The rumor mill at Gray Stone U. had it they told their son they would disinherit him because he disgraced the family. Many inmates believed that was the first time the boss hired Casper, to make sure his parents wouldn't live to change their wills to cut him out.

Anyway, when paroled from prison a few years ago, Smokey and the boss started this gang. About a year ago, Smokey said he wanted to quit before they got caught. The boss smiled, "You don't have to quit, you're fired!" and put a bullet through Smokey's heart. As Smokey fell from chair to floor, the boss claimed survivor rights to overall control of the caper.

No, the boss had a really poor sense of humor about even joking that you wanted to quit. It showed in the cold way the boss got rid of Smokey's body, and they had been friends.

Since that day, the boss could bring Stretch up short with just two words that carried a thinly veiled threat, "Remember Smokey?" Of course Stretch remembered Smokey. Some days, he wished he could forget, even if just long enough to sleep through a half night without visits from that ghost.

Stretch helped take Smokey's body to the boat. He expected they would just tie some weight to the corpse and dump him overboard, like a burial at sea. Instead, he watched with churning stomach while the boss used the bait grinder to turn Smokey into chum, then dumped the chum into the sea near the reef a few miles offshore. After he fed Smokey to the fishes, the boss promoted Stretch to head the shipping department because he had connections on the docks.

Advanced from warehouse to front office, as it were, Stretch was fully involved in the business now. The boss thought Stretch held a vital position in the organization and would never let him leave on his feet. Just the hint that Stretch wanted out would be fatal for him.

Even with only the education gained on the streets, Stretch knew he wasn't irreplaceable. His job could be filled by any other thug who knew a few ships' captains with a larcenous streak, or had the muscle to coerce the reluctant ones.

Another had the really pivotal job. The business wouldn't work without Toad, although you didn't ever want to call her that to her face. She ran procurement. Despite a venomous personality, somehow, someway, she found an inexhaustible supply of the commodity they exported without a license. Stretch wondered how Toad found so many good-looking young women. It surely wouldn't be at church. And, just as surely, they all didn't volunteer for the job.

It didn't matter where they come from, Stretch shrugged as he drove, as long as they bring twice more per pound than pure heroine, and the customers are satisfied enough to place repeat orders. Even after expenses and bribes, they made a very good living, a good enough living to kill for.

The boss wanted to kill the woman, like they killed her friend, for that very reason, but he also said that he wanted the women dead to settle an old score. Stretch knew a lot of convicts who threatened police, District Attorney, or others who put them in jail. Most of the time, the threats were just so much hot air, blowing off steam. The boss was one of the few who meant to carry out the deadly promises he made after his conviction.

Stretch felt mixing business concerns and personal grudges was bad tactics. Threats were an arrow pointing right back at them. Maybe not right away, but, sooner or later, a smart cop would put two and two together. How would the boss like that knock on the door?

He didn't need to compound his problems by asking the boss that simple question. Stretch figured he already had enough trouble. That was reason enough to do as told, provided, of course, that he decided to stay in this cruel business. He had some little nagging second thoughts lately, an unusual and unexpected attack of conscience.

Outside a gas station that wouldn't open for eight hours more, Stretch spotted a phone booth. He parked near it and placed the call.

"Nick? So you finally answered. This is Stretch. Where were you?"

"In the drunk tank. Just got out. Sorry I wasn't there."

"Too late to worry about that now. If you're game, I need your help. It went badly this afternoon. Have to try again. Take both of us to pull it off."

"When?"

"Tomorrow. Meet me at Fong's, one o'clock. That gives us a second chance on Tuesday if we need it. Okay?"

"Sure, Stretch. Meet one o'clock tomorrow afternoon, Fong's restaurant. You can count on me. I'll be there."

"See you then." Stretch hung up.

After he smoked a cigarette and took a swallow or three from the bottle of liquid courage he carried to help him through such contingencies, he had to make a second call. He had to tell the boss before the boss found out from someone else, or risk losing his life.

That was something else about which the boss showed no sense of humor, or understanding. Tiny had tried to hide a mistake from the boss, and the boss fed Tiny to the fishes, too.

Stretch shuddered at the vision of ending up as shark shit on the ocean floor. The worst thing about ending up that way, Stretch figured, was that the ones you left behind thought you just ran out on them. Tiny's wife committed suicide when he disappeared because she thought he had abandoned her.

His wife and daughter deserved to know that he loved them to the end. Stretch brooded. Maybe his only out would be to turn himself in. He could try to cut a deal to turn state's evidence for a reduced sentence, and the witness protection program after he finished his time. Even if the boss or somebody hired to make the hit got to him while in prison, at least his women would have a chance to bury him.

He nearly dialed the police right then. Instead, he decided there would be time for that next Saturday if things didn't work out before then. During recent weeks, Toad hinted she wanted to take over. She was ready to make her move this week if the rest of the gang didn't object. He could slide through another week, witness the hostile takeover that would change management before the boss decided to kill him. Then he only had to stay on Toad's good side.

Stretch remembered his own half-thought-through plot. It slipped out while he talked to Nick. Possibly, if Toad didn't take over this week, he should make a move. It would be a sure way to protect himself from the boss's rages, and hers. He concluded that loyalty among thieves, at least these that some evil star had cursed him with, was a rare commodity.

Once past the bullshit in the movies and legend, self-interest drove them. It drove him nearly to making a preemptive deal with the law if it meant his survival. When he decided against that choice, he almost decided to take over. Stretch didn't really like this enterprise, but the machinery could export stolen cars as easily as they exported girls. That way, he could get rid of both the boss and Toad, and save his own hide to boot.

Stretch took another long swallow, then checked the level in the whisky bottle. Much as he didn't want to do it, it was time to call the boss. He smirked to himself as he thought the rest of the unutterable plot. If he took over, he would report one last time, and this was as good a time as any for that.

* * * *

When the movie ended, while the tape rewound, I gave Bruno the remote control and the same instructions he gave earlier, "Find something good. I'll be right back."

As he channel-surfed, I excused myself to call Mom. It was time to make the weekly reassurance to each other that we still existed, and each thought of the other. But there were secrets between us. Getting shot at today was something I would never tell her. I steered the conversation skillfully and listened patiently to Mom's recital of ordinary things. Sometimes, finding myself in the middle of a storm, I forgot the ordinariness of life for the rest of the world. Compared to my tempest, they plodded along in relative sunshine. When I hung up and rejoined Bruno, I decided that I'll have to try that someday, if I live long enough.

The movie he selected had an appropriate plot for the day. Bogart and Greenstreet vied for the Maltese Falcon, but neither won. The statuette they hold is but lead under the paint. Hammett, or at least the director of this version, never let on whether it was statue or legend that it was made of gold which was counterfeit. I hoped to more adequately conclude the murder of my friend with incarceration of the white slavers I judged and held responsible. I wouldn't be satisfied with less.

Still, nestled next to him with his arm across my shoulders, I felt secure. Nagging unrest faded for this little while. When the movie ended, it was Monday morning. "Time for bed, Bruno."

"See you in the morning." Bruno lay back on the much-too-short-for-him sofa, started to stretch out to make himself comfortable.

I took his hand, "Not this time, sailor. Come with me."

His eye lit up. "Are you sure? If you're not sure, well, I've slept on harder bunks in worse places."

I confirmed the invitation, "I'm sure. I told you when we met that I didn't do one night stands, but this feels like it will be a long term friendship... Come on."

He sprang to his feet, took me into his arms, and carried me into the bedroom. We turned back the covers, undressed, and joined in the middle. His gentle touches electrified me, thrilled me beyond my expectations. Before the last kiss for the night, I knew daylight would come too soon. Or maybe not soon enough if he would give an encore then.

His parting toast that night we met ran through my mind as a welcome refrain, "For old shipmates and new bunkmates." I reveled in the possibility that I had met a new bunkmate to share my life and who would let me share his. I dozed with the sweet dream that it would be so.

My nap ended an hour later. I forgot something important enough that it woke me. In a moment, I remembered that my purse was still in the kitchen. It wasn't the purse I missed. That had spent many nights resting on the counter next to the coffee maker. It was the equalizer inside it.

I wriggled from Bruno's embrace without waking him, slipped on my robe, and went to the kitchen. Finding the purse without turning on the lights, I secured the pistol. Against any potential foe, its two pounds of machined steel would serve far better than any security blanket, no matter how warm the fabric.

Back in the bedroom, I placed pistol and a spare magazine of ammunition into the night stand drawer, hung the robe in its usual place - on the hook on the inside of the door - and returned to bed. Before sleeping, I gently kissed Bruno just because he was there. He stirred slightly, then his great arm held me close to him once again. Now both could sleep, although I wouldn't sleep completely free of care until this case ended. All the ordinary nocturnal creaks and groans of the house assumed an unfamiliar and ominous note, no matter that they had been normal noises on previous nights.

Minor Monday

ONCE AGAIN, GENTLE GURGLES FROM THE coffee maker woke me before the alarm clock sounded its harsh reveille. This time, waking without concern that some intruder violated my home, I lay in bed for minutes longer, listening to cooking noises clinking-clanking from the kitchen.

Finally, drawn by pleasant aromas and the anticipated pleasure of his company, I rose, pulled on robe and slippers. After pausing at the dresser mirror to brush my hair, I joined Bruno in the kitchen. This time, he offered more than just a cup of coffee and a doughnut.

He served a full breakfast, really brunch by the hour shown on the clock. Two identical places - a glass of orange juice, two eggs over easy, a rasher of crisp, browned bacon, and toast buttered to the edges - waited, mirrored each other across the table. As if chaperoning, a jar of orange marmalade stood watch between them.

At table's end, he once again prepared the third place setting, unserved, unoccupied. I teased him, "I take it that extra place is for the friends who just drop in. I know a couple of guys who can smell a free meal from across state." Privately, I considered the deeper reason. If we stay together long enough, perhaps he will tell me about the lost friends he honors with the extra plate. This tradition may become part of my life, but it isn't the time to ask direct questions, not yet.

Bruno broke into my musings, "As promised, I made breakfast this time, even though we're at your place instead of mine. Hope you like it." He hovered anxiously, awaiting favorable review of his culinary efforts.

Although I rarely eat a large breakfast, I was rather impressed. The aromas coming from the plate indicated a tasty meal awaited, and the kitchen was still clean. Some of the guys I knew over the years were hard pressed to make a bowl of cold cereal without making a mess. "It smells good. My mouth is watering already."

Bruno relaxed with the reassurances, then sat across, at the plate he made for himself. He grinned, "Thanks, but you haven't tasted it yet. You may be jumping to conclusions."

Thus prodded, I tasted, then ate. It was as good as hoped. I told him so, "This IS good. You could spoil me with such treatment, Bruno. I could get used to this."

"Nah! You won't be spoiled. I only cook on Mondays, Thursdays, and for special occasions, like Christmas, or the first time a woman visits me." He chortled, "Besides, I don't wash dishes."

"So, you've got a big budget for paper plates, huh?" I should have looked up before speaking. The wisecrack had been poorly timed, caught him just as he drank his juice.

I heard the muffled, sputtering, coughing laughter, glanced up to see him wipe juice from his nostrils and beard, and almost choked on my own food as I started to laugh too. "Bruno, we must be soul-mates," I babbled between giggles, "to laugh through a shower of orange juice."

When finally finished with the meal, I offered, "If you do the dishes, I'll do the laundry we just made."

He protested, "Goes against my grain. Haven't washed anybody else's dishes since boot camp." He grudgingly agreed, with a stipulation, "But it sounds fair, as long as you have a dishwasher."

"Dishwasher is right over there." I pointed. He loaded his assigned machine while I started a load of wash. The machines whirred a duet to accompany another cup of coffee at the table. Some questions would remain unasked for now, but others needed answers. To gauge my predecessor, I asked, "But you're nearly domesticated for an old bachelor. What was she like, your first wife?"

Bruno hesitated, then the story broke through his reserve. He said, "She was a good woman, but not cut out to be a sailor's wife. I was on an extended deployment, so wasn't around enough to see how unhappy she was. After ten years and a son together, she filed for divorce when I re-enlisted rather than take the job her father offered. That was about ten years ago."

"Do you ever see her or your boy?"

"No. That's the really sad part. Both of them were killed. A drunk ran a traffic light, crashed into them broadside. It hurts most because they were coming to visit me in the hospital, after I was injured during that shipboard explosion and fire. He would have been 18 this year." Bruno sighed, shuddered, nearly sobbed, then composed himself.

Woefully inadequate, I knew, but said it anyway, "I'm so sorry for you!"

He gathered himself, controlled his grief, strength of his will tested nearly to breaking. Having opened the door, I had to answer when he asked, "What about you?"

I started, "Married after college, then divorced because she was cheating on me." He blinked. I knew the question would come up sooner or later. I continued, "Nearly married a second time, but, before we set the date, I went into surgery, came out quite different. Just haven't found anybody I liked enough who'd have me since." It was near enough the whole truth. Yes, I wanted to marry Norma, but couldn't after I became Michelle. We stayed friends, close friends, but that was about the time I began to wall away my emotions. It took this big, rugged sailor with the scar and patched eye to bring me back from those dark reaches. "Not until recently, anyway."

He asked, "Same sex marriage wasn't even allowed in the liberal states until recently, so when you say married, you mean civil union?"

I answered, "Good thing you're sitting down. This is a little complicated, so hear me out." He nodded. I continued, "In a life before this one, I was a woman inside a man's body. Wasn't really happy, but didn't know why. Then I was wounded while on the job. The Police Department paid to have me patched up, and arranged for a psychiatrist to help me with the recovery. During those sessions, the shrink asked some questions, and then some more questions, and got me to go way back in memories of childhood. We discussed this and that, and other things. Finally, he hypnotized me to get the whole story." I took a drink of my coffee and finished the story.

"He told me that I said I wanted to be a woman while in the trance. We spent a number of sessions discussing it. At his suggestion, I bought a few clothes and dressed while inside my house. I found a new peace that I hadn't known before. He brought my girlfriend in for further sessions together. After a while, I dressed and went to dinner with her. I started hormone treatments, dressed full time, went out to find how I'd react and finally had the surgery to make the change. That was six, almost seven years ago."

He was silent as he though about it. Finally, he said, "Must have been tough, going from he to she. Based on the experience last night, you've done it." The soft gaze from his one eye gave the answer that I hoped for, even though he never said the words, "We'll see how it works out." That's all anyone can ask for when two people try to make it a couple.

* * * *

Nick arrived at Louie Fong's café on schedule. He suffered through a cup of awful coffee before Stretch came through the kitchen door and joined him in the back corner booth. He greeted his comrade, "Hi, Stretch. How ya doin'?"

"Not bad, Nick. Have you ordered yet?" Stretch returned.

Nick said, "Not yet, just got here myself. Don't know if I'm hungry. What are we goin' to do next?"

"Will that help you figure out if you're hungry?" Stretch shot back, with some wonder that they were friends. Stretch admitted that he wasn't a rocket scientist, but, compared to slow old Nick, he was fairly brilliant, even if he said so himself. But he liked Nick enough that he never said it to Nick's face.

"Kinda. If this is my last meal, I want to order somethin' nice. If I'm goin' to be around a while, the lunch special will do. That's all I meant." Nick pouted.

"Then have the blue plate today. Unless the walls fall on us, we should have plenty of time to choose something really nice twenty years

150

from now." Stretch lied. Everything had to go exactly right during the next day and a half, or they were cooked as thoroughly as the food served in here. The boss told him that earlier this morning in just so many words. Nick didn't need to know that. In fact, it would be far better to let Nick think everything was fine. He screwed up whenever he got too nervous or spooked.

"Thanks, Stretch. I feel better now. But, still, what are we going to do?" Nick pleaded.

Stretch watched Madam Fong approach, deferred answering until after he ordered lunch, "Two blue plate specials." When she went to the kitchen, he outlined his plan. He kept it simple, so even Nick understood, "We stake out the broad's house. When she comes out or gets home, either way, we dust her with a load of buckshot. After that, we don't have to worry that she'll bust our caper, and the boss will be happy with us again."

"But what if it don't work, Stretch? What then?" Nick whined the embarrassing question.

"Nick, are you trying to spoil my lunch on purpose? Or are you just scared of your shadow since that guy beat us up last week?"

Riled, Nick professed, "I ain't scared, Stretch, just worried a little bit. I know the boss ain't happy. People disappear when the boss ain't happy. I don't want to disappear."

"Trust me. I know what I'm doing." Stretch said, as much for himself as for Nick. He thought back to the meeting with his mouthpiece this morning. "If the boss gets me, us, before we get him, he'll go down anyway." The instructions to the attorney were as simple as the plan he just related to Nick.

If Stretch didn't call his lawyer every day before 9:00 to say that he was all right, his lawyer would deliver the signed confession to the Assistant District Attorney who was his fraternity brother. That personal tie between the two attorneys would ensure the law came down on the boss like a ton of bricks if the call didn't get made.

Nick and Stretch talked about the good old days, and their plans for the good new days ahead as they ate their leisurely lunch. By the end of the meal, both were in far better spirits. It was nearly 3:00, time to drive to the reporter's house. Unless she stopped for groceries or some silly thing, she would be getting home around 4:00. By 5:00, they'd be at Sweeny's Bar and Grill, knocking back a few to celebrate.

* * * *

Dish and clothes washers finished their cycles, signaled by the duet of bell and buzzer. I hoped Bruno would have said something more romantic, but the words which emerged were, "Saved by the bell."

We bent to separate chores. After that, we probably wouldn't recapture the earlier romantic mood this Monday, but I wasn't ready to quit either. I just needed time to adjust. Spinsterhood had been the best I looked forward to for a long enough time that any conjugal alternative nearly overwhelmed me. I found our stories similar, so predicted his reaction from the way I felt. If pushed, I would reject the prospect that somebody cared. It was something that had to grow on me, on him, on us.

Bruno showed this momentary confusion too. He didn't want to be pushed or pulled, but he liked this woman. He wanted to be around long enough to work it out. The first question asked after dishes were stacked in the cabinet again, after the clothes were dried, was hardly romantic, but showed the intent. "Are you working tonight?"

"I am. Gwen said the regulars stop in to watch the game. She figured there would be enough business to keep three barmaids busy tonight. I'm supposed to be there by 6:00." He knew my plans, so it was my turn to probe, "Will you stop by tonight?"

"Sure, I'll be there. Couldn't keep me from it without torpedoes." Bruno stumbled into an invitation, "We've got a few hours. Would you like to see my quarters? Bring a bag so you don't have to come back here alone?"

I considered his offer. Because I didn't accept immediately, Bruno advanced additional personal and tactical reasons why I should spend the night, several nights there instead of here. "Besides the fact that I'd enjoy your company, it'll be safer to stay at my place. Whoever tried to shoot you yesterday won't know where you're staying, not right away."

"I'll have to tell your brother, in case he has more questions for me, and Gwen, but sure, okay!" some strange woman spoke as I listened in complete surprise, but realized it must be my own voice. It had to be me. I was the only woman in the room.

Bruno, too, showed initial astonishment that I accepted, but recovered quickly. His jubilation burst out, "ALL RIGHT!" The Seaman Recruit calmed again and the old Master Chief Petty Officer instructed, "You can make the calls from my place. Get your stuff together, and let's go."

I packed light, only one medium suitcase and a makeup case, partially because the clothes I would wear to work at the Blue Onion didn't weigh much, didn't take much space, but I had enough to last the week if I mixed and matched outfits. Besides, I can always come back if I need more clothes, and I can replace any forgotten sundries at the supermarket.

We were on the way to Bruno's apartment by 3:00, and arrived by 3:30. He gave the grand tour of his small, one-bedroom flat. By 4:00, he left me alone while I prepared an early supper, then again when I changed for work.

For our last time alone together until my shift ended, he escorted me during the short stroll to the bar. Were we still in high school, my Mom would say that I was seeing a young gentleman. Our ages were far past that stage, but the emotions flowing through us were that young.

Those emotions and his presence nearby buoyed me through the night. Even after the full shift, my feet didn't hurt during our walk back to his apartment the following morning.

* * * *

At Midnight, Nick whined, "Where is she?" That annoyed Stretch almost as much as having his plan foiled by the Fates once more. Nick insisted, "Well, where is she, Stretch? Huh?"

Stretch conceded, "I don't know." He calmed himself, masked his own annoyance. "She should have been back hours ago. We'll just have to try again tomorrow. Take me home, Nick, and go home yourself. Get some rest."

Nick complied, and wheeled away from the curb. They drove to the nicer neighborhood in the surrounding hills where wife and family waited for Stretch.

Lately, Stretch's heart finally got his brain's attention. When they started this caper, Smokey and the boss explained this was just like shipping stolen cars to people who wanted them. Under that impression, Stretch went along with their idea. After all, while the law said shipping stolen cars overseas was wrong, it was merely illegal. No one was really hurt, only inconvenienced until their insurance settled and they found a new car.

But this thing wasn't that clean. Kidnaping and sending young innocents off to pander to some foreigner was wrong, as wrong as it could be. It was so wrong that Stretch didn't want to do it, was more wrong than he could be a part of any more. And, Stretch wondered, what would the judge, the one who said that he was a hardened, irredeemable criminal at the last sentencing hearing, think about this change in him? What would that judge think of the boss and Toad, who showed neither shame nor pity, only remorseless greed?

Stretch recalled his daughter's nineteenth birthday two weeks ago. The recent acute attack of conscience began as he watched his pretty princess dance with her young beau, when he grasped that the boss and Toad would send her to some far land if he wasn't there to protect her. Unless something changed drastically, he knew the load of double-ought buck in the shotgun lying on his lap would be used by Thursday Night. If he didn't unload it into that reporter, rapidly becoming the less favored choice, he would unload it into the boss. In defense of his daughter, he would eradicate both evil pariahs before they disposed of him. He convinced himself that was the best next step.

"Here you are, Stretch. Right to your door." Nick beamed at the minor victory of safe arrival after the string of humiliating defeats. He thought about it during the drive over. He had decided to follow the advice Stretch gave him, pass up the night in Sweeny's, go home to rest. "See you what time tomorrow?"

"Figure somewhere around 4:00 in the afternoon, unless I call with a different plan." Stretch paused with the door open, feet on the walk. "On second thought, just wait for my call, Nick. May take a little while to find out where she's gone to ground if she isn't staying at her house. Maybe Weasel can ferret her out." Stretch got out, closed the car door, and walked into his home. He faced a night of mortal combat with his conscience, and knew the outcome was far from a sure bet. He only knew that either his old self or his conscience and, with it, his soul would die tonight.

Nick drove to his place. He didn't know what bothered Stretch, but he knew something upset his friend. They had been together far too many years for him to miss the changes, but he had done enough thinking for one night. If he thought about anything more, he knew it would give him a headache. He figured that whatever Stretch decided to do was good enough for him. For now, a half-tumbler of good whisky brought untroubled sleep.

Something Smells

SHORTLY BEFORE NOON TUESDAY, VOICES IN the living room roused me. I had the bed to myself, although his side was still warm. I listened to hushed yet urgent chatter, but, through the walls, couldn't understand what they said. I wished they weren't so considerate for a sleeping guest, not if the conversation involved me. Soon, Bruno spoke my cue, "Do you want to tell her? ... I'll get her. She's in the bedroom."

Soft footsteps on carpet traced his path to the door. I was partway to my robe when Bruno came through. "Oh! You're already up." He appraised what he saw and passed judgement, "You look good in the morning light."

Certainly, I had no reason to be self-conscious that he caught me while wearing only my birthday suit, not after the last two nights together, but I blushed. He eased my embarrassment as he gently helped me into my robe. "Chet's here. Has the Coroner's report, and something he found out yesterday that he wants to tell you. Join us in the kitchen as soon as you're ready, okay?"

"Be right there. Just give me a minute to comb my hair." I answered. Many questions flit through my mind as I organized to meet the unexpected visitor. While he was family to Bruno, he was still someone I met just recently. I wanted to put my best foot forward, at least the best foot I could. I wouldn't make the impression that I wanted to leave, showing up in my bathrobe, so pulled on sweater and slacks. In minutes, I joined the brothers around the small kitchen table.

"Hi, Mickie." Chet greeted. Without pause for an answer, he started,

"I told you last week that we suspected foul play. During the autopsy, the doctor found the injuries from the fall were serious, but unlikely to cause death. Dr. Samson, the medical examiner working the case, also found a bruise on Norma's hip. The location indicated somebody injected her with something, so he ran a toxicology screening. I got the results late yesterday. The tests showed a massive, probably lethal, dose of tranquilizer in her system. Those lab tests point to murder rather than an accident."

The news didn't surprise me. It supported the assumption held since Sid first admitted he and Norma were investigating a case. The idea gained strength when the detectives first mentioned the possibility of murder. With this additional evidence, I was certain. "Because she was killed, it's important that I remember what the sailor who bumped into Norma looked like, isn't it?"

"It is. But I've got some pictures that may help. Do any of these guys look anything like him?" Chet spread a half-dozen mug shots across the table. He leaned against the chair back as he let me study the photos, front and left profile. Several held numbers across their chests.

After several minutes study, I fingered the possible murderer. "He's older now, but this looks like him when he was younger, maybe." A second face in the array seemed familiar. "And this one looks like the tall, thin man who keeps popping up at all the wrong times." said pointing to another. "I don't recognize the others."

Chat didn't smile visibly, but victory resonated in his speech, "Thanks, Mickie. Let's see who you picked out." He turned over the first picture. "Hmmmm, Paul 'Casper' Campbell, questioned as best suspect in a half dozen murders-for-hire in the past six years. We never had enough evidence to take him to trial." Det. Sgt. Grabowski thumbed through his note book, then continued, "Something else interesting. His parole officer notes that he lives pretty well for somebody who works as a handyman at the marina. He was in the same cell block at State Penitentiary as Art Limburg for a few years. There's a rumored connection between the two. Again, never enough evidence that he associated with a convicted felon to revoke his parole, or Limburg's either, for that matter."

The Cheshire Cat never grinned so widely as Chester did when he read from the back of the second mug shot and additional information written in his notebook. "This one is a likely suspect too. Thomas Lincoln, also known as Stretch. He's been in trouble since he borrowed a car without permission for a joy ride when he was a juvenile. Since then, he's done two stretches for grand theft auto, and suspected in other thefts. The first time cost him a dishonorable discharge from the Army as well as five years. The second time was six years of a ten-year sentence before being paroled for good behavior. By coincidence, he was in the same cell block at the same time the other two were there. The Street says he's into something bigger than car theft this time."

Bruno rose from his chair. Silent while he considered these facts, he brewed another pot of coffee. Finally, as he brought the pot to the table, he asserted, "I don't do this sort of thing for a living, like you do, Chet, but it seems there's a real connection just waiting to be proved. That's your job. Do it."

Chet rumbled like a nearing storm, "I intend to. But let's get it straight. I need to know what each of you knows, just like you need to know what I have." He paused to refill his cup. After the first sip, he turned to me, spoke with an edge to his voice, "First, Mickie, I've seen Sid and the photos. It sure looks like my partner is dirty, damn him. Thinking back on it, there were a few times Jim seemed to detour us around the missing girls. If he's on the take, I'm alone in this. But, under department rules, I can't go to Internal Affairs about him without getting pulled off Norma's murder investigation too. I'm stuck unless you and Sid go to I. A. as suspicious civilians. You can get him pulled off the case, out of my way, and I get to stay on the case. Will you help?"

"Sure, Chet. I'll do what I can. I'll call Sid as soon as we're done here." I assured.

"No need to call him. He'll be here shortly. He said you are working on this together. I asked him to be here while we talk. That way, you know everything is on the up and up, and we all find out what the others know." Chet revealed unexpected knowledge about my role.

Clearly, the revelation surprised Bruno, who looked at me, head cocked quizzically to one side. Questions that he wanted to voice burned through his frown, yet he kept silent for now. I knew he'd ask them before the day ended if the talks with Sid and his brother didn't answer them this afternoon.

At the sound of footsteps on the stoop, Chet glanced at his watch, reported, "In fact, that should be him now." He rose to let Sid into the apartment.

Returning to the kitchen table after the greetings and introductions ended, Bruno sullenly spoke, "I guess I'm supposed to go to my room now, and stay there until you're all done talking?"

Sid exclaimed, "No, stay! You have as much right to know what's going on as anybody. Once you took Mickie under your roof, you volunteered to serve for the duration, whether you knew it or not. And Chet says we can trust you to keep it quiet as long as we need."

Bruno sat erect in his chair. Once Sid invited him to stay, he leaned slightly forward. "Fine! ... Well then, what are you waiting for? I'd like to know what I've stumbled into. Something smells. I just don't know yet whether it smells like rotten fish or roses."

The detectives told Bruno background he could know no other way, but he quickly steamed ahead of them. Bruno heard the drums beat to quarters, the boatswain's pipe sound the call to arms, while the others heard only silence. He identified the enemy while the rest barely saw smoke on the horizon. He mentally girded for a battle soon to be joined before the others saw a ship below that smoke.

We reviewed Norma's thesis that a gang kidnaped young girls, then sold them as concubines for the wealthy. After weighing the evidence, we decided it was a good working hypothesis, and explained the facts better than alternatives which relied too heavily on coincidences.

Sid recapped, "Some girls probably stay here in the United States, while others are sent to foreign lands. Thanks to Bruno's suspicion when he heard about a passenger, we took photos of a girl dragged aboard just before the *S.S. Flying Fish* sailed last Saturday morning. My source at the Port Authority say the ship's headed for Bordeaux, France. It fits if the gang smuggles the girls overseas on tramp steamers. They have no fixed routes, and don't draw the attention of customs officials when the crew disembarks for shore liberty, even if the crew is a few short when they come back."

Bruno listened attentively. During the third pot of coffee, he contributed to the discourse, "Then there are two girls on her... Don't look so surprised. Manny said a girl was taken aboard Thursday, plus the one you saw taken aboard Saturday morning. Even I can add."

Having grabbed their attention, he continued, "Norma spoke to Gwen before she died. Gwen told me that Norma thought she knew enough about a big crime that her life was in danger. I didn't believe it until she lay dead on the barroom floor. Listening to you folks, I only guess how much she meant to you. I know she meant a lot to Gwen, too. I'll do whatever I can to help put this scum out of business." When he finished, Bruno checked the clock. He ended the session, "But right now, Mickie, you need to get ready for work. It's almost time. A good spy is never late."

Sid challenged, "And you know that from personal experience, I take it."

I was ready to scold Sid for unleashing his acid tongue when all worked toward the same goal. I didn't need to defend Bruno. Before I said a word, Bruno silenced Sid with an emotionless declaration, "If I told you about that, I'd have to kill you."

Chester reinforced Sid's open surprise when he added the ominous affirmation, "He means it, Sid. You don't really want to know. Take my word for it."

And I wondered who this man was, this big sailor who stormed my castle of solitude, and captured my heart. Whoever he really was beneath the veneer, I was glad that he was on my side.

* * * *

Manny and Jeff made their rounds at the change of watch. So far, all the hatch covers were still secure and tight. That was better than they found below decks. Sunday, two days ago, they found a pair of rivets sheared off the hull plates below waterline in hold # 3. During this inspection, they found three more sheared off at a different frame. The leaks weren't an immediate danger, at least while the bilge pumps could keep up, but popped rivets meant their old girl would spend time in dry dock soon.

"Will the owners pay for repairs, or just scrap her, Manny?" Jeff wondered aloud.

"You mean if she doesn't sink first, right?" Manny shot back over his shoulder. When he turned to face his young helper, he saw undisguised concern on Jeff's face. More gently, Manny continued, "Don't worry, Jeff. She'll have to lose a lot more rivets than that before she's in danger of sinking. Still, this may be the last time I sail on her. If they check all the rivets to find out how many more are rusted partway through, then replace all the bad ones, she could be in dry dock long enough that I'll have to find another ship, or, maybe, take it as an omen and just retire."

Manny neared the rail, looked over the side. The angle of the bow wake to the hull confirmed his suspicions. The Old Man is pushing it this trip. The *S.S. Flying Fish* traveled above her best speed. She's a lot faster empty than they sailed presently, but with cargo aboard nearly to her capacity, her best speed was quite a bit slower. Manny wondered what cargo escaped his notice that justified use of so much extra fuel, not to mention the added wear and tear on the ship. Nothing on the manifest, at least not the pages of the manifest he signed as they loaded her, was noted as perishable or priority enough.

"Jeff, did you sign for anything perishable, or rush delivery?"

"No, Manny. Now that you mention it, though, I could ask you the same thing."

"Skipper is sure pushing it. We may be in port a day early, if nothing in the engine room breaks." Manny paused, "Then the question is whether those passengers paid enough for fast passage to justify the rush. If they were in that much of a hurry, why did they take a tramp steamer rather than one of the fast cruise ships, or, bite my tongue, an airplane?"

"What passengers, Manny?" Jeff questioned in surprise.

Manny looked into Jeff's eyes and saw the real concern, "You didn't know we've got two women, young blondes, up in officer's country, then?" Jeff shrugged his shoulders with open palms forward, gestures which confirmed that he had no idea about the fares aboard.

The Old Salt didn't like this one bit. Any normal passenger would have been on deck for a breath of air and to watch the sea roll under the keel sometime during these last four days. They hadn't been out during his watches, but he figured they had been out during Jeff's turn on deck. It just wasn't right that they stayed in their cabins this long without one trip into the daylight.

Manny needed some time to think about this, but maybe retirement was the best next move for him. He heard stories from the old timers, back when he was as fresh as Jeff is now. If that's what this is all about, he would leave the ship when they got back to the States. He didn't want any part of THAT. Even if it wasn't white slave trade, the *Flying Fish* would be in dry dock at the end of this trip, or at the bottom if they didn't repair her before she sailed again. Maybe, he thought, this was time to buy a part of that small cruiser Bruno owned. They could take tourists out for a day trip around the bay, or fishermen out to the reef to try for a wall-hanger for their dens, and he'd get to spend his nights with Wanda.

Manny brought himself back to the present. "Well, Jeff, I've got the deck watch now. You're relieved. I'll report the three new missing rivets to the bridge." As an afterthought, Manny entreated, "If you can manage it, come up a little early and we'll check the holds again. She's old enough to take a little extra watching when she's pushed this hard."

"Sure thing, Manny. See you again in four hours." Jeff turned and went below decks to his bunk. Two cruises together taught him something about Manny. His senior became worried about something while they spoke on deck. He'd ask what bothered his mentor at the next change of watches, down in the holds where they'd have privacy. Whatever it was, he understood, anything that bothered Manny ought to bother him. But Manny wasn't worried about the ship for now. After Manny's assurance, only five missing rivets out of the thousands that held the ship together was not enough to keep Jeff from sleep, even if they are below the waterline and they were taking on a little water.

Still, with winter coming on, Jeff knew the North Atlantic would not be kind to shipwrecked sailors, even at these middle latitudes. It was only common sense to keep his coat and trousers folded nearby, and to check that he could find his waterproof survival suit and floatation vest, just in case, before he climbed under the blankets and closed his eyes.

On deck, Manny decided that he'd tell Jeff about his concerns at the next change of watch. Jeff was a good kid. He didn't need to be in this crew if things went as badly as Manny feared. He shrugged deeper into his coat with the chill wind that he noticed so much more now that he was getting old enough to gray. His old wounds and injuries twinged agreement, but he smiled with a new thought nevertheless. Besides, Manny and Bruno would need a younger fellow to help crew their boat. Young legs, and arms, and back to do the things Manny felt too old to want to do anymore, even though he still could.

Manny strode to the bridge to report the new discovery that three more rivets were missing. For now, his only concern was whether this new Captain would understand that sheared rivets warned of the stresses this speed put on his old girl.

After he reported, Manny returned to the deck. His guess had been right on the money. Surely, even the young Skipper must know that ahead-two-thirds, the engine room telegraph indicator showed that, was far too fast for this old girl when loaded this heavy.

As he made the prescribed rounds, checking for anything loose that should be tied down, he recalled that he joined this ship for her first voyage after the last time she was dry docked. It was fitting that he leave her when she went to dry dock again. He felt at peace with himself and the sea, but not with the cargo they carried this trip, or the people who shamed this fine old ship with skullduggery and contraband cargo. Serve them all right if she sank under the weight of that shame.

* * * *

Almost one thousand miles astern, the ship's new owner called the hired help. "Casper, Art here. I want you to get rid of that damn private eye tonight. He's getting too close."

"So, what do you want me to do, Cheese?" Casper demanded.

"No finesse, no excuses. Just kill him tonight! Use a damn shotgun if you have to." the boss ordered. He bridled every time Casper called him Cheese, but Casper was the only man who ever made him afraid for his life, still scared him too much to complain. "Did you hear me?"

"I heard you. It costs extra to meet deadlines that tight, and to try an open hit rather than sneaking in and out." Casper countered.

"Fine. Double the money if you do it tonight." Art Limburg capitulated to the judgement and demands of the specialist he needed so badly. His own people had proven ineffective, incompetent.

"Done deal. I'll call you to arrange picking up my money when he's cold." the triggerman agreed. The phone clicked dead. And Casper almost burst with mirth. Cheese would come unglued if he knew that call was now on tape. Yes, if Art, or, for that matter, any of his other clients, ever tried anything to silence him, the shelf full of recorded conversations, phone ordered executions, carefully stored at his lawyer's, would exact full retribution on the self-important pukes who made others call them boss.

Casper devised the contracted frontal assault quickly. If the target wasn't at home, he'd be in his office. Casper liked his simple plan. Just crack the janitor on the head, take the keys, open the office door, and eliminate one snoop. He gathered all that he needed for this effort: a gray shirt and slacks, surgical gloves to prevent leaving behind fingerprints, sawed-off double barrel shotgun and six shells carrying buckshot, all wiped clean. No fingerprints meant that no one would be able to tie him to the crime, at least not prove it to a grand jury. That meant no indictment to worry him.

* * * *

Chet and Sid were gone by the time I washed, put on my face, and dressed. Only Bruno sat at the table. This time, he wore a scowl instead of his usual smile as he played with the half-full cup.

Outside, beyond the window behind him, squall clouds gashed the sky. I sensed there would be a squall blow through here in a minute, too. I went to him and put my arms around him. "You look glum, Swabby. What's the matter?"

His eye flashed with controlled anger as he turned slowly to face me. Bruno fired the first salvo of sarcasm, "Thanks. Thanks a lot. It's SO nice to know I'm trusted. That you and Sid and Chet finally decided you could tell me what's going on." He paused, then railed on, "I suppose you only got friendly because it's your job. God, what a load of crap!" He turned to stare at the middle of the table.

I stepped around the table to stand directly in front of him if he looked up. "Feel better, now that you got that off your chest?" I waited, but he said nothing more. I needed to explain before he pulled away, and my heart nearly broke again at the fear I might lose him before I really found him. "I trusted you, but this has already cost me one friend. I didn't want to get you involved if you didn't need to be put in harm's way. Everything has been on a need-to-know basis. Until this afternoon, the others thought that you didn't need to know. There's one more thing, besides what Sid and Chet told you, that you need to know. I got friendly with you, as you put it, because I like you a lot. That has been, is, and will be, something that's strictly personal, just between us."

If that didn't explain it to somebody with things in his past that he had to kill you if he told you about them, then we weren't on the same page of the hymn book at all. We might even be in different books. My whole future suspended during the minute he thought it over. If he rejected the explanation, our future together would become two separate futures alone. I wondered if he understood that as well as I did.

Finally, Bruno looked up from the table, spoke softly, "I'm sorry. Ten years ago I wouldn't have told this to anybody. Five years ago, I might have told my brother, but no one else. Somehow, I think I can tell you, that you'll understand." He rose, took me in his arms, and just held on as he confessed without whining, "I'm not myself since I met you. I worry that you'll leave, and scared that you'll stay. I don't know which I want more. I'm confused."

I hugged back. "I know what you mean. I'm confused the same way." I admitted it aloud for the first time. We swayed to music that no one else could hear. Only two lovers could hear it well enough to dance to the tune. For us, the song was a slow waltz, not a polka or a two-step. This was the kind of song that lasted a long time, and that we wanted it to last.

Outside, sky and skyline reddened with the setting sun. The squall line passed without damaging winds. The storm inside was over, too. There were no guarantees that we wouldn't sail through other storms more damaging, but at least we weathered our first one.

Bruno relaxed his gentle hold. "Getting time for you to go to work. If we hurry, Harvey can burn some burgers and fries for us before you have to start." He smiled, "This way, neither of us has to wash dishes." He released me and, because he had been in charge of men and other important things for so many years, his new tone of voice unconsciously instructed, "Okay, get your coat. Let's go."

I recognized a bit of my Dad in that manner, did not take offense. He was a gentle man, in need of the chance to let it show. I shrugged a little to myself, then grabbed coat and purse. He stood behind me as I suggested, "Maybe, if we hurry, we can see the rainbow." As I turned to face him again, he shoved a Government Model pistol into an inside-the-pants holster worn on the cross-draw side. He didn't say anything, but my curiosity showed. "Where did you get that rig?"

"From Chester. He said I should carry this for a little while," Bruno reported, "just in case the bastards stay beyond arm's reach. It's a little insurance that we'll get the chance to see a lot of rainbows together... Ready?"

"Yes, as ready as I'll ever be."

Walking to the Blue Onion, we enjoyed the fresh smell of the city after a Fall shower, and the pleasure of each other's company.

* * * *

Cluttered desk stared back, mutely accused him of sloth, disorganization, a slow mind, and all manner of failings which counted as mortal sins for someone who billed himself as a good detective. Somewhere in the piles of data, he would find the proof for the theory. The key to understanding all the other pieces and how they fit together hid in plain view, Sid told himself once more.

Despite self-administered pep talk, Sid felt he wouldn't, couldn't, find it tonight. Too much new data poured into the mix at the afternoon meeting with others seeking the answer just as ineffectively.

If only Sherlock Holmes, Nero Wolfe, Hercule Poirot, Sam Spade, Mike Hammer, or even Miss Marple were real, he'd gladly pay their consulting fee. They sometimes made a wrong turn, but always prevailed by the last chapter, before the closing credits. Where were they when he needed them?

Was his counterpart, Chet Grabowski, up to the job that faced them, like Lieutenant Columbo would be? Or would he bumble along like Inspector Clouseau of Pink Panther infamy?

Sid decided that only his fatigue led him into this melancholy diversion. It was unfair to judge either himself or Chet by fictional detective standards. After all, neither of them had a script which gave them all the answers, nor a writer who started with the solution and worked backward to the crime so the hero character could solve the case.

By objective standards, they weren't doing badly. They had a tolerably good idea what the crime was, how it was carried out, and who some of the underlings were. They were close enough to ending it that somebody hired a hit man to kill his partner, and threaten him. True, they still needed proof to skim off the brains of the outfit, whoever that was, but the muscle had been identified as Thomas 'Stretch' Lincoln.

Sid almost laughed at the cruelty of nicknames, particularly those given by one juvenile hood to another. Then Stretch grew tall to boot, doubling the appropriateness of his handle when he stood inches taller than the varsity players while still only on the juniors. Yes, Sid knew the story because his coach used the example to enforce his lectures against dumb choices. It was commonly accepted that Stretch blew a career in basketball when he went to prison instead of college.

But that side trip down memory lane was a distraction. He forced himself to take another try at the clues. If only he could get a handle on the rest of this case, Sid thought to himself. But he drew a blank. He decided to call it a night. A good night's sleep would do wonders for his ability to concentrate.

As he piled papers into neat stacks, then folded them into a manila folder, someone pounded on the outer door. A premonition made him shudder. The secretary went home hours ago, so Sid was alone, all alone, except for his .45 caliber companion. As he shouted, "Hold on. I'll be right there." Sid checked that there was a round in the chamber, the magazine was full, and this instrument of last resort was cocked and locked, ready for instantaneous use if needed.

Sid realized his mouth went suddenly very dry. And why not? The Boogeyman was still out there, contracted to kill him. But he had a name now. After Mickie picked his mug shot from the array of likely suspects, Sid knew the killer probably was Paul 'Casper' Campbell.

If Casper or anybody else from that gang found the file, the investigation could be delayed or thwarted. Sid spread a closed case file across his desk as a decoy. As he crossed the outer office to answer the still hammering visitor, he slipped the real file into his secretary's desk.

Sid opened the door cautiously. The wizened, wiry ancient slipped between door and frame. Sid guessed this visitor wore his total wardrobe, topped it with a gap-toothed grin gashed into the gray stubble below steel gray eyes. The old man, wringing an old cap in his arthritic fingers, warmly greeted, "Hi, Sid. Thought I'd drop by. It's been a while since I've seen you."

"About three years, Weasel. What do you need this time?"

"Nothin', Sid. You saved my ass that last time. It's my turn to save yours. I've got somethin' you need to know." Weasel countered.

"In my office." Sid invited in a tone far warmer than the words. When he re-locked the door, Sid asked, "Still take a wee dram to ward off the chill?"

"Sure do, Sid. Three fingers of the good stuff, if you don't mind. Scotch if you have it. No ice, please. Thanks. You've got a nice office. This sure is a comfortable chair." Weasel chattered as he crossed the reception area into Sid's office and chose the best visitor's chair.

As Sid poured, he knew two things before the grand master of all snitches opened his mouth again. First, Weasel didn't lie. Whatever he said was the truth as he knew it, and he knew nearly everything that went on near the docks. Second, while he might not tell you everything if you talked to him on the street, if he came to you and accepted a drink, he told you everything he knew even if you didn't ask the right questions. Sid handed the old man four fingers of the best Scotch he had in the office, the brand he served to important clients and prospects. "Hope that meets your expectations, Weasel."

Weasel took the glass, slyly held it to measure the portion with his fingers. His eyes confirmed that Sid poured liberally. "Thanks, Sid. This should ward off the chills and keep the wolf away from the door." Weasel sipped. His nose and palate confirmed the quality. Yes, he was right. Sid treated him right. Not at all like that pushy thug who pestered him today, or the handyman at the marina who grilled him for a couple weeks now. Neither of them ever offered a decent drink, just cheap wine.

"Take your time, old timer. There's no rush to send you back into the cold." Sid offered cordially. And, he admitted to himself, really, there was no rush. No reason to push the old man into the cold again. Not since Mary called it quits, packed her things and disappeared into the night with her new boyfriend.

Weasel knew the offer was genuine, but felt his claustrophobia crushing in. He remembered the cold night in 1950 spent buried by rubble in Seoul. North Korean artillery collapsed the house onto his squad. He lived, the only one of twelve good men to escape. Even after the V. A. shrinks worked with him to overcome his guilt and fear of being inside four walls, the cursed malady got the best of him, cost him a good job thirty-some years ago. Now that he couldn't hold a job on the docks, he was used to his three-sided shipping crate hovel. He spoke calmly, "Thanks for the offer, Sid, but let me tell you what I've got. Then I need to go. Get back outside where I belong."

"Okay, Weasel, spill it. I'm all ears." Sid prompted in good humor.

Weasel recounted, "First, two weeks ago, the handyman at the marina started asking questions about you, Norma, and some woman ex-cop. Stuff like where you go after work, have I ever seen you with a woman I don't know. Then a tall hard case looks me up today, starts pumping me about a new woman working anywhere in the dock area. Possibly she's a new agent you've hired, he says."

Sid looked up as a key turned in the outer door. The entering janitor's uniform caused no alarm, not until Weasel stage-whispered, "It's the guy from the marina." When Sid took a second look, he saw that the janitor wore surgical gloves. Then he saw the shotgun's double muzzle rise from behind the waste paper stacked in the canvas cart. Just before it exploded its lethal message, he dove for cover.

Too slow to avoid all the pellets, Sid felt the sting as some cut his back, but he knew the different feel of shallow and deep wounds. Sid knew these were shallow. And he knew that bastard would feel the unpleasant counter argument that 230 grain hollow points would make to his load of buckshot. Shotgun roared again, shredding the desk inches from Sid's head as he drew pistol from shoulder holster.

The assassin opened the shotgun to reload. Casper had made but one error in his haste to fill this contract. He didn't try to get the extra shells out of trouser pockets while he wore surgeon's gloves. Now, he fumbled as his pocket turned out with the friction of latex on cotton, spewing shells onto the floor. That slowed him during the reload, but didn't worry him. He didn't expect that Sid was still able to resist. He never missed from this close range, not with both barrels.

As Sid recognized the shooter paused to reload, he rolled to a firing position, acquired his target, yelled "You're dead meat, asshole!" He put four shots into the assailant's chest before the first ejected case hit the floor. The dispute was settled. In the gun-smoky room, Sid kicked the shotgun from Casper's grasp, stood over Casper's last-gasping, soon-to-be-corpse. "What for?" he demanded of the dying man.

"Cheese's orders!" The last words Casper wheezed before he reported to Lucifer for his next assignment, stoking the furnaces of Hell for eternity, made no sense.

Sid checked on Weasel. The old man was seriously wounded, but alive, and would live if he got to a hospital. Sid pushed a handkerchief under the old man's coat, used it as a pressure bandage to stem the flow of blood. "Can you sit up and hold this against the wound while I call help?" he asked. Weasel weakly groaned but complied.

Then Sid made two calls. Weasel's condition demanded that he first call 9-1-1. A normal response interval would give him enough time to make the other call after he started police and ambulance on their way.

* * * *

About 10:00 P.M., Gwen answered the phone on the back bar. She spoke curtly. She listened for a shorter time. Then her knees buckled as she abruptly lowered the phone from her ear. She caught herself, braced herself against the counter with her free hand. She stood again by the time I reached her and questioned, "Gwen, what is it?"

Gwen was still wobbly, so I took her arm to help steady her. She dropped the phone and held my hand with clenched fingers. When I tried to return the phone, Gwen's ashen lips murmured, "No, you take it."

I put the receiver to my ear, and joined the already started conversation. "Hello? Who's this?"

"Who are you? What happened to Gwen?" the voice countered.

"Sid? What's wrong? Whatever you told Gwen nearly caused her to faint."

"Sorry I didn't recognize your voice right away, Mickie. Yes, this is Sid. I just called 9-1-1. Weasel and I are wounded, not badly, but we'll be in the hospital as soon as the ambulance gets us there. The shooter isn't doing so well. He's headed for the morgue."

It was Gwen's turn to hold me up when my knees gave way.

Sid continued, "I called to warn you. Before the shootout, Weasel said a tall thin guy - sound familiar? - started asking about you today. Watch your back. They don't know where you are, but they're looking. And it sounds like they're looking in the right neighborhood to find you sooner rather than later."

A second voice sounded in the background. Sid announced, "The ambulance is here. I have to go. I'll call from whichever hospital they take me. I'll need a ride home after they sew me up. Say 'Hi' to Bruno and Chester for me. So long." The phone clicked dead before I could say anything, ask anything.

I felt everything moved in slow motion, even if I knew it weren't so. By this time, Harvey hovered behind his Lady Gwendolyn. Gwen recovered enough to contend for control over the minor disaster. She suggested, "Better sit down, dear. You look as awful as I feel. Then I'll get you a brandy. Aw, hell! ... Harvey, get us both a brandy!"

Bruno came from the men's room as Gwen and I moved to a table near the bar. He stormed over, accosted us, "You don't look well, either of you. What's wrong?" At least that would save telling the story over and yet again to each new audience.

By the time Harvey poured and served the brandy, Sharon and Kim joined us. When Gwen started her report, she had to speak loudly for those at the back of the growing crowd. Midweek regulars and a few who strayed in, now two deep, encircled us. While some didn't know Sid, everyone knew Weasel. He was the unofficial mascot, by acclamation of the members, for this loose-knit fraternity.

The news that Weasel was wounded brought outcries of anger. The news that he was on his way to the emergency room for treatment drew queries about which hospital. The revelation that the would-be executioner was himself headed to the morgue brought cheers. Gunny, a retired Gunnery Sergeant, even bought a round of drinks for the house to celebrate swift justice that slick lawyers couldn't unravel in Appeals Court. Even Wanda and her girls agreed that anyone who shot Weasel deserved that end.

With so many customers to serve, my brief rest ended. Waiting tables displaced the shock, but if Sid was seriously hurt, it probably would have done nothing except expend my nervous energy.

Three hours later, the phone rang again. Gwen relayed Sid's report. They were at County, and were repaired as well as emergency room staff could manage. Weasel faced additional surgery as soon as the orthopedic specialist scrubbed. One pellet shattered the humerus. Since fragments endangered the nerve, a specialist needed to put the pieces together if Weasel were to use that arm again. Even with an optimistic prognosis, Weasel faced several weeks sleeping warmly between clean sheets and having regular meals and baths. The crowd reacted with mixed laughter and cheers at that announcement.

When the crowd finally quieted, Bruno volunteered to gather Weasel's meager belongings and safeguard them until his return to the docks. That earned Bruno a cheer, and some promises to buy drinks when Weasel retrieved his gear.

During that minor uproar, Gwen received Sid's report of his condition. He was released into an outpatient status, and ready for a ride home. He wanted to be there rather than in the hospital when the analgesic wore off and he began to feel the stitches that closed his wounds. She relayed the report privately after the throng dispersed, returned to their tables.

Then Gwen decreed, "You and Bruno better take off." She explained, "Sid gets impatient when he has to wait too long." As I gathered coat and purse, she added, "Tell him Harvey and I wish him well, a speedy recovery… See you tomorrow, six o'clock as usual."

I turned to Bruno, "I'll drive Sid to his house, but I'd like you to come with, ride shotgun."

Bruno launched from the barstool like a Jack-In-The-Box jumps when you crank to that part of the tune, agreed instantly, "Sure, let's go. Let's get him home so we can go home too."

As we walked back to Bruno's apartment where I parked my car, he asked, "Did you ask me along because you're worried that a wounded man will make a pass that you can't resist?"

"No, that's not the reason." I explained, "When he called the first time, Sid warned that the tall thin man was looking for me. From what Weasel told him before the shooting started, the thin man was close, might already know where I am. I really want you along so he can't catch either of us alone. Besides, more than that, I like your company. I like having you near."

Bruno smiled gently, "That's all I wanted to hear you say." A few steps farther, he confided quietly, "Just so you don't feel all by yourself, I like you too, a lot. I'm glad you asked me to come along."

Shortly, we reached the car, loaded up, and drove to County Hospital with an empty rearview mirror. That, I took it, was a good omen despite all the threatening possibilities. Soon, we found Sid in the waiting room. He sat with back arched to keep shirt and jacket away from his freshly sutured wounds, eyes closed in semi-meditation to keep his mind off the discomfort.

If I knew Sid, he focused on our next moves. We must carefully negotiate the slippery slope between court imposed restrictions on police efforts, and freewheeling disregard for law that too many fictional detectives displayed. If too cautious, we would get nowhere. If too bold, any capable lawyer could void our efforts in court. Either alternative to the pursued goal were totally unacceptable.

Gently at first, louder and firmer until he responded, I hailed him from wherever his mind took him for relief, "Sid … Sid … SID!" Finally, he blinked himself back into our world. "Welcome back. Ready?"

Sid rose quickly, but stiffly. His priorities reflected in his greeting, "Let's get out of here before they change their minds about letting me go home! Hi, Mickie, Bruno." He already strode toward the exit as he spoke. Bruno and I rushed to keep up.

Once outside, Sid became uncertain which way to go. Despite the hour, many cars still filled the lot, too many others to spot my sedan without knowing where I left it. He slowed. We closed, then overtook him. I answered the silent question spoken with his eyes, "I'm parked over here, Sid." Then I led the way to the car.

A half-hour later, Bruno and I followed Sid into his small house. What began as a short visit to help him settle in safely for the night turned into a longer session when Detective Sergeant Grabowski arrived soon after. We gathered in the kitchen after the greetings, and, in deference to Sid's wounds, I started a pot of coffee. It seemed the appropriate beverage for the impromptu meeting.

Chet opened the session while we waited for the fresh Java, "Congratulations, Sid. You're one of the few who has lived through an attempt by Paul Campbell, and the only one who had a chance to shoot back, draw blood. The fingerprints show it really was him that you bested."

Sid sat silently for a moment before answering, deep thought showed on his face. Seriously, he observed, "I thought it was some lunatic on a mission from God. Now you tell me it was Casper, a hired killer. If that's true, why did he say that he did it on 'Jesus' orders'? Some kind of sick gag?"

"I don't think it was a gag. Are you sure that's what he said? Could it be something that only sounded like that?" Chet grilled.

Sid testily admitted, "Maybe it was something else." He defended the possible mistake, "You try to hear a dying man's last gasp after two shotgun blasts and your own return fire, all in a small room. Tell me what you hear while your ears still ring."

Serendipitously, I opened the refrigerator to get milk for the coffee, to tame the caffeine at this late hour. Next to that jug, the wrapper around the cheddar proclaimed cheese, and the old joke, which played off the similarity between those two words when spoken, came to mind. "What he said was 'Cheese's orders'. But who the hell is Cheese?" I wondered aloud.

Sid glared at me like I had lost what little mind I had left, but Chester remembered the joke and understood. He answered, "I don't know … yet. But I sure can find out. It's not much, but it's better than no lead at all."

Chet continued, "By the way, you folks have stirred up a hornet's nest. The stronger you build the case that a gang abducted coeds and sent some of them overseas, the more people notice. Took a call from an F. B. I. Agent I know. They have to reopen a number of cases closed with the conclusion that no crime was committed, not kidnaping at any rate. Because there were no ransom demands, they were sure the girls were just runaways. Now, they're not so sure they figured it right."

Bruno commented glumly, "Don't forget boys. For some people, boys are used the same way you think these girls are being used, to pander to some rich old fart's sexual appetites."

Stunned silence greeted his observation. I guessed the possibility eluded the others, as it evaded me. I blurted, "Somehow, we always think only girls and young women are targets for sexual perversions. Why don't we worry about the boys? Don't their pictures show up on milk cartons too?"

Sid spoke first, "Damn, Bruno, that idea probably doubled the number of people we're looking for. I hate to say it, but you're probably right! People are not guaranteed sainthood because they were born into good families with money and power. Most of them are probably good eggs, but the rotten ones have the resources to be really rotten."

Chet opined, "Yeah, we can't say all of kids who disappear are snatched for sex, but we can't ignore the possibility that some of them were. Wait until I remind my friend at the Bureau this is not just about girls. The Feds will be at each other's throats because nobody there figured that out themselves." He shook his head as he commented, "And they worried they'd run out of things to do after the Cold War ended and everybody said they didn't have to worry about Russian spies anymore."

Sid snorted, "If the Feds spent more time tracking real criminals, they wouldn't have so much time to hassle honest, if a bit wacky, citizens. I'll bet most theories about government conspiracies to take away our rights would fade if people heard about them busting real gangs rather than stuff like Ruby Ridge and Waco."

While they argued politics and police work, I tuned them out. I listened to my heart instead. Norma died in the line of duty, died fighting the good fight against evil unspeakable. Even if she didn't know how big this case was, could be, when she started, the people in this kitchen certainly knew it now. We only had to find enough proof so others would know it, spend the effort to end it. I owed Norma, and all the kids already lost, an end to this before any more were hurt. I had to do this one for an old friend.

Sid signaled to Chet and Bruno that their sidebar debate was ended. "Let's get back to the point of the meeting."

I rejoined the discourse, "Do we know who owns the *Flying Fish* yet? Where she's registered? That might give us more to work with, help us find an answer."

"My Port Authority contact says Black Lines, an offshore corporation, owns her, and leases two more of the same type." Sid reported. "All three sail under the Panamanian flag. I put Nelda on the job of finding out who the people are behind the corporation. She knows how to dig out the names, but it will take her some time if they made any effort to hide behind holding companies and other blinds."

The conversation ended about a half hour later, while the clear dark sky still sparkled with stars.

* * * *

In an expensive downtown penthouse flat, part of the estate inherited from his parents, Arthur Limburg couldn't sleep. Even at this midnight hour, he paced the floor instead. At last, he pulled a heavy robe close around him against the night chill, and stepped into the roof garden. He was always able to think things through better in these surroundings, especially after the time in prison. The city lights seemed to mirror the stars in the sky, but such frivolous thoughts were not on his agenda tonight. He had more urgent matters, important to his own survival, to occupy every brain cell at his command.

Art, despite the throbbing headache, considered what he knew and what he suspected. Casper, that festering thorn in his ego, should have reported success by now. He never let the clock deter his reports, his taunts, his demands for payment. Could Casper have failed for the first time?

If Casper failed, who could the boss find to execute the ruthless death orders now? Neither Stretch nor Nick was very good at that specialty. In fact, Art had already decided to kill Stretch. The signs were clear. Stretch was no longer a reliable soldier, but a possible threat, like Smokey had been. That this was still mere suspicion might stay his execution, but Stretch would not survive the week unless needed very badly.

And that hideous woman, Stretch called her Toad, had to go too. That little indiscretion with the teenager would die with her. Why had the Fates placed her at the dock when he sailed with the boy aboard, and kept her there until he came back to port alone? There had to be another woman ready, for the big money, to take Toad's place, to become the procurer of innocents to satisfy the lecherous.

The boss faltered in mid-stride. His enterprise sounded evil, even in his own mind, when painted that way. He had never been at a loss for clever justifications for his transgressions, including the hired murder of his parents. He shrugged it off in a moment, but even he could do so only after he redrew the portrait of the business that paid so well. He finally decided that he gave youngsters, who would never leave the state if he didn't intervene, the opportunity to travel the world and to taste other cultures.

Still, this might be the right time to take a vacation, suspend operations. The captain of his ship wired earlier this evening to report that she needed repairs possible only in dry dock. He could suspend operations while she was made seaworthy again rather than find another boat to continue the trade.

He leaned toward that decision because he would be free to eliminate the weak links in his organization immediately. After he eliminated Stretch and Toad, he could take a few weeks or a few months longer to build a new gang of competent henchmen. When the *S.S. Flying Fish* came out of dry dock, even if it took a year to reopen his business, the market would still be there.

The market for fresh flesh had always existed, even if ignored by polite society, as had the market for works of art and other antiques sold without benefit of provenance, those documents which proved the origin and authenticity of articles. He observed, even participated occasionally, when such items traded for high dollars. The required common thread was that buyers and sellers shared disregard for whether acquisition was legal, or whether or not the girls and boys wanted their new experience.

Art decided that was the course he would follow. He could sleep now, even with the uncertainty whether Casper succeeded or failed in his task. He could stand the headache until the medicine worked.

...If You Sign on With Me, Mate

"WAKE UP! I NEED TO DO something, and you should come along." Bruno insisted as he shook me.

"Bruno, has anyone ever told you that you have way too much energy to be retired?" I stretched awake and checked the clock. It was 6:00 A. M. We slept for only 5 hours.

"I'm only retired from the Navy, not from life. I own a small day cruiser. It's only a thirty footer, but I stay busy taking tourists for rides around the bay during summer. I need to check on her after the storm last night. Make sure she's still berthed where I left her." He explained with a quiet chuckle. Noting the question in my eyes, Bruno added, "You need to get used to this if you sign on with me, mate."

"You're not going to wake me this early without offering coffee, are you?" I beseeched.

"Get dressed, warm clothes. By the time you're ready, I'll have it on the table." The mattress rebounded as he rose to rush the kitchen. Between the clangs and bangs of bustling between cupboard, sink, and counter, Bruno interrupted the task. He called back, "You'll have to settle for instant. Don't have time to wait for the brewed version."

Wearing two sweaters under a wind breaker, jeans, and wool socks, I felt the apartment soon would be too warm. His rush became mine, too, and the coffee went into insulated mugs to take with rather than dawdle at the table. We drove to the pier in the comfortable silence shared by friends.

At the gated parking lot, the key card admitted the skipper and his crew of one. Others were already checking their boats as he pointed her out, "There she is, right where she belongs." In the middle of a row of glistening white fiberglass hulls, one boat stood out in varnished wooden splendor.

"She's beautiful in the dawn, isn't she?" Bruno asked with undisguised pride. "I put the rush on to make sure we got here when she'd look her best. Now that you've seen her, let's go aboard. I'll introduce you to each other."

"I'm almost jealous." I teased as we walked down the quay toward *Virginia*. "So, which girlfriend did you name her after?"

Bruno nearly blushed, "I didn't name her after an old girlfriend. If I were Barry Fitzgerald, I'd gush in my best Irish brogue that I named her after 'me sainted mither, rest her soul'. The truth is that's the name she wore when I bought her, and my mom is still alive. I probably bought her instead of the other boat that was for sale when I was looking because she was named after my Mom, as much as for the wooden hull and that the price was right."

We clambered aboard, and he directed the tour, from bow to stern, and beam to beam. I needed to relearn the language of sailors, their ships, and the sea, yet remembered enough from Dad's stories to qualify as a recruit rather than a complete landlubber.

"Can we take her out?"

Bruno smiled, "Sure. I usually stretch her legs at least once a week this time of year, just to keep her tuned up." He selected and removed a key from his key ring, then handed it to me. "This fits all the locks except the engine starter. It's yours for as long as we're together. Check the locker in the cabin for the rain gear in case we get another squall while we tour the bay."

"Check the locker for rain gear. Aye, aye, Cap'n!" I opened the cabin and started below. Suddenly, feeling quite mischievous, I grinned with glee. For no reason that I could explain, I turned and tried to deadpan. "What's a locker? And what does a rain gear look like?"

I knew I didn't pull it off when Bruno smiled and shook his head. With pretended seriousness, he used an officious tone to explain, "Harrumph! You 'lubbers call them closets and rain coats. I'll explain the rest later. But whatever under God's blue skies ever prompted you to sign on as Cabin Boy - uh - Girl in the first place? Harrumph!" Our laughter rang through the boat, from bridge to cabin, and beyond to other boats still tied.

Going below, I found the raincoats, ensured there were no visible holes, and tried them on until I found one which fit comfortably over my jacket and sweaters. When I returned to the bridge, Bruno explained the procedures followed to leave the dock, and mentioned that he ran the fans to exhaust potentially explosive fumes from the engine compartment before starting. He checked his watch and announced a simple itinerary, "We'll run out a few miles past the harbor buoy, come back to port, then top off the fuel tanks. After we tie up, I'll take you to lunch. We should get back to my place in time for you to take a nap before work tonight, even with a stop to pick up Weasel's stuff." The starter growled, followed by the rumbling thrum of big engines at low rpm.

"Cast off fore and aft mooring lines… Stand by to cast off spring line." The orders pierced the morning calm. Bruno eased *Virginia* forward against the spring line restraint to swing the stern away from the dock. Throttles at All-Stop, he ordered, "Cast off spring line." then backed out of the slip. Once clear of the other boats, we set course for the harbor mouth. While out of reach of land, we could relax our vigil against attack, although we had to remain wary of the other traffic. It wouldn't do to collide with another vessel in port.

* * * *

As he sipped his coffee, Art Limburg, the boss, looked down on the harbor. A lovely old boat worked through traffic toward the open sea. He voiced his envy to the winds, "Lucky bastards. They're going for a boat ride, and I have to work my butt off, try to save my own ass and salvage something from this wreck." He winched from the stabbing pain of a migraine coming on fast.

Jim Philips, his man on the inside, source of timely warnings when the investigations got too close, called Stretch. The news relayed to him just minutes ago was not good. In fact, the tidings were bad enough to spoil Art's breakfast. This coffee was the only thing he could stomach until all these fraying ends were raveled back together, or he calmed down again. He reviewed the list.

Internal Affairs visited Philips at his house. They relieved him of gun and badge, then told him that he was suspended without pay. The investigators promised fair and full inquiries. Philips knew the payoffs swelled his bank accounts far beyond what the city paid. He couldn't explain that away. Flight would be as good as an admission of guilt, but, even if he stayed, it was very likely the judge would put him in the same prison where Art did time. Several toughs now spent time there because Philips was a good cop, except for this transgression. As a convicted dirty cop, he feared he wouldn't make it through his first year. That was what he told Stretch. Philips also said not to call him after tomorrow, that he would call Stretch after it all blew over.

Art knew that Philips, deep down, wanted to rabbit. He also figured that Philips couldn't run fast enough to avoid capture. Police and FBI had telephones, radios, faxes, computers, and all the other modern tools of communication at the ready to help chase him down once he took the first step.

Once caught, Philips didn't have the nerve to take the heat. He'd cut a deal, turn State's evidence rather than go to prison. Clearly, if Philips stayed alive, he was a danger to all of them.

That's why Art had Stretch arrange the meeting for this evening. Art promised money, cash, to help the discovered bad cop escape to Mexico. That was the bait. At the meeting, Art would offer to take Philips to a ship waiting offshore. Really, Jim's one-way ride would end at the reef. Stretch wouldn't come back either, if he didn't go along with the plan more enthusiastically than he had done lately. The fish would eat well tonight with double servings.

That resolved to his satisfaction, Art turned his attention to the next problem. The morning paper announced results of the gunfight between hired killer and local detective. In the face of that setback, he must try again. Sid Koenig had to die before he stumbled across any more evidence that jeopardized the enterprise that allowed Art to live so well. The only real question was whether the attempt would be through another, hopefully more competent, agent or by his own hand.

He opened and smoothed the newspaper crumpled in his initial anger. The headline, "Them - 0, Us - 1", had been in poor taste as far as Art was concerned. The pool of possible candidates to attempt this ticklish task was small. Only a few of them would apply with such headlines. The best of the local lot was in the morgue. Pride aside, Art knew he was not as good as Casper had been.

Art had to import some help. He recalled names heard during conversations with some of his domestic distributors. Among those with the best reputations were Grits from Atlanta, Reaper from Chicago, and Smoker from Detroit. Any one of this trio had ample experience enforcing someone else's will on the reluctant and unwilling. As a bonus, they charged modest fees for the large service rendered.

Surely, one of them could resolve his problem with the detective. He only had to contact them, find the one who would take the contract. As long as the hired gun was in town already, perhaps Art could arrange to pull the other thorn from his side for not too much more. Art decided to offer two contracts, one to eliminate Koenig's interference, the other to have his revenge on Stevens.

Meanwhile, Art would eliminate the easier targets. Philips, Toad, Stretch, and Nick wouldn't expect him to take direct action. It wasn't his usual style to act himself when it could be hired done. That gave him an edge over these incompetents.

Art smiled with decisions made. He returned to the kitchen, and warmed the congealed breakfast in the microwave. He decided it would be a better day, now that clear resolve replaced the clouds of uncertainty. Even his headache receded, and the voices quieted.

* * * *

Habitually, Randall Osgood IV, junior partner in the firm of Osgood and Osgood, listened to the messages on the answering machine when he reached the office even before he scanned the morning paper. One of his clients with arrangements for post mortem revelations called, but not both of them. That unmade call, the broken custom, shattered his routine and caused near panic.

Randall keyed the intercom, instructed his secretary, "Trisha, pull the Campbell and Lincoln files. Reschedule my morning appointments.

No calls or visitors until I review their instructions." In moments, Trisha delivered two sealed heavy envelopes. As he sat at his desk, the morning paper's headline caught his eye. The lead story confirmed his obligation to implement the contingency plan.

First, he called the surviving client, "Thomas Lincoln, Randall Osgood here. If you saw the headline this morning, it may be time to turn yourself in. Let's talk about it, say 10:00 this morning"

Then he called the Assistant District Attorney, invited him over to receive the collection of incriminating tape recordings. The Sword of Damocles began its fatal fall. By noon, a great - in the sense that it was large, not that it was good - criminal organization would be in mortal peril.

Randy quietly hoped that the courts would do their job this time. Only his belief that even Judas deserved the best defense that could be honestly prepared within the law kept him representing such wicked clients. He shivered as he thought, "Thank God they never told me anything before it happened!" That foreknowledge would have converted him from defense counsel into co-conspirator, possibly one of their cell mates at State prison.

Panic passed, and Randy shrugged. At least the fees would be worthwhile, all the way through the appeals to stay the execution, provided his remaining client had the money to afford him after the government confiscated money generated by criminal activities. This might wind up a case represented for no fee, just the satisfaction that he did what he felt a lawyer should do. After all, he had other clients who paid quite a bit for his services. He could afford to take some cases just to keep the system honest.

* * * *

For the first time in many days, I slept until the alarm clock rang. True, it was only a nap after lunch, but I got the rest needed before work at the Blue Onion tonight. Three factors contributed to the slackened tension. First, I was tired following the late meeting last night. Second, I breathed a major dose of sea air while we toured the bay on Bruno's boat. Lastly, I had a transitory attack of selective amnesia which allowed me briefly to forget that the thin man hunted me while I hunted him.

I also forgot, until I finished my shower, that Norma died just one week ago. To blunt the pangs of having lost a close friend, I found a new one, Bruno. At least in my case, the Lord had given in equal measure for what He took away. I was grateful for the favor. It doesn't always work that way. Mom still hadn't met the special someone who could take Dad's place.

As I finished putting on my face, I wondered why I always had such weighty thoughts when too busy, too involved in the world, to give them the serious consideration they deserved. I felt like a photographer who saw something really wonderful but fleeting while I changed the film in the camera.

Time for peripheral thoughts ran out as I dressed. The front door of this little sanctuary opened into a free-fire zone. When we eliminated the threat, I could explore those thoughts in safety. Until then, I had to focus on the physical dangers to live long enough for these thoughts to matter.

In the living room, Bruno napped in the recliner. From the kitchen door into the living room, I called to him, "Bruno, wake up! It's nearly time."

He unnerved me once again, as he did every time he seemed to waken into full alert from deep sleep in one blink of the eye. Some day, I would ask how he does that. Was it something he was born with, or something he had learned during his life? I almost felt that he never slept, just closed his eyes and feigned slumber to lure his prey closer. "Why are you out there?" I asked.

Bruno shrugged, "Seemed to be a good move, in case we had uninvited visitors." He threw off the Afghan with his left hand, revealing the pistol held in his right. He grinned as he slipped it into the holster, "Chet was right. This is a hell of a security blanket." He pulled the chair upright, leaned over to put on his shoes, then asked, "What do you want for supper? Cold cut sandwiches here, or burger and fries at the bar?"

"Well, at least the sink will still be empty if we eat at the bar. I guess I can face another burger, but with onion rings this time." I declared my preferences. Laughing a little, I added, "I can almost feel my arteries hardening just saying that."

Bruno laughed, "Then try the fried shrimp. Just let me change shirts and get my jacket, and we'll go!" He disappeared into the bedroom, and reappeared in a clean shirt and, what else would I expect, a navy blue blazer.

By 5:30 P M, we sat at the back corner booth while Harvey prepared our meals. Gwen drew two drafts, a schooner of best dark for Bruno, and a mug of pale ale for me. Waiting for the food, my feelings found voice, "This is only our first week anniversary, Bruno. Hard to believe we've grown so close so quickly. It's like we are meant to be together, not just be two ships passing in the night." I expected that he'd fidget, or show some other typically male reaction to the prospect of serious relations.

Instead, Bruno gave his best effort at a serious answer, "It's a little scary, isn't it? Never figured I'd ever have anything but the *Virginia*, not with this scar and patch. How did you look past that anyway?"

"You asked me to, remember? That first time, you said you were a nice guy once I got to know you." I smiled. "I felt I owed you the chance to prove it. Something clicked that first night that let me see into your soul rather than get hung up on the first layer. As far as I can tell, you are a nice guy."

Gwen served food and drink as Bruno struggled for words. She asked, "How are you two getting along?"

"Meet my new Cabin Girl, Gwen. I predict Mickie will make a tolerably good sailor in ten or twelve years, if she ever figures out what a locker is. She will if she stays with me." Bruno smiled broadly. "After that, she should make a fine First Mate." He took my hand, proposed, "Provided you're willing to sign on for that long."

He hadn't gotten down on his knee, or offered a big ring, or even asked in the usual way shown in all the movies, but I knew he meant it. Despite having attained an age when I should be cautious, I blurted out my answer in front of Gwen as witness, "Should we call the Chaplain, or have the Captain marry us at sea?"

Before Bruno could answer, the real world crashed the party. Chester Grabowski didn't ask what he interrupted when he broke into the conversation. "Gwen, get me a beer, please." He turned to us as Gwen hustled away, "You two better hold on to your hats. When we searched

Paul Campbell's rooms, we found a tape recording of the phone call when Art Limburg hired Casper to kill Sid last night."

"So that makes Art Limburg guilty of conspiracy to commit murder, right?" I asked.

"Better than that. Limburg can be charged with murder. Campbell died committing a felony." Chet beamed. Excitedly, he continued, "On top of that, Campbell left a collection of tapes with his lawyer. He recorded the phone calls when he was contracted to kill somebody. He instructed that, if he were ever killed, the lawyer was to turn the collection over to the District Attorney. All of a sudden, twenty-some murders over the past four years are solved. A half dozen thugs, including Art 'Cheese' Limburg, face the death penalty if convicted. What do you think of that?"

"I think we should get the Chaplain. Makes it more official." Bruno answered my question. Then he answered his brother's, "I think that makes a great wedding present, best man."

Detective Sergeant Grabowski is nobody's fool, but it took a minute to shift gears, grasp what Bruno said. His eyes lit with pleasure for his brother and sister-in-law-to-be. If he pounded Bruno's back any harder, he might have caused injury, "Congratulations! When?"

"When we can. Got to find a Chaplain and chapel, take the tests, all that. But I'm going to take the groom's prerogative, and let Mickie worry about the details." Bruno chortled, "Wouldn't want to cheat her out of that ulcer!"

"Oh, thanks a lot!" I laughed back. But I counted on Mom's good intentions, interference, and help to make the planning a unique experience, as daunting as the hunt this past week had been. If mother and daughter didn't come to blows by the wedding, we would have gotten along better than my mother and sister did after preparing for that wedding.

There was one question left before their celebrations could be more meaningful than the half time show at a high school junior varsity football game. I threw the cold water, "Chet, have you rounded up all of Limburg's gang yet?"

Chet's face darkened, smile sagged into frown, and he admitted,

"Not yet." Mirth and merriment abruptly ended. It wasn't over by a far sight, and wouldn't be over until Art and his henchmen were jailed.

* * * *

Across town, Internal Affairs detectives visited the house again this evening. They searched for Jim Philips. Mrs. Philips asked why they wanted him. The detectives revealed that, according to bank records, her husband took a hundred thousand dollars from some crook over the past four years. Adding insult to the injury she felt, they grilled her about whether she knew how he earned those payoffs. Finally, they accepted that her surprise was genuine. In truth, she never knew they had anything more than his salary to live on. He hid that tainted income, that blood money, from her. She felt crushed when they told her that he made the money protecting a gang that kidnaped children, sold them overseas.

With supreme act of will, she managed to maintain a calm demeanor during the visit, but broke down when they left. When she went to her bed to cry, she found the tiny little note on the pillow. Helen Philips read the note from her husband, and wept, sobbed, cried once more.

Her tears soaked the scrap of paper that said it was over. She and Jim had a good life together for fourteen years, and children, and family, and friends. He threw all of them away, threw her away. He ran away without telling her face to face. He just left a note on a scrap of paper which said she'd be better off without him. At least until he reestablished himself somewhere else and called for her.

Her sadness gave way to anger at this final insult, this final betrayal. After their years together, he still didn't know her. Her father and brothers were officers, policemen. She wouldn't, couldn't, ever follow Jim again, not to the wrong side of the law, not even down the grocery store aisles, not anymore. She was hurt, and angry, and stopped crying in her quiet rage. She just wished him a speedy death, if only to save herself and the children the pain and disgrace of a divorce.

* * * *

Yvonne didn't know it, but she had the better man, although he was going up-the-river, to prison, soon. He told her, face to face, that he was in something so dirty that recently, as he realized how dirty it was, his flesh crawled when he thought about it. Stretch confessed everything to her, begged her to forgive him, asked her to wait for him while he served his time. He concluded with the promise that he'd go straight when he got out, take an honest job, even if only pumping gas at his brother's station in Council Bluffs.

Then he left for the attorney's office for the second time today. Together, crook and mouthpiece would go to the D. A..'s office. Only the lawyer would leave tonight. In ten to twenty, when he got out, he and Yvonne would start a new life far from the ocean. No guarantee was given, but it might be sooner if he could earn the witness protection program through his testimony. Either way, even twenty years hard time beat The Needle, the lethal injection established as the penalty for capital crimes like murder or kidnap.

* * * *

Randall Osgood IV waited for his client. During the day, after their first meeting, he negotiated a voluntary surrender to the Assistant District Attorney, with the real possibility that his client might qualify for witness protection. Under the circumstances, that was the best that could be done before Stretch confessed, gave details that would unravel the web of the crimes. And he even managed to include Stretch's friend, Nick, in the deal.

At the appointed hour, Stretch and Nick entered the building which housed Osgood and Osgood. In his office, Randy outlined the options. At first, Nick was reluctant to go back inside voluntarily. Then Stretch graphically described Smokey's demise and disposal. Nick wasn't usually squeamish, but the story made his stomach revolt, reject the supper just eaten. By the time he flushed his discomfort, came back to the office from the bathroom, Nick decided that it really was the best idea to tell the D. A. everything. The two friends would serve their time, make the best of it. It was their only way out now that the D. A. had Casper's tapes, now that the boss was clearly the lesser threat.

Stretch, Nick, and Randy took the elevator to the first floor and left the building. Stretch never heard the shots which laid them low, but neither of his companions had time to react before the rapid fusillade of buckshot relieved them from their earthly cares.

"Damn wimps. Tried to go State's stoolies on me, did you? Serves you right!" Art gloated as he sauntered back to his car. As he drove away, he decided that no, he wouldn't try to take anybody good enough to beat Casper, but these bums were easy marks. If Philips and Toad were as easy, maybe his headaches would go away too.

He wondered if Toad would still help him if she knew he planned to kill her. Earlier this evening, Toad relayed rumors going around the paper. She related that some reporters, at the D. A.'s office to cover another story, overheard a phone conversation between an Assistant District Attorney and the lawyer for some members of a gang who wanted to turn State's evidence. They wanted to corroborate tapes turned over earlier for lighter sentences and protection.

Even if the rumor wasn't true, or was about some other gang, Stretch and Nick had become liabilities instead of assets. It was all the excuse Art needed to bump them off now rather than waiting.

All he had left to do tonight was meet Philips at the safe house. If that fell through, they would meet at the marina. Once Art got Jim in his sights, whether on Calabash Street or aboard the boat, he'd crush that threat too. Soon, he'd pay off Toad with the same currency, some double ought buck shot, that he used to settle with Stretch and Nick, maybe as soon as tomorrow morning. Art realized that his blood was up. Besides, only spilling others' blood would give him the chance to escape, the only chance to escape. If he left enough corpses littering the landscape behind him, the cops would trip over them. Art believed he could find sanctuary with one of his clients before they followed him again, since he didn't know that INTERPOL was in the hunt too.

* * * *

Chet declared, "I'm not going to let any thugs make me waste the night my big brother proposed. Mickie, we'll catch them. It's just a matter of time." He raised his glass to toast, "For my brother, and the woman he loves." Slowly, with effort, we reclaimed the earlier happy mood.

By this time, Sid entered the bar and joined Gwen. They hovered nearby for a little while, then approached the booth.

"I understand that congratulations are in order. Best wishes to both of you." Sid seemed genuinely pleased for us. He sighed, "Guess you won't need the job I offered."

I looked at Bruno. He looked at Sid, then surprised all of us. "Mickie can give up detective work no more than I can give up the sea. I suspect I couldn't keep her from it even if I tried. If she wants to work as a private detective, it's all right with me."

Bruno turned again to me, "But, Mickie, if it's all the same with you, I wish you could do it just part-time, for big cases like this one. Can't learn about the sea if you're always ashore."

"Oh, Bruno." I responded to the insight and the entreaty, "If Sid only calls when he needs help, I can do that for you."

Sid agreed, "Sure! That's fair. Besides, part of why Mickie is so good at it is that she's not one of my full timers. Not many people know her, and she learns things that my regulars never hear." After a moment's thought, Sid continued, "Okay, Mickie, I amend the offer. How would you like to be a reserve operative?"

"Sounds like I'm getting the chance to have the best of both worlds. I'll do it." I looked into Bruno's face, saw the reluctant approval. "I love you, Bruno."

Gwen spoke, "In that case, dearie, take the night off to celebrate both your engagement and your new job. I probably won't see you in here again unless you come in with Bruno, ... or looking for him."

"Thanks, Gwen. Hope it doesn't leave you short-handed."

Before Gwen answered, somebody's pager went off. Sid drew first, found the display blank. He looked up and grinned at Chet. The police detective checked his. He turned to Gwen, "Can I use the phone in your office? I have to call in."

Gwen motioned him to follow, and led him to the cubicle under the stairs. She unlocked the door, flipped on the light, and instructed, "Turn off the light and pull the door shut when you're done. We'll be outside if you need anything."

When Chet returned, his expression was dark, accented by furrowed brow. "I've got to go. Somebody just perforated our two star witnesses and their attorney. Left them for dead on the steps."

"Then they're not dead?" Sid asked.

"Stretch Lincoln is dead, no doubt about it. Nick Filbert probably won't live through the night. But, the lawyer may come around before he checks out. It's touch and go in his case. Depends how much blood he lost before the medics got to him." Chet related. "I have to start the hospital vigil in case he can tell us something. Stay close to a phone, here or at Bruno's place. Okay?"

"Sure thing. Looks like the pimple is about to burst, and I want to be there when it does." Sid agreed instantly.

Bruno declared, "Chet, we'll be at my place, as soon as we finish supper. Sounds like something may happen that we'll face better on coffee rather than booze." He turned to me, "Looks like we'll have to delay the party for the night. Do you mind?"

"Yes, I mind, but there isn't anything else we can do." Earlier, I worried about throwing a glass of cold water over the festivities, but it seemed the Fates had planned this deluge far in advance. Mere mortals fought the Fates at their own peril. It was far better to go with the flow.

"Okay! I'll let you know what I find out." Chet rushed out the back door, leaving his nearly untouched beer behind.

"Sid, you better order take out and we'll just sit it out at my place." Bruno confirmed the plan. He called Gwen to our table, and changed their orders to take-it-home. "Can't expect every thing to go our way, but I wish it didn't seem so much went wrong."

Sid instructed, "Gwen, a hamburger with everything and an order of fries, in a doggy bag." As she relayed the order to Harvey, Sid rose, explained, "I have to call Bill, let him know about the change in my plans. By the way, he and Al are watching the house where we got the photos. Jim Philips let himself in late this afternoon, and hasn't left yet. If he moves, I want to know about it. Bruno, is it okay to give them your phone number?" Bruno acquiesced with a reluctant nod.

* * * *

In a dark room overlooking the house at 1313 Calabash Street, the ringing cell phone broke their vigil. Bill answered. He spoke little, listened a lot, jotted a note. After he folded the instrument into his pocket once again, he turned to his companion. "Al, that was Sid. A big chunk hit the fan tonight. Maybe more will later tonight. We're supposed to double our watch, make sure that nobody gets in without us seeing it and getting photographs. If Philips leaves, we're to follow."

"I hope it does hit the fan tonight, Bill. I'm starting to wear down, tire out. Getting too old for this stuff, or some such crap, I guess." Al conceded. He wished aloud, "I sure would like to get a good night's sleep sometime this next year."

Bill teased as he crossed the room to his observation post, "Be careful what you wish for. You may just get it. Anyway, what are you complaining about? You know you can't afford your girlfriend without the overtime." Through the camera viewfinder, through the telephoto lens, he watched the other house like a cat watches a mouse hole in the wall. All quiet, and, like in the poem, not even a mouse stirred, certainly not the rat hiding across the street, or the head rat they hoped would visit the little rat.

He suspended his vigil long enough to look at his comrade, "Take it from me, Al, this isn't so bad. Be glad you're working something other than a 9 to 5 job. Those can wear you out just as badly, leave you feeling just as tired and frustrated, but it's your soul that gets tired, not your body."

As the older one of the pair, Bill also felt tired, but they would soon have a rest. They would hand off to the official police after they had enough nails for the crooks' coffins. His wife would like it if he could spend a little more time at home, at least for the little while between cases. After this one, though, tracking wayward spouses would seem so very tame, routine, almost boring. But missing person cases would never be boring again. Surely, this wasn't the first nor the last of gangs who played this game.

Bill alerted his partner, "Hello! What's this? Haven't seen that car here before. Al, visitor."

"I see it, Bill."

Both felt renewed. All the fatigue of long fruitless hours evaporated.

Bill remarked, "Adrenaline is a remarkable thing. Too bad we only taste its benefits in moments of crisis."

* * * *

"Detective, I think the patient passed his crisis." Dr. Whatever-her-name-is reported. She was one of many trauma specialists who learned as much about burns, blunt trauma, knife, gunshot, and crushing wounds at the emergency room of County Hospital as any doctor assigned to a Battalion Aid Station during a very hot battle of a shooting war.

Sgt. Grabowski stopped counting blue tiles in the floor, blinked himself alert. He acknowledged the information. "Thanks, Doctor. Can I see him now?" When he looked up, her name tag identified Dr. Susan Fox inside the surgical scrubs. Chester noted the deep blue of her eyes and her beauty, undisguised by lack of makeup and lack of sleep.

She allowed, "His vital signs are stable. You can talk to him for a little while, but try not to excite him. Looks like he started to turn away, because the wounds were in his upper arm, not the chest like the other two. He's lost his left arm, but he doesn't know it yet because of the pain killers and anesthetic."

Chet felt a little guilty, but Dr. Fox was so pretty. Would Norma understand if he filed away his observations for later consideration, later actions, later relations? He felt that he owed Norma an honest mourning, but past experiences, his own and his brother's, and some of his friends', taught that he also owed himself a life. He felt guilt only because the two, losing one and finding another, came too close together at only a week apart. For now, for Norma, he would keep this a professional relationship. "Okay."

"Follow me, please. Don't straggle! And don't forget your visitor's pass." Dr. Fox instructed, and led him to the recovery room.

Chet followed quickly. Just because Randall Osgood IV's vital signs were stable five minutes ago didn't mean that he was past danger. If he lost the will to live when he noticed the stump where he once had an arm, he could still decide to give up, to just shuffle off this mortal coil. He would be very hard to question then.

* * * *

Bruno cleared the table while I made coffee, and grappled quietly with apprehension. I knew we were not completely safe as long as Art Limburg was free. He held and carefully nurtured a grudge against me because I helped put him in prison. He threatened my life as the bailiff led him from court.

My friends were at peril, too. Sid threatened Art's current enterprise, as Art's order to Casper testified, so wouldn't be safe either. Bruno, new friend, could find himself in the middle, possibly an unintended victim of Art's revenge.

Only Bruno seemed calm while I fussed with the coffee maker. Sid, visibly tense, paced, sat, rose to pace the floor again. Despite our efforts to retain a positive outlook, a black mood fouled the air. We waited for the other shoe to drop, for something to happen even with the full knowledge, with the expectation, that what happened might not be good. It's not a pleasant interlude.

Within the next few days, we or the police had to find and capture the miscreant, or chance that he would make it underground. If Art escaped, successfully hid from his pursuers, he could come back to haunt us, attack when we least expected it. That was an unpleasant and dangerous prospect.

At least this week, we were ready, on full alert because we expected Art to move. That gave us a chance to prevail. If we dropped our guard, like Stretch and Nick had done, we could find ourselves lying on a sidewalk some day in the future.

Sid broke the silence, but not the tension, "I wish I knew what was going on. This waiting is the hardest part. It's almost over, but far enough from it that I can't relax."

Bruno watched him pace again. Finally, his patience exhausted, he ordered, "Sit down, Sid. That doesn't help at all, and you're wearing out my carpet."

The coffee maker sputtered its last hissing drops through the grounds. We gathered around the kitchen table to hide behind mugs of fresh perked coffee. Despite the company of others, each seemed detached, preoccupied with private thoughts. The question could not spoil this already foul mood, so I asked it, "Has the Coroner released Norma for burial yet?"

"I'll check in the morning. They should release Norma soon if they're not finished already. The results of the tox screen showed it was murder. I don't think they need to run any more tests, so we should be able to bury her properly fairly soon." Sid answered.

"Make sure you tell Chet what arrangements you make. He liked Norma. That's why he takes this case so personally." Bruno revealed. "We had a long talk, nearly emptied a fresh bottle of whisky talking about it. Her death hurt him badly."

"She was a good friend." I toasted, "This is only coffee, and she deserved better, but for Norma, one for an old friend." I couldn't speak for the others, but felt glum. I wanted action as an antidote for my melancholy. Then I realized we solved the crime, and nearly all the gang members were in jail or the morgue. Only two roamed free. From Norma's theory as starting point, we followed a twisted trail, and almost reached its end. My depression lifted. Only the tension of a hunt in progress remained.

The phone rang. Bruno answered at the second ring He listened, then handed the handset to Sid, "It's Bill."

Bruno rejoined me at the kitchen table, curiosity burning our ears as we listened to only half of the conversation. We gained no clue. Sid received information, not issued orders. It's impossible to know what's going on when all you hear is, "Yeah. Uh huh. Really! Okay. Hmmm. Do that. Be right over." between long pauses.

Yet, like a spark in a room filled with gas, the phone call caused an explosion of action. Sid grabbed his jacket. Bruno and I learned nothing. Sid only said, "Got to go. Something just went down at the gang's safe house. Bill called the cops already, and thinks that I should head over there. See you folks tomorrow if your lights are out when I come back past here." He headed out the door without a backward glance.

* * * *

Chet left the hospital without looking back. Randall Osgood IV related the conversation between Stretch and Nick which convinced Nick to turn State's evidence. Dr. Fox, with them to monitor her patient, became uneasy when he recounted Stretch's tale how Smokey had been fed to the fishes, and she had seen a lot of mayhem during her years in the emergency room. Even Chet felt queasy as he listened, caused partly by the mental picture of the act, more so by evidenced cruelty of the perpetrator. It fueled his concern for the safety of his brother and his soon-to-be sister-in-law.

The detective understood that there would be no trial until the criminal was in custody. As long as Art owned a long range cruiser for an escape by sea, he wouldn't be cornered easily. This case wouldn't truly end until Art Limburg was captured, jailed, tried, convicted, and executed.

Yet, now that he knew Art owned a boat, Chet could track it down, put it under surveillance, cut that escape route as his orders cut escape routes by air and land. As he drove away from the hospital, Chet planned to stop at the Port Authority office, then the Yacht Club. Art would anchor there with private craft rather than the commercial fleet.

Chet radioed his plan to headquarters, but the dispatcher directed him to 1313 Calabash Street instead. Some poor sucker just suffered a fatal case of acute lead poisoning when a 12-gauge shotgun forcibly introduced double-ought buckshot into his body.

Chet confirmed the destination, and that there wasn't any rush to get there. He would drive quickly, but neither light nor siren was necessary. The victim wasn't going anywhere until the ambulance crew took him to the morgue, and they wouldn't do that until he had a chance to inspect the scene.

While on the radio, he had the dispatcher call the Port Authority and Yacht Club. Other officers could start the search for Art's boat, and stop him if he tried to get out of port tonight. That way, when finished with the unlucky stiff, Chet could follow up immediately, as if in mid-stride rather than from a standing start.

Two stop lights farther, Chet realized why that address, 1313 Calabash, sounded familiar. That was the house where Stretch handed Jim Philips the envelope fat with payoff money. He wondered if Jim received enough money to ease his conscience, to face prison as a dirty cop, and whether Jim knew it was all for scum like Art Limburg.

Chet decided there wasn't enough money in circulation to pay him to endure that disgrace, not the way his family would treat him after. If the strength of his convictions ever faltered, or he even looked like he might stray from the straight and narrow, Bruno would gladly pound some sense into him. He would do the same for Bruno, although Bruno wasn't in the way of many temptations to go crooked. It was the promise they made to their Dad before he died. That wasn't a promise broken on a whim.

* * * *

Fourteen hundred miles toward the rising sun, during this sunrise watch, Manny decided, "I'll leave the ship if I see them sneak those women ashore." He checked with his friend on the bridge, promoted from the ranks to serve as Third Officer, and found the old *Flying Fish* averaged 12 knots for the trip so far. If they kept it up, this crossing would take only six and a quarter days, just a day and a half longer, until they reached Bordeaux.

There was only one reason to push this old lady so hard. The Skipper wanted to deliver some contraband cargo over the weekend when the fewest number of port staff would be on duty. Manny would forego his Friday night shore leave in this port to watch what happened after the crew left the dock. It was small enough price to pay for a clear conscience. There would be other ports-of-call where he could party hearty some other day.

After all, if he saw nothing suspicious, he could stay aboard after they offloaded the hold-full of legitimate cargo addressed to merchants here. A winter spent trading between ports in the Mediterranean appealed to him.

On the other hand, if anything looked wrong or crooked, he could make himself sick enough to go to a hospital. Detergent dysentery, a trick used by goldbrickers and slackers, mimicked food poisoning. He'd have all the symptoms and the doctors had to observe him until he recovered. He'd need a week in bed to miss sailing without inventing an excuse to jump ship legally. He heard that lemon-scented liquid dish soap, just a coating on a teaspoon, went down easiest if mixed with very sweet orange soda and rum. Manny shuddered at the idea, but then laughed to himself, "Heavy on the rum, really heavy, and I'll have to drink a bottle of whisky, a quart bottle, so my taste buds have passed out before I try it."

Manny resumed touring the deck, checked hatch covers at each hold, booms and winches, ensured all were secured. For now, the hull was secure too. The old girl hadn't popped any more rivets since yesterday morning. The count reached seven then, but those holes were spread around the hull. No point weakened enough to threaten the ship. Even so, Manny was glad he remembered a damage control trick learned when in the brown water Navy and their hull was perforated by machine guns along the Mekong's banks. They carved short lengths of mop handles into tapered plugs. Hammered into the empty rivet holes, the plugs stopped the leaks, gave the old *Flying Fish* time before she went into dry dock for permanent repair.

Manny noted the paleness at the eastern horizon. Jeff would come on deck soon to assume the watch. As they shared information, Manny would share his plans. They had already concluded that it wasn't normal for passengers to stay in their cabins the whole voyage, that their reclusiveness indicated something wasn't kosher.

Two nights ago, testing whether he could trust his young shipmate, Manny recounted old sailors' tales of the white slavery trade. Manny was relieved when Jeff became concerned by the possibility the women were headed into sexual servitude for somebody else's profit. It was the reaction he expected from anyone who drank coffee and stayed faithful to his wife even while on shore leave far from home.

They would watch through the first night in port. After that, Jeff could stay or leave the ship as his conscience dictated, but Manny was sure of the youngster. If Manny left, Jeff would too. Besides, if both had the green-apple-quick-step after a liberty, the doctors would more likely diagnose them as victims of food poisoning. That would give them an unarguable reason for leaving their ship in a foreign port. They'd be free to sign on some ship headed home after release from the hospital rather than paying for passage. Best of all, they wouldn't need to answer a lot of questions from officers and new shipmates.

Home. Manny suddenly felt very old, for the word home had not brought a lump to his throat for so many years, not since he was very young. Manny accepted that too many years had passed to feel young, so it must be time for the return leg of his voyage. Like the ships which circumnavigated the globe, he was coming full circle.

In his youth, he left the land for the sea. He neared the time that he would leave the sea for the land. At least his decision would be voluntary, not like Bruno's retirement, forced by injury.

* * * *

My thought found voice almost as quickly as it formed. "Bruno, I haven't been home for days. I need to check my answering machine and mail. It's still early, compared to the hours we've kept the last few nights. Come with me. Please?"

"Sure. It beats sitting around until they decide to tell us what's going on. Sid and Chet are busy. We might as well get something done." Bruno shifted from neutral to forward. "I'll just call so Chet knows where we are."

"Let's get some beer and chips on the way. I've got a comedy on video that should give us a laugh, dispel the gloom." I vamped, as if Mae West spoke, "Pack your bag besides, sailor. Who knows? ... You just might get lucky."

Bruno laughed, "Already got lucky, the night I met you." Still, he accepted the suggestion, packed a pair of jeans, clean shirt, skivvy drawers and T-shirt, socks, and shaving kit. With a flourish, as if boasting that there was room to spare, he shoved a sweater into a satchel barely the size of my makeup bag. He was ready to go while I still packed. He watched as I struggled with getting my clothes into the suitcase, then teased, "When a guy packs light, it's measured in pounds and cubic inches. When a woman packs light, it's measured in tons and cubic yards."

I wanted to be angry. I packed for a week while he packed for one night. But there, side-by-side at the foot of the bed, my bulging suitcase dwarfed his partly empty valise, and I didn't even have that many changes of clothes. Instead, I retorted, "That's the price guys pay because you want your women to look good all the time. We've been taught to pack lots of outfits to keep you interested."

"Point well made and taken, Mickie. But, I see I'll have to help you unlearn it so we don't sink the *Virginia* when we take our honeymoon cruise." He roared with mirth as he engulfed me in his arms.

I knew he was not a superman, just a mere mortal. Nonetheless, I felt shielded by his strength, and affection, and warmth, as safe and secure as anyone marked for death could feel. We didn't make it out of the room, let alone to my house. Still, we did make it, out of our clothes, a special evening together. Both of us just got lucky.

* * * *

Chet lifted the blanket covering the corpse. He feared seeing friends, even those who went bad, when he looked under the blanket or into a body bag. It was disturbing enough when the dead were strangers. This time, Jim Philips' mortal remains would soon be wrapped in one of those zippered black plastic bags. He turned and asked, "Did you know him, Sid?"

"No, Chet, I didn't. I only knew of him because we got his picture during surveillance on this place." Until this instant, Sid believed he was a hardened detective, inured against revulsion, but this man was hashed by multiple loads of buckshot. He didn't look a second time.

Chet lowered the blanket over his fallen partner, eulogized, "It's a shame he ended like this. He wasn't a bad guy. Wonder what turned him crooked?" The detective stood to full height, "I guess we just got lucky, Sid. Not often that professional detectives, even the private kind, get to watch a hit. It's even rarer that they have the camera rolling to tape it. How did they know to watch this place tonight?"

Sid explained, "My people weren't here just tonight. I've had a team watching this place since Norma found it. I would have told you that my guys saw Philips let himself in early this afternoon, but I didn't get the word about that until after you took off for the hospital to question the mouthpiece."

Chet recapped the witnesses' statements. "Your guys said a man, wearing a raincoat and fedora, drove up, went up the stairs, knocked, and Philips opened the door. They acted like they knew each other, but the visitor pulled a shotgun from under his raincoat and let fly, six times. Philips went down inside the house, and the raincoat drove away in the car he came in."

Sid, Al, and Bill confirmed that summary. Bill even commented, "That's what you'll see when you play the tape."

"Did either of you get the license plate number and a description of the car? Or do I have to wait until I get to a VCR and TV?" Chet grilled. These guys were old enough hands that they couldn't have forgotten to note that basic information, or they had gotten lazy, depended too much on technology.

Al offered, "Detective, as near as I could tell under these street lights, he drove a dark metallic blue 1997 Explorer. Front license plate was shadowed, or maybe covered with something. I couldn't read it, but might have got the rear plate in the frame when he drove off. By the time I put the camera down, the car was too far away for me to read the plate without binoculars."

At his car, Chet radioed to check license numbers for vehicles owned by Art or Arthur Limburg, or by Black Lines Shipping Company. Computers answered within minutes. An Art Limburg, Penthouse, Limburg Towers, owned a car matching Al's description. Now they had a place to start the search. And a vehicle description with license numbers for the all-points bulletin.

"Sid, we just got lucky again. My hunch was right." Chet beamed as he shared information, "Your guys saw Limburg's car here. That means it's likely he did the shooting. If we find him before he washes off the residues, we have him dead to rights."

* * * *

"I just got lucky." Art Limburg admitted to himself. Philips never suspected that he would be shot in the safe house. The crooked cop agreed to the meeting there because he wanted help, money to run away. That was the break Art needed to throw another corpse into the path of the pursuing police.

Art stopped at a gas station several blocks away. After he filled the tank, he called Emma. She agreed to meet him in the parking lot of the doughnut shop near her office at 8:00 A.M. tomorrow. Toad wouldn't expect he would try anything there, not after he dangled an irresistible carrot in front of her. He said he'd hand the controls to her while he left the country. Only hours remained before he obliterated her threat, finished that ambitious, traitorous woman before she got him, or the Law did.

Art also made another important call. He confirmed that Grits accepted the contracts to murder Sid Koenig and Michelle Stevens. He owed the one for present inconveniences, the other for past insult. Art believed the time in jail had been an insult to him and his family. After all, they had money, position, social standing. Why had that detective been so tenacious, searched so hard to find out why that insignificant night watchman had died in the fire? Well, this would be payback.

Finally, he arrived at a place where he could hide out for a little while. After a few hours sleep, if the headache and the voices let him, he'd be free of all the loose strings that might lead to him. He could fuel his cruiser, and sail for distant ports. In a year or so, he'd come back.

Giving Chase

WHEN THE ALARM SOUNDED AT 06:30 (Navy talk seemed to come more naturally the longer I spent around Bruno), I forced dread and foreboding from my mind. There were too many pleasant thoughts that I wanted to consider instead. This was morning, a time for showers, coffee, and small talk with the man who took me to the stars last night, and safely brought me home again. That was all I wanted for now, but, once again, what I wanted and what I had to do were different things.

"Bruno, I still need to go to my place, check my mail and messages and things. Let's do that first, all right? Instant coffee here, then brewed Java with breakfast at my place. Sound all right to you?"

"Sure sounds good to me. Don't forget to add some doughnuts to the shopping list."

Suffering from first-thing-in-the-morning amnesia, or taken by surprise by a decision he made without me, I asked, "What shopping list?"

Bruno laughed quietly, "You know, frozen pizza, beer, chips, and doughnuts. All the necessities for a balanced diet." He hesitated, then introduced more evidence that, in his mind and heart, this was not a temporary liaison, a passing infatuation. "Maybe we should talk about getting us a place, not yours or mine, but our place. It could be a little place, where you can write, or be a detective, if it's close enough to the *Virginia* that I can keep an eye on her, and take care of my charter business."

I knew what he meant. While welcomed here, I felt that I was only a visitor. He likely felt the same at my house. In our house, both of us could feel that we belonged. "I volunteer my computer to keep your books and records. I'll show you how to use it. You show me how to handle the boat." I laughed agreement, "And we'll split the housekeeping!"

It seemed to me that both had been alone long enough. Certainly, I had been. Perhaps both were ready to sail into a new relationship at full speed, to open a new chapter of our lives. It would explain why we already had a conversation that other couples took months, even years, to hold.

"Guess we'd better buy a paper with the doughnuts. We can start checking the listings at breakfast. Let's just agree before we start that we don't need to rush into buying some place that doesn't meet what we want." he negotiated.

We loaded the car and drove to my house. There, I quickly went through the phone messages and mail. None of the phone calls required an immediate answer, nor did any of the letters and bills in the mailbox.

Scanning the morning paper filled time as we waited for the coffee maker to finish the cycle. The real estate for sale section listed several houses which might meet our combined needs.

I fingered an ad which caught my eye and pushed it to Bruno, "Look at this one." The listing for an old house near the docks sounded interesting. It belonged to a ship's captain before current owners turned it into a rooming house. We could revive it as a single family dwelling. I imagined space for our combined possessions, and still having room for guests. Intriguingly, it was priced so it would be a trade. What I should get for this house in the current market would buy it, and leave some money to fix it up a little. If he had any savings left at all after buying his boat, we would be in business. The Fates seemed to treat us more kindly this morning than they had for quite a while.

I teased him, "It's even near enough that we could still visit the Blue Onion. Now that I know the people there, it really is a good place to spend an evening or two … once in a while… Old Gwen will have kittens if I show up in a peacoat and bell-bottom dungarees faded by the sea and sun." He smiled.

But the morning paper also recorded two shootings which killed three and wounded a bystander. Then I read about Stretch, Nick, their lawyer, and Jim Philips. These were more germane to the situation. As I read the stories of mayhem on the streets, I observed that even the legitimate news showed heartless disregard for survivors' feelings. Callous questioning and intrusions into the lives of Yvonne Lincoln, Helen Philips, and the Randall Osgood III's showed through the prose. The reporters must have wakened those poor women and parents in the middle of the night for the interviews to appear in the morning edition, and on the local morning TV and radio news.

While working for the *National Rag,* I tired of insinuating myself into others' lives when they only wanted to be left alone. It seemed I still faced that onerous task even if I went with one of the reputation papers. Sid's offer of part time work at his agency acquired an extra measure of gentility as I considered my future there and compared it to alternatives. While part of a detective's job would be to pry into others' lives, I wouldn't be required to make their closeted skeletons known to all the world.

"Bruno, thanks for understanding. I know your macho instincts were to make a big fuss last night. Instead, you backed me when I took the part-time job with Sid. I'll like doing detective work better than going back to work as a reporter." The rest just flowed, somewhat wistfully, "But, I'd like it best if your charter boat earns enough that I can join your crew full time rather than be a part-time detective."

While Bruno knew what I meant, he teased, "Harrumph! That's interesting talk, coming from an apprentice Cabin Girl." With a lilt in his voice, Bruno offered to fill the day with more pleasant diversions, "Come on. Shake off your blues. Maybe you'd like another cruise in the bay, get another seamanship lesson, now you found all your stuff is still in one piece, huh?"

"Sure, let's go. I'm ready." The newspaper fluttered to the kitchen table as I sprang toward my coat and bag. I showed him clearly that I wanted to spend the day with him rather than starting the story about Norma's death and the bigger, far more disturbing story about white slavery revealed during the following investigation. In passing, I checked the clock and projected, "We should be ready to sail by nine, ten the latest, don't you think? That means we'll need to take a lunch with us."

Bruno was close behind. He nodded to confirm the plan, and suggested, "I know a diner that caters to the yacht sailors. They serve good take out, packed to stay warm until we're ready to eat." He went around me, noting that I stopped and hadn't yet taken a single step to his several. He turned and ordered, "Now, quit your skylarking and move!"

I was ready for the cruise, after we stopped to load one cooler with lunch, and the other with beer. It struck me, one of the little mysteries of life, "Bruno, why do we call them coolers? They're insulated containers. The insulation keeps hot food warm as well as cold beers cool."

He looked at me like I really had an extra head, then burst into laughter. When the belly laughs trailed off into mere chortles, he said, "Sometimes, I think you live on an entirely different world. At least you'll put the food and beer into different coolers. My ex thought they worked by magic, not insulation, and put the chicken and beer into the same one. Oh, she was angry when we had both lukewarm chicken and beer. Spoiled her picnic." He grinned, "I don't guess it helped any when I laughed."

* * * *

Detective Sergeant Chester Grabowski sat at his desk, listening to a ringing phone that no one answered. "Where did they go so early in the morning? Damn it, I told them to stay near a phone."

He tried the second number. Again, no one answered, just the answering machine. He left brief instructions to call in, but feared they wouldn't get the word until it was too late.

This wasn't doing his digestion any good at all, not when he had already insulted his stomach with too much over-strong black coffee. This news was too important to trust the Fates that they would be safe.

He dialed the third number. At last, a real person answered. He listened while the receptionist recited the greeting. As soon as she finished, he spoke, "Detective Chet Grabowski, I need to talk to Sid. Is he there?" She transferred the call to Sid's private office.

Without the usual pleasantries, Chet immediately asked, "Sid. Did you hear that Emma, receptionist at the *National Rag*, got the same payoff this morning that the others got yesterday?"

"Buckshot again?"

"Yeah. Guy in a metallic blue Explorer shot her in the doughnut shop parking lot near her office."

"Shit! That means no one is left to testify. He left a pile of physical evidence, but no one from inside his gang can explain how it worked. If he gets away, he can start up again after this heat cools." Sid noted the overt actions were unusual for Art, typically the deep background mover and shaker. "What's got into him? This isn't anything like the Limburg I expected after checking on him."

"Yeah, I expected him to hire it all done while he sat in a sun chair on a beach somewhere in Argentina, building a bombproof alibi." Chet agreed. He shared his concerns, "Now that Art has killed all of the other known gang members, he only has you and Mickie for targets. If he hired Casper to kill you, like the tape recording tells it, he isn't likely to forget you. And I read the transcript from his trial. I don't think he's the type to walk away from that promised revenge against Mickie."

"So, what do you want me to do?"

"Watch your butt. You're handy to have around in a pinch. I don't want you to get hurt because you got careless... Do you know where they are? I've called Bruno's place, and Mickie's house. I don't know where they went, all I got were answering machines." Chet pressured for an answer to relieve the pressure he felt.

Sid didn't know Bruno as well as Chet did, but he knew Chet well enough to guess that fraternal concerns caused a temporary mental block. A little helpful guidance should help his friend think it out. "If they're not at either house, and it's way too early to go to the Blue Onion, where would Bruno take her?"

There was a long pause as Chet sorted it out. "Thanks, Sid. I should have realized they'd go to the *Virginia,* especially with a forecast for light winds and sunny skies." Chet realized that his frenzy was no friend of logic, a lesson relearned all too often, just now once again. "If you're not busy, meet me at the police launch. We'll try to intercept them. Watch yourself."

Sid confirmed the plan. "I'll be there within the hour. Sounds better than sitting around here waiting for something to happen." Conversation ended, he readied for the mission. On his way out, he stopped at the locked closet.

When he opened the door to take out the long case, Sarah, the secretary, grasped her employer faced potential serious danger. She asked, "Will it get that bad?"

"I hope not," Sid responded, as lightly as he could with misgivings riding so heavily on his shoulders, "but I'd rather have it with me and not need it, thank you very much!" He swung the case onto the sofa, opened it, and checked the contents. All was in order. He took a case of ammunition, and spare magazines, then closed the closet. As he left, he smiled and said, "See you soon, Sarah." He added as an afterthought, "Just pray it's all over when I get back tonight."

* * * *

Grits confirmed the plan with his wife. He would drive over for his business early tomorrow. He should finish in time to meet her at the airport Friday evening, and they would spend a pleasant weekend on the coast. If he had taken care of everything by Monday, they'd drive back together. If he still had further consultations, she would fly home and he'd return as soon as he could.

Grits wondered whether she even dreamed what he did for a living. It wasn't really important, but he wondered nevertheless. Still, whenever anyone pressed for an answer, she recited the cover story he told her, that he was a security consultant. Until that day when he slipped, or, if she knew more than she let on and accidentally spilled the beans, that would just have to do.

There were other people that he had to worry about. He shrugged. He prided himself on the impeccable professionalism he brought to the trade, the eradication of threats to somebody's security. Why did some of the survivors take it so personally? He felt their grudges were wasted energy. They should spend their energy and time furthering their agendas and businesses. As a free agent, he worked for the high bidder. If they shed their grudges, he might work for them someday.

Well, it was time to leave. He faced a twelve-hour drive. Flying would be faster, but, unlike some cities where he worked regularly, this was his first visit to this destination. He spent days in a new, unfamiliar city finding a weapon when he had the time. This contract gave him no excess time. Driving, he would be ready to start work as soon as he took a nap after the long drive. He could take one from his own arsenal and not have to answer a lot of questions at the airports along the way.

Grits loaded the car and went back to the house. They had been married a long while, but he still loved her. He gave her a long kiss that would last him until she joined him.

As he entered the flow of traffic east bound on the Interstate highway, Grits mused that he must be getting soft in the head. Art, the man for whom he would make the hit, insisted that he would transfer the entire contract fee after, and only after, success was confirmed.

Well, anyone as high profile as a Society Private Eye and an ex-police detective who works for a scandal sheet should be easy enough to find, especially after Art named them and assured that they were listed in the phone book. In his twenty years doing this work, Grits decided that the challenge was finding the target. The actual hit was easy after that, a done deal, unless the victim had more luck than anyone had a right to have.

* * * *

Art gathered the water and aspirin bottles from the picnic table and strolled back to his Explorer. This headache had been the worst one yet, and he was nauseated too. He knew that stopping for some medicine, waiting for the pain to ease, put him behind his plan's timetable, but he had to do something before his skull split with the pain.

This corner of the park was enough like his roof garden that he paused here until the pain ended. Blue sky, white clouds, the different greens of pine trees and grass, contrasting reds and yellows of fall flowers and hardwood trees, soothed his mind in synergy with the aspirin, and allowed him to think.

By now, he knew, the police searched for him in all the dark and closed spaces where he usually lived, rousted out all the known associates that he hadn't killed. Out here, he had been nearly invisible among the others sitting at picnic tables in the morning sun. Do the opposite of what they expect, and you can get away with a lot. That's what the voices advised, and, so far, they had been right.

Now, the voices insisted that he follow the plan laid out in such haste, yet as carefully as it needed to be. Three days ago, he transferred all his money to his offshore account, using the excuse that it would be easier to draw during an extended vacation. Two days ago, he had the marina attendant start his boat to make sure it would. Yesterday, he contacted the black market arms dealer, picked out the shotgun and bought more than enough ammunition. Even after the barrages fired into proximate foes, he still had twenty shots to dissuade pursuers. Today, he would leave for the Virgin Islands, refuel and restock the galley there, and then disappear into the sea, into the world. In a year or so, new henchmen selected, he would rise from these ashes to resume the lucrative trade in innocent flesh.

That was the plan, confirmed by those damnable voices heard above all the words spoken to him by real people. As he drove to the marina, Art speculated whether they were his personal demons, or some otherworldly guardians. In the deeper analysis, it didn't matter, for the present case dictated the cut-and-run tactics he used. It was the only action that made sense.

* * * *

From her lookout's perch in the office atop the Yacht Club, Madeline scanned the harbor. Very few members took their boats out this morning. The typical weekend sailors would descend on the bay tomorrow and Saturday and Sunday. It would be much busier then.

She put the binoculars on the window sill, and thanked the Power-Who-Is that she was in the right place at the right time to get this job. And, yes, she also owed this job to those kids who stole that half-million dollar yacht for a joy ride. It was a real shame they ripped out her bottom on the reef, but that boat's theft and sinking gave her this chance. After that, the members voted her job into existence. Undoubtedly, this was the most interesting job she ever had in her young life. It let her meet all the right people, and didn't stress her out despite some rare excitement.

In fact, just after she started, Madeline once called the police in time to foil an attempted theft. She found the elation of a participant rather than merely a spectator in the stands cemented her fondness for the duty. Her action also won her the little medal pinned to her blazer. The Yacht Club Commodore himself awarded it during a formal ceremony in front of all the members.

To her mind, it was a constant symbol of her own worth. She had been shaken so badly that she flunked out of college when her second fiancé walked out on her, not that she expected much more from him in hindsight. She needed to know that she was good for something more than a one-night stand, or the demeaning but necessary one-hour stands, tried under Wanda's tutelage.

Hooking earned enough to keep body and soul together after Daddy disowned her in a fit of anger, cut off her allowance, but it was hard on her self-esteem. Working that oldest profession had almost devastated her fragile ego, then she lucked into this job.

Every time Madeline donned the issued uniform of dark navy blue blazer and skirt over white turtleneck sweater and black heels - a classy uniform for a classy job in a classy place - the glistening little badge confirmed to her and all the world that she was competent, courageous, and quick-witted. The perception buttressed her fragile ego. And, the hours were so much more to her liking than working the bars when the sailors got a liberty ashore.

Madeline recovered from her reverie with a sigh of contentment. She took up the binoculars and scanned the anchored yachts once more. All was quiet.

After she lowered the binoculars again, she read the previous watch's entries in the logbook. She noted the phone call from the police logged in hours earlier. This must be the one her predecessor meant when he called over his shoulder as he hurried down the stairs, "I'm late. Read the log. Call from the police. See you tomorrow."

She read it again. "02:15 - Police called. Art Limburg wanted for questioning. Let them know if he goes aboard the *East Wind*, especially if it looks like he'll leave port."

Madeline focused her gaze on the slip where the *East Wind* usually berthed. The cabin cruiser was tied to the dock, and, Madeline noted, wore the canvas mooring cover which kept the weather out while the owner was ashore. She saw no one aboard, but really wouldn't if they lurked under that canvas. She would ask whether the alert were still in force when she checked her radio link to the police harbor patrol on the hour.

* * * *

As Bruno and I topped the hill and drove down into the harbor area proper, after all the times I came here with eyes unseeing, I consciously studied the port for the first time in a long time. Men-of-War, dressed in their somber gray, claimed the best anchorages in the deepest waters by force of their muscle, size, and speed. Because all their names began with U.S.S., United States Ship, they gave the neighborhood undeniable prestige, as Amazon warriors conferred dignity upon their lesser sisters.

Their nearest neighbors were the big freighters, entitled to wear names that began with an S.S., steam ship. These oceangoing merchantmen claimed the next best quays, built to entertain commerce rather than to facilitate the defense of a nation.

For now, the commercial wharfs bustled under a bright sun, while the martial docks were serene. I hoped it would stay so always, but remembered Dad's stories of darker days when it wasn't a world at peace but at war. Sorrow and pride mixed, blended, at vivid visions of brave men who sailed their brave ships into harm's way, and other brave men, like my Dad's brother.

One sunny day, he marched up a gangway to fight ashore in some faraway place, and didn't come home. He wasn't alone. Others willingly matched his sacrifice in the past, in the present, and, given human nature, likely would be called upon to do so into the future as well.

I dabbed tears from my eyes. To dispel the sudden blue funk, uncalled for under this bright blue sky, I turned my attention to the little knot of bobbing white hulls. Farthest away, just inside the headland which marked the harbor mouth, expensive yachts, toys of local society, kept their distance from the real ships. Twin arms of stone breakwater encircled the yacht basin, as if to perpetuate distinctions of class based solely on money. Those who went to sea to earn a living were thus kept at their proper distance from the shore bound owners who only played on the sea.

Between the landings allocated to the freighters and the yachts, among the commercial boats, the fishermen and the charter cruisers, *Virginia* awaited. On her, Bruno and I soon would spend the afternoon giving chase to our dreams, our future, beginnings of our happiness.

I confided, "Bruno, my Dad was a sailor. I think I would have been a sailor if I were a boy instead of a girl. Do you think it could be reincarnation, or is it in the genes?"

"I've seen you in jeans, and I guarantee, you would have been an asset to any crew!"

I punched his arm lightly.

"Ouch! After that, I think you could have been a pirate, Long Mickie Silver."

"That's funny, coming from somebody who almost looks the part. All you need to complete the picture is a pair of big gold earrings!" I laughed gently, and he laughed too. And the sea-breeze brought the pleasant aromas of fish and kelp, gulls and ducks, varnished wood and tarred ropes, fitting perfume worn by the plans we made for the day, to replace the stifling exhaust fumes of the city.

We parked in his designated spot, and transferred coolers to *Virginia* without breaking a sweat. Bruno talked me through lesson one, pre-start ventilation of fuel storage and engine compartments. Then he gave me the key and had me start the engines. The engines warmed to operating temperatures accompanied by their powerful thrum while we prepared for departure.

* * * *

Above the Yacht Club basin, Madeline returned from an authorized coffee break. She looked out from her watchtower, scanned her charges with affection. They were all such beautiful boats.

The piers were still uninhabited, except for the attendant at the fueling dock where somebody wanted an early start for the weekend. Whoever it was planned a long weekend, or a long cruise, judged by the length of time spent taking on her load of fuel. "Which boat is that?" she asked herself, then reached for the binoculars.

First, the name came into focus. Someone prepared the *East Wind* to sail. Then she found the figure who scurried about on the bridge. She met Art Limburg only once before, but the man on the boat looked enough like him that she decided that was the solo sailor.

The fueller rolled up the hoses as his customer began the start-up routine. When he finally went inside his cubicle with eight C-notes, $800, to make change, his customer started the engines as the call came from the lookout's office. He fumbled with the receiver as he lifted it to his ear, and at last spoke, "Fuel Dock, this is Jerry."

"Jerry, this is Madeline. Was that Mr. Limburg on the *East Wind*?"

"Yeah, he just topped off all the tanks, 750 bucks worth, and told me to keep the change. He said he'd see me the next time he was in port, and the tip was to make me remember him. He's pulling away now, as a matter of fact."

"Thanks, Jerry. Just wanted to make sure nobody was stealing his boat." Madeline lied through her teeth, as instructed, because the Commodore suspected Jerry helped those little ruffians steal his beloved *Santa Rosa*. She reached for the handset and pushed the preselected frequency which offered instant communications with the police.

* * * *

At the police dock, Sid caught up as Chet boarded the harbor patrol boat. He handed over the long case, then jumped aboard as the little craft bounced in the waves. To answer Chet's sideways, questioning glare, Sid joked, "I never go to a party where they may ask me to play without my fiddle."

Recognizing that a civilian who brought his own weapon onto the official department vessel breached regulations, Chet instructed, "Just keep it cased unless we really need it. It's bad form for anybody to join this band without being asked." But, once aroused, Chet's curiosity had to be assuaged. "Okay, Sid, What is it?"

Sid confided, "The rifle I use to compete in service rifle matches, a commercial copy of the M-14 I carried my first tour in country, in the 'Nam. If Art still has that shotgun throwing buckshot, this gives us standoff, about 100 yards out of his maximum range. If we weren't likely to be bouncing so much, we'd be able to engage from farther away."

In the background of their conversation, the Sergeant in charge, the Chief of the Boat, carried on his own conversation over the radio. When he signed off, he called, "Hey, Detective, you got aboard just in time. The Yacht Club lookout just reported. The suspect just left the fuel dock after filling all the tanks."

"What are you waiting for? An engraved invitation? We're giving chase. Get on his tail." Chet barked back as he closed the gap between himself and the Chief of the Boat.

"How far do we chase him?"

"To the limits of our jurisdiction. Since this is hot pursuit of a suspected felon, that means to the ends of the earth if we have to. You understand?" Chet set the rules.

The Chief of the Boat grinned widely, then turned to the helmsman, "Terry, boy-o, are you ready for this?"

The young officer, eyes wide with surprise, nodded that he was ready, then called the order to Smitty, the deck hand, "Let go all lines."

The Chief of the Boat turned again to the helmsman, "You heard the man. Follow that fucker!"

Mars light flashed, siren wailed, and they maneuvered through the harbor traffic at a speed which made Chet and Sid hold on for dear life, whisper prayers for safe delivery under their breaths. The big engines, rarely given the chance to display their full horsepower, soon had them following in the wake of the *East Wind*, and rapidly closing on their quarry.

The Chief of the Boat noticed his passengers' green gills. He staked his claim to command the chase, "You two stay out of the way. Once we left the dock, this became my show. We'll do it my way." He turned, saw the junior member of the crew holding on for all he was worth, and roared, "God dammit, Smitty, let go the friggin' rail and get the boarding party gear ready. You're finally going to earn your pay."

While the crew prepared to board the fugitive vessel, Sid appraised the situation. He reported his concern, "Chet, we're catching up to him too fast, too easily. I don't like it."

"Relax. Maybe he doesn't realize that we're after him. And I think this is the faster boat anyway." Chet reassured as sincerely as his own misgivings allowed.

"The faster boat in the harbor, but what happens when we get to open water? Waves out there are a lot bigger than in here." Sid countered.

The Chief of the Boat, who overheard, butted in, "If we don't catch him in the harbor, we only have to keep him in sight. I've already called in the Coast Guard to help. But we should be able to board her in about another minute. Stay out of the way."

In thirty seconds, he bellowed through the loud-hailer, "Ahoy, *East Wind*, heave to and prepare to be boarded." He watched the yacht's wake, determined she was slowing. "Terry, take us alongside. Smitty, with me, in the bow."

At twenty yards, they could hear that the yacht's engines only idled. She drifted forward without anyone at the helm as she shed headway. Sid saw Art peek over the engine compartment. "There he is!"

At ten yards, the Chief of the Boat and Smitty prepared to clamber aboard the *East Wind*. At five yards, Art stood up and leveled the shotgun at the boarding party.

The Chief of the Boat never knew what hit him. He just felt like he had been kicked in the chest by the biggest mule on his grandfather's farm. Then he passed from this world. Smitty caught up to his supervisor just outside the Pearly Gates.

St. Peter let them in. Stupidity brought a lot of folks here early, but, in His mercy, God had never made stupidity a sin. Heaven would be an empty place if he had.

At the third shot, the windshield in front of Terry shattered. He had already spun the wheel hard to port and slammed the throttles full-astern. That put most of the lead pellets wide of the mark, so Terry escaped with only minor cuts, and only one shot pellet embedded deeply in his left upper arm.

But the maneuver brought water over the stern. Seeking the lowest level, the water found the air intake, and suffocated, drowned, the police launch engines.

As the powerless harbor patrol boat drifted with the currents and wind, the *East Wind* powered up and motored away. Adding insult to injury, Art taunted over his wake, "Boarders repelled, Aye, aye, Sir!" His mad, cackling laughter haunted the scene.

* * * *

As *Virginia* entered the channel and crossed the wake of the harbor patrol launch, Bruno remarked, "Somebody is in trouble. I've never seen those boys go after anyone at full throttle before." He gauged the relative directions and speeds of the two boats, added, "If they don't wreck or break down, we should pass them just after they stop the boat, cite the owner for whatever it is they're chasing him for."

A few minutes later, he called, "Hey, Mickie. Come up on the bridge, watch this. They've caught up to him."

Bruno handed me a pair of binoculars, pointed out the yacht and patrol boat close together, "There. Just starboard of the bow. See them?"

I focused on the scene as the two officers took the full charges aimed against them. "Oh My God! Bruno, the guy on the yacht just shot them!"

"What? Let me see those glasses!" He snatched the binoculars and focused on the aftermath. "Son of a bitch! Hang on." Throttles reached full-ahead and the *Virginia*, despite her age, gathered her long skirts above her knees, leaped forward, and ran through the water to reach the injured while they might still assist the wounded rather than count the dead. As we flew across the tops of the highest waves, Bruno radioed for help.

I scanned the patrol boat for signs of life. The binoculars brought them close enough to see two men in plain clothes tending to the one officer's wounds. I reported, "Bruno, Chet and Sid are on her. They look like they're all right, but the rest of them, one looks hurt badly, the others aren't moving."

We quickly covered the distance, and slowed as we neared the launch. Bruno hailed, "Ahoy, harbor patrol! Can we help?"

"Get over here, Bruno. I need a ride." Chet called back.

"Be there right away, Chet." Bruno hollered encouragement. Then he turned and instructed, "Take survivors aboard, midships port."

I stood dumbfounded. Bruno explained, "Go to the port side, open the hatch in the gunwale so they don't have to climb over it. Take a rope. In case one of them falls in, you can throw it to him." I moved but he didn't think I moved quickly enough. He snapped, "Jump to it, woman. Lives are at stake, maybe even our own."

As he maneuvered *Virginia* alongside the launch, I found the latches and swung the hatch inward, then secured it against swinging with the chop, slamming in the face of the survivors coming aboard. Even with good seamanship, the gap remained too wide for the men to jump across up onto *Virginia's* deck and keep their feet dry. I yelled, "Bruno, what do I do now?"

"Take a heavy line, like one of the mooring lines. Put the looped end over the cleat nearest the hatch, and throw them the other end of the rope. They can pull themselves closer." Bruno instructed.

Frustrated because I spoke a different language, I tried to follow instructions. I had to learn a lot about this boat, and the man who ran her. This wasn't the atmosphere I wanted to learn it.

Finally, Chester grabbed the rope, and, with Sid's help, closed the gap to an easy step up and across. Sid came aboard first. Chet handed over the long case, then came aboard.

"What about the others?" Bruno demanded.

Chet answered, "Terry will stay with the boat and his friends. We're the only ones going with you. Proverbial pregnant pause, then he added, "It was Art Limburg. Can we catch him?"

Bruno answered from the bridge. "Of course we can catch him. This old lady was built as a rum runner, and I just put new engines in her last Spring. Never thought I'd get to say this, but clear the decks, every one to battle stations!" He didn't say it loudly, but I was close enough to hear him mutter, "GAWD DAMN! But I feel just like John Wayne!"

Judging we drifted far enough away from the harbor patrol boat, Bruno shoved the throttles full forward. Obligingly, *Virginia* once again complied with her Captain's demands for actions above and beyond the call of duty, seemed to revel in release from the drudgery that was her fate as a charter boat.

As we flew across the tops of the highest waves, skimmed across the surface as the gulls when searching for something to eat, Bruno talked his raw crew of landlubbers through the preparations.

"Don't just stand there. Gather up loose lines! Close the hatch! Get a move on!" Bruno paused to peer through the binoculars, adjust course to the best angle for pursuit. "Mickie, come up here."

Not very Navy-like, I joined him at the helm and asked plaintively, "What?" Confusion and fear put an edge on the question that struck a chord in him.

He looked at me, recognized imminent panic, whispered encouragement, "Don't fall apart on me now." Louder, he instructed, "Take the wheel. Steer ahead of his bow. If you steer at where he is, he won't be there when you get there. Aim for where he's going. Yell out if he changes his course, then adjust ours. Be right back."

Bruno jumped down to inspect his boat's readiness. *Virginia* was as ready as any impressed sailor had ever been for battle. Then he checked on his crew. With 'lubbers aboard, he needed to make them really ready. What they didn't know about boats and sea battles could get them all killed. "Sid, Chet, how are you doing? Are you ready for this?"

"Not doing too bad, but I'd rather be in a car chase." Sid quipped.

Chet just grunted. A little green showed in his complexion.

Bruno began planning the battle, "What's he got?"

"Shotgun with buckshot. At least that's what we saw. He might have something else, but he hasn't used it yet." Chet reported. His color returned to more normal as his mind thought about something other than his seasickness.

"What do we have? Just the gun you loaned me and your service pistol, Chet?"

Chet nodded, opened his coat to reveal the holstered pistol. "9 mm semi-automatic. One spare magazine. It'll do if we can get aboard."

Sid interrupted, "Got my service rifle in the case, Bruno. And ammunition, 7.62 mm NATO ball. Should be able to hit the boat from maybe 300 yards away, even if we're bouncing too much to hit him. That gives us a range advantage."

"Okay, Sid. Go below and get ready. Forward cabin opens onto the foredeck. That should give you a place to shoot from." Bruno watched Sid gather the gun case and go into the cabin, then turned again to his brother, "Anything goes wrong, use the radio, get help. Take care of Mickie and Sid."

"What are you going to do?"

"Nothing stupid, I hope!" Bruno called over his shoulder as he climbed back onto the bridge.

"How are we doing, Mickie?"

"He's still headed out to sea, east-south-east, and it looks like we're getting closer."

Bruno stared over the bow, considered, then agreed, "We are closing. I can make out some of the bigger details without using the binoculars." He watched a bit longer, then advised, "When you can see him, and he looks about an inch tall, holler out. That's when we'll be close enough for Sid to start shooting. Maybe Sid can keep his head down so we can close in and board her without getting shot."

He put a hand on my shoulder, encouraged, "You're doing fine. Be right back. Need to check the charts." He ducked into a small compartment, emerged with a map. Bruno spread it out, reached across the panel and pushed a button, then smiled as he read the instrument display, "Might have a bit of luck here." He weighted the map with the binoculars, turned to call, "Chet, does Sid have a pistol with him?"

"He doesn't go anywhere, not even the bathroom, without one. I can't believe he doesn't have one with him now. Why?"

"We should be close enough to start shooting soon. I want to try to force him to the northeast. The more lead we lob at him, the more likely he will go where I want him. Come up to the bridge, and I'll show you the chart. Have Sid come up too."

The crew assembled for orders. The Captain did not disappoint them.

"Sid, how many rounds did you bring?"

"I've got six boxes, 120 rounds, but only three magazines. That means I can only take 60 shots without reloading the magazines. And I can't put enough holes in the *East Wind* to sink her, even with all 120 cartridges."

"I don't expect you to sink her, just make him keep his head down." Bruno looked up and across the sea, "We're still a bit far, but can you take a few shots for ranging after I tell you my plan?"

Sid nodded that he'd try.

Bruno continued, "Target the engines first. Knock out one or both to cut his speed. Take a few shots at the bridge, too. Any hits near him will shake him up, at least a little bit. Chet said that you're an old grunt, so you know what I mean when I tell you to use sustained rate. Not more than one magazine on the run up, not more than one magazine when we're in close, and use the third to keep him pinned down when we turn away... Don't forget to set your battle sights."

"My range notes say 12 clicks elevation for targets at 300 yards. That should do for a target as big as a 50-foot yacht rather than a 12-inch X-ring on a target." Sid smiled.

"Yeah, but paper doesn't shoot back. Don't get cocky." Bruno turned to Chet, "We're faster by about five knots. When it looks like Sid has made him duck, we'll dash in close enough for you to use that pistol of yours. Again, one magazine only. Just shoot up the bridge. Chase him off. Then we'll pull away to reload. I'll overtake to his starboard, so take a position on the port side. Use the cabin for cover. It should stop buckshot."

Bruno searched his crew's faces for unasked questions. Reasonably certain they understood, he finished, "Here's the payoff. We'll pull ahead to block him, make him turn to the northeast." He pointed to the chart, "We have a shallow draft compared to his. I want to run him across the reef. I think he'll just lose the rudders and screws, but he might even hole her bottom. Either he gets shot when we close the range, or he swims. If he tries to swim with the shotgun, we just wait it out until he gives up."

"Or the bastard drowns." I heard myself say it, but didn't believe that I really had said it aloud until Bruno looked at me.

He turned back to the others, "If we have to board her, we'll need your pistol, Sid."

"I've got a pistol, and two extra loaded magazines. We can use it too." I volunteered.

Bruno ruled, "That arms the boarding party. Sid, on the second run, use only two magazines. That leaves your last one to support the boarding." Bruno looked through the windscreen, and gauged the distance between *Virginia* and *East Wind*. "We're almost close enough. Everybody, take your places."

When the others left the bridge, Bruno turned to issue my orders, "Mickie, go below, reload the magazines as Sid empties them, but don't give them back to him until we're going in on the second run. In your spare time, get your pistol ready. I'll take the helm for this maneuver."

"You're not just getting rid of me because I'm a woman?" I demanded.

"Hell no. I'm not sending you below because you're a woman. That just happens to be the best spot for you." I didn't budge, so Bruno explained, "If you know how to load pistol magazines, you can load magazines for Sid's rifle. You can steer a boat well enough when there is room for mistakes, but in close, you'll need more practice. It's my boat, and I know what she can do. Sid brought the rifle, and Chet wears a badge. Nope, the best place for you is down below as Sid's loader. Besides, it'll give you something to do instead of worry if we take fire. If it makes you feel better, take a few shots at him yourself, but make sure the rifle magazines are reloaded before we make the second run."

"Go below and load magazines, Aye, aye, sir." I complied, swayed into reluctant submission by logic. Bruno was right, this time anyway. Even if he weren't right, I didn't want to mutiny on the high seas. That was only a little less serious than piracy. "And take a pot shot or two if I have time. Aye, aye, Sir!' I muttered to myself as I made my way below deck.

* * * *

"Piracy, that's what it is." The voices explained to Art. "First, you had to repel those pirates in blue uniforms when they tried to board this boat. Next, you'll have to keep those new pirates off her."

Art looked back over his shoulder. The smaller boat was gaining, no doubt about it. Every time he turned a compass point to run straight away, she steered onto an intercepting course. With her greater speed, she kept getting closer.

223

But that played into his own plans to spring a trap. Soon, she would be near enough that Art would be able to pick out targets among the crew. When he let fly with the buckshot, they'd know it. All of them except whichever one he shot first. After all, buckshot and pistols had about equivalent effective ranges. When they got close enough to shoot at him, he'd be close enough to them to shoot back.

Art leaned down to check the small bag which held his extra ammunition. Sharp, sonic crack of something very fast passing very near his head was followed instantly by the sound of something striking the instrument panel very hard. Shortly he heard a distant gunshot. That brought him erect again.

The shattered glass lens over the port engine oil pressure gauge evidenced what happened. In a second, Art realized they had something able to reach out while he was unable to respond in kind. He screamed in indignation, "You're not cheating fair!"

Beside him, another sonic crack passed to his right, and whatever-it-was hit the water about five yards off the starboard beam. A thud sounded from the engine compartment cover, again followed by the reports of distant shots. With this insult, Art passed from indignation to anger.

He wheeled *East Wind* hard to port. He saw another small geyser, like someone threw a small stone at him, erupt ten yards off his right shoulder. Two more thuds came from the hull somewhere behind him. Each impact sounded more and more like somebody pounded a hammer against his fair vessel. Art's anger grew to rage.

The voices advised him to shoot back at the pursuers. If nothing else, it would give them pause, give them something to think about twice before they came any closer. With seventeen shells left, Art decided that he could afford three long range shots. The rest were for closer range.

He picked a spot in the air above the pursuer's helm and fired a salvo at his tormentors. He lowered the shotgun from his shoulder, and watched the helmsman disappear from view. Art reloaded as he muttered, "There, you bastards, take that!"

* * * *

A shot shattered the laminated safety-glass windshield near his head. Instinct caused him to duck below the solid bulkhead. Slowly, Bruno rose again to his full height. He surveyed the multiple spider web patterns in the cracked and crazed glass, mere feet from his face. "Damn! That was close."

To be heard above the throaty roar of the engines, he bellowed, "Sid, Chet, get ready for the first run. Make him keep his head down." Bruno protected his hand with his cap, and pushed the broken window from its frame to clear his vision again.

Below decks, Sid continued to fire from the forward porthole, deliberate shots, aimed as well as he could from a launch which bounced across the waves, directed in the direction of another craft which also bounced in the sea. I felt *Virginia* strain as Bruno pushed the throttles forward the last margin.

"I'll take her about 25 yards off her beam. We'll make the pass now." Bruno's voiced carried the edge of tempered steel honed to razor sharpness.

"Mickie, hand me a full magazine, open one of the windows on the port side, then stand on the other side. I'll move there when we're nearer so I can get a better shot." Sid instructed. "Want you to know what I plan so I don't trip over you, or have you get in the line of fire. I think Bruno would beat me to a pulp if you got hurt by friendly fire." he expanded.

Sid fired twice more, then turned to me. "And you better watch when I change magazines. This is the short-short course on how to make this rifle work, in case I'm knocked out of action."

Bruno cajoled *Virginia* to try harder, "Come on girl!" He ran the arithmetic in his head. Five knots faster was nearly 170 yards per minute if they traveled a straight line. Because the quarry zig-zagged, he estimated they closed at only 100 yards in a minute. From 300 yards behind to 300 yards in front would expose them for just less than six minutes. It would feel like a lifetime if Art was still able to shoot back. He pushed the button on the Global Positioning System (GPS) unit to get a current position. "Come on, girl. Just a little bit more. That's all we need." The reef was only two minutes ahead.

* * * *

"That reef is around here somewhere." Art tried to guess his position. He had been a little too distracted, a little bit too busy to keep careful track of the navigation. The GPS unit was just so much scrap now, a lucky shot that hit the dashboard rather than him. He had to depend on dead reckoning, and he reckoned he'd be dead if he wasn't careful, wasn't lucky.

Art felt surprisingly calm, resigned. The voices had abandoned him in this hour of need, but the quiet was welcome. It really was uncomfortable to have all of them jabbering inside his head all the time.

He looked over his shoulder. That persistent little boat was getting nearer again. It might be worth a few more shots to dissuade her from following so close astern.

Art eased the helm around to let *East Wind* run in a straight line while he fired at his unwelcome pursuers. As he walked to the stern, he smelled fuel. The wind carried the odor behind him while he was on the bridge. He only noticed it when he stood aft of the leaking fuel tank.

Art decided that was sufficient reason to move forward again, and to put out the smoking lamp. With enough ventilation, the fuel-air mix would not reach explosive proportions. By like token, he didn't want to check how much gas was in the tank by the light of a burning match.

He felt the wasp sting, so vicious that it tore the shotgun from his grip. When he reached for the weapon, he noted the stump of his left ring finger bled freely. "Damn, this is getting bad." He wrapped his hand in his handkerchief, and returned fire until the shotgun clicked on an empty chamber.

Art noticed the wisps of steam, maybe smoke, rising from now perforated engine compartment cover as he reloaded. He sensed when his boat lost speed even before the overheating warning light for the starboard engine flashed. "Soon, now," he thought, "they'll pull alongside. Then I'll have them right where I want them. When I see her mast even with the cabin, I can blast them to perdition." Art crouched in the ladderway from cabin to bridge, protected from sight by a total one-half inch of fiber reinforced plastic in the hull and inner bulkhead.

* * * *

"He's losing speed. Get ready… Steady… Now!" At Bruno's command, Sid, Chet, and I loosed a broadside fusillade into *East Wind*.Suddenly, she fell astern rapidly, much quicker than we had gained on her. "Did she hit the reef, or did we knock out her engines?" Bruno asked for information necessary to plan the next pass. Easing back the throttles, he gave *Virginia* her first respite in nearly two hours since we began the chase.

I reloaded my pistol, then fumbled cartridges into the empty magazines that Sid kicked over. Finally, I rested too, all three magazines refilled, and looked up from my task. "Sid, you're bleeding! … Bruno, where's the first aid kit?"

* * * *

Art thought it had been a good plan, except they came in shooting, not at all like those other pirates. The fiberglass shattered all around him, directly in front of him, before he could stand up. Even wounded thrice more, he managed to fire a few shots before his boat slowed, stuttered so abruptly that he fell backwards down the ladder into the cabin in a heap. He reached for the first aid supplies, but his fingers went limp. His heart beat a few more times before it, too, went limp as his body collapsed into the large pool of his own blood.

When Art asked directions from the next person he saw, St. Peter directed him to the other place. While true his madness excused some of his recent transgressions, Art already earned his eternal punishment long before.

* * * *

Bruno called directions from the bridge. "In the galley. The cabinet above the cook top." After a few seconds, the question followed, "Who's hurt? You or Sid?"

"Sid. He's bleeding from the head." I answered as I retrieved medical supplies and went to Sid's side. I swallowed hard, knew I paled at the sight of so much blood. Steeling my nerve, I tried my hand as a combat hospital corpsman.

"Take it easy, Mickie. It's not that bad. Scalp wounds always bleed a lot, look worse than they are." Sid assured quietly. "And I know it's only a scalp wound because I can't find a hole in my head that I wasn't born with."

"Sit still while I bandage it. You're getting blood all over the place"

Bruno looked in through the hatch, "Got it under control?"

"I think so. Where's Chet?"

"As soon as you're done down here, we need another one patched up topside." Bruno pulled back from the opening before I could ask.

Two gauze pads and a half dozen wraps of bandage stemmed the flow. Done with Sid, I hurried onto the afterdeck. An iridescent dark spot on his gray suit showed the wound was in the leg. Chet had wrapped his tie around the thigh to hold a handkerchief as a pressure bandage against the puncture.

"Can't be too bad, Chet. That's a long way from your heart, if you have one." Bruno teased, aggravating his brother's discomfort.

"Easy for you to say. You don't feel seasick too." Chet got in a lick of his own as we helped him into the cabin to keep Sid company.

As I tended to the wounded, Bruno watched the adversary for signs of life. After ten minutes, I went on deck. He voiced the judgment, "She must have been holed. She's settling by the stern. If he doesn't come out soon, either he's dead already, or he's decided to go down with her."

"What do we do now?" I queried.

"Wait. One way or the other." Bruno ruled, "And we search her if she stays afloat." Soon, he spoke again, "Mickie, watch her. I've got to check for our own damage."

When he came back, he had good news. "There's nothing below the waterline, although the port side of the cabin is chewed up badly. All the portholes on that side had the glass shot out of them, as well as on the bridge. Got a lot of patching to do before the tourists will hire her." Bruno paused, looking toward the other boat. He spoke with a strange blend of victory and sorrow, "Well, Mickie, relax. We won't have to board her after all. There she goes."

The *East Wind* slipped below the waves. She took her owner's husk with her to rest in Davy Jones' Locker.

Just visible on the horizon, the Coast Guard cutter steamed into view. Bruno called her by radio to make the report. Then he turned *Virginia* for home.

* * * *

Grits awoke from his nap. He tuned in the local news as he loaded the gun he would use. The first story reported that Art Limburg had been killed during a shootout while attempting to escape from police. He shrugged, thought, "Damn, that was close. I was almost headed out to kill those two. But, no one to pay me, no contract. They get a by this time. And, if they're this lucky, I couldn't have done it anyway."

He unloaded the gun, and secured it deep in his valise. Well, at least he could enjoy the weekend with his wife.

When All Is Said

SID AND CHET WERE TREATED AND released to attend Norma's funeral during the afternoon. They would join Bruno and I this Friday Night at the back corner booth of the Blue Onion for the wake. Yes, it would be a wake, albeit after the burial, one for an old friend named Norma Winslow.

Waiting for them, I entertained my own thoughts. We evened the score for her, but there is no joy in it. Now that it's over, when all is said and done, there isn't the feeling of triumph that I expected. The sadness at her loss still lingers.

True, we found the man who ordered Norma's murder and sent Art to hell. His henchmen joined him because they got careless and cocky, or because Art became frightened of them. But there were those missing children who would stay missing forever.

Sid held the door as Chet hobbled in on crutches. They joined the wake already in progress.

Sid reported that Weasel was doing well. The psychiatrist who worked with him had hypnotized him, got him to tell why he feared being indoors. With a little tender loving care, Weasel would be just fine, and had been transferred to the VA hospital for extended care of both physical and mental injuries.

After drinking a toast to Weasel, Bruno turned to Chet. "You're smiling like the Cheshire Cat. Don't tell me they're going to give you medical retirement for a piddling little flesh wound?" Bruno chided.

"No. Got good news, though." Chet reported, "Interpol and the

French police intercepted the Captain and First Mate of the *Flying Fish* while they tried to sneak the girls ashore. The police got there late, but your friends, Manny and Jeff, tackled them at the foot of the gangplank. Held them until the police got there. The Captain doesn't know everything, but he knows enough to start tracking down some of the earlier cases. We might be responsible for a few kids getting back with their families after all."

"Good Old Manny!" Bruno cheered.

Chet added, "Seems the century old Mann Act will get a facelift as a result of what we found. The two coeds, Manny, and Jeff will be back in town soon, compliments of the Feds. They'll be flown back to testify before Congress."

"That's good. I'll need Manny around to help repair *Virginia*." Bruno took my hand, "And I'll need you to help, too."

At least for this conversation, I decided to let Bruno have the last word. I just hoped he wouldn't expect to have the last word every time.